DANGEROUS DUEL

Alexandra had felt no fear when she faced the odious Giles O'Hara in a duel at dawn after that drunken gentleman had accused her of cheating at the gambling table. The duel was with pistols, and Alexandra was even handier with them than she was with cards. Even if the weapons had been swords, Alexandra would have had the skills to meet the challenge.

But now in the carriage home, she faced a far graver peril. Hit by a stray bullet, Alexandra's shirt had become stained from the flesh wound. Without asking and without warning, Lord Wrotham stripped the shirt away to assess and salve the injury.

Alexandra saw his eyes widen as they took in her creamy skin. She felt his fingers pause on her naked shoulders. And she realized that adept as she was with cold steel, warm flesh was quite a different matter— and though her life was safe on the field of honor, she could not say the same for her virtue in this man's arms. . . .

Lady Alex's Gamble

Evelyn Richardson

A SIGNET BOOK

SIGNET
Published by the Penguin Group
Penguin Books USA Inc., 375 Hudson Street,
New York, New York 10014, U.S.A.
Penguin Books Ltd, 27 Wrights Lane,
London W8 5TZ, England
Penguin Books Australia Ltd, Ringwood,
Victoria, Australia
Penguin Books Canada Ltd, 10 Alcorn Avenue,
Toronto, Ontario, Canada M4V 3B2
Penguin Books (N.Z.) Ltd, 182–190 Wairau Road,
Auckland 10, New Zealand

Penguin Books Ltd, Registered Offices:
Harmondsworth, Middlesex, England

First published by Signet, an imprint of Dutton Signet,
a division of Penguin Books USA Inc.

First Printing, February, 1995
10 9 8 7 6 5 4 3 2 1

To Janice Franca,
who offers me so much support
and encouragement.

Chapter 1

The rain drummed ceaselessly against the window, as it had for days, its incessant rhythm broken only by intermittent gusts of wind that rattled the leaded windowpanes, forcing the lady watching by the bed to clutch the paisley shawl even more tightly around her shoulders. The man on the bed stirred and moaned and the lady bent over to apply a damp cloth to his sweating brow.

He was a handsome young man with dark auburn hair, finely penciled dark brows, a broad forehead, patrician nose, and generous mouth, but the puffy skin around his eyes and lines of dissipation running from nose to mouth spoke of a dissolute life that was beginning to rob him both of his looks and his youth.

He moaned again and twisted his head from side to side under the damp cloth. "Damn you, Alexander, be still," the lady muttered fiercely. "I must do this to cool the fever." She dipped the cloth in the basin of water, wrung it out, and applied it again to his forehead. "For if you die, I shall murder you," she added rather illogically. It was just like Alexander to land them in the basket, she thought angrily to herself. And it was just like him too to leave her, his long-suffering twin, to sort it all out.

With the exception of a complexion unmarred by the effects of drink, late nights, and an unhealthy predilection for every other sort of debauchery, Lady Alexandra de Montmorency was the spitting image of the man in the bed. She had the same thick dark auburn hair, delicately arched brows over eyes of such deep green as to be almost emerald. It was an interesting face rather than a beautiful one, the high-bridged nose and generous mouth giving it far too much character to be acceptable in a society where pale blond beauties with retroussé noses and simpering rosebud lips were all the rage. However, no one who had seen Alexandra de Montmorency was likely ever to forget her. Like her brother, whose six-foot form lay sweating under the covers, she was tall and long-limbed, but slender, and she moved with what in a man would have been called athletic grace. Such assurance in movement and bearing could be a trifle unnerving in a woman and had been known to intimidate the shorter, less confident men she had encountered at the rare assembly she attended in Norwich. But in truth Alexandra did not care. Since her father's death, she had had her hands too full of more important things to waste her time on balls and other such frippery affairs. And truth to say, one man was already causing her enough headaches to keep her from wishing to waste her time worrying about the impressions, negative or otherwise, that she might be making on any others.

Alexander de Montmorency, Earl of Halewood, had come into his inheritance a scant four years ago, but in that short time he had managed to gamble it into nonexistence. At first his twin sister had not been aware of his ruinous propensities, but of late, she had begun to sense that the gay and reckless lad she had grown up with had somehow changed. The generous, fun-loving nature of youth had slowly disappeared, to be replaced by a wildness and a desperation. As a boy Alexander had always included his friends and family in one lark after another; now he seemed heedless of their very existence. More and more frequently he returned home drunk and angry, to apologize briefly—if he apologized at all—before going off again.

Alexandra could never say precisely when the change had come about. Certainly he had gotten in with a bad set of fellows at university, where he had begun to gamble so much that he was forever at odds with his father over money. The old earl, who had enjoyed a riotous and misspent youth of his own, had not been so upset at the gambling as he had been unable to understand how any son of his could lose so consistently at games of chance.

"It is not that he does not have a head for faro," her father used to complain to Alexandra, "it's that he does not have a head for anything—whist, piquet, loo, macao, or even hazard—not that one needs much head for that. I cannot understand it, a child of mine . . ."—and he would shake his head in genuine perplexity.

Certainly their mother's death, three years before their father's, had not been the cause of Alexander's decline, but it had increased its velocity. The countess had exercised the same steadying influence over her eldest son as she had over his father. Gentle and beautiful, she had run the household so smoothly and easily that no one was aware of the organization and hard work that had gone into it. Unfailingly kind, she never criticized, but set such an example of love and charity that people could not help but follow her lead, while her sense of humor and her delight in life had kept her from seeming sanctimonious. She had been universally loved and her eldest son had adored her.

Alexandra sighed. Perhaps if she had been more like her mother her twin would have remained the passionate, but essentially good-hearted youth he had been. But it was no use repining. Certainly she had always longed to be as good and beautiful as the Countess of Halewood, but somehow Alexandra had fallen into scrapes as often as her brother had. As a child she had been as adventurous as he, and with her twin to support and encourage her in every whim, she had gone from one escapade to another. Then too, she did not possess her mother's gentle nature, being more like her father: loving and kind, but passionate and unwilling to live a life that tamely accepted everything without questioning or understanding it fully.

And without a doubt she had done her share of questioning her twin's behavior after her father died. Alexandra had not hesitated, as he gallivanted off to this race meeting and that mill, to point out that fences needed mending or the tenants' cottages wanted repairing. She had not meant to nag, but her brother had seemed to live as though the entire estate existed for nothing more than to finance his mania for betting on anything and everything. Alexander would often exclaim testily, "Oh come off it, Alex. *I* am the Earl of Halewood, not you.

Nor are you my mother." She had been aware she was making a bad job of it, but she had not known how else to go about it other than to pester him when there was no money for the servants' wages or household expenses.

For a while things had improved when Alexander, whose temper had been deteriorating rapidly, seemed to take a turn for the better. He had set about at last to pay the servants and attend to the immediate necessities. She'd soon found out, however, the real reason for his renewed optimism. One night he came to her bedchamber; it was so rare that he consulted anyone about anything, so rare that he was even home before midnight that she had been quite astonished. When she happened to look up and see him lingering awkwardly in the doorway, the book she had been reading had slid to the floor with a bang.

"Alex," he began carefully, tentatively, "may I come in?"

"Why of course."

He sat down heavily on a chair in front of the fire and stared into the flames for a moment before glancing up with a half-guilty, half-pleading smile. "I have been rather, er, ah . . . rather unfortunate," he began, looking so much like the old Alexander who had just gotten into some scrape or other that she could not help but smile in return. She had missed him, the fun-loving Alexander of her childhood. "You never wear Mother's diamonds, do you?"

"Why no," she replied, mystified as to what he thought she'd do with them, when he knew she hardly ever went to assemblies, and certainly wasn't about to have a Season at her age.

"Good. May I borrow them?"

"Borrow them?" she had asked stupidly, not even trying to imagine what her brother would do with the elaborate necklace, matching bracelets, and earrings.

"Well, you see, as I say, I have been rather unfortunate lately and I, er, need to raise a little wind so I thought perhaps I could take them to Goldfarb in Norwich and he could give me something to help me out of my, er, difficulties."

"You must have been very unfortunate indeed," she had responded dryly.

Alexander flushed. His twin sister always made him feel inadequate. She sat there looking at him coolly as though *he* had been the fool, but he had not. Nimrod could not have failed to win. Alexander knew the horse's owner and had talked to the lads who exercised it. That horse had been the sure thing that was going to win him back his gaming debts. How was he to guess it would wind up close enough to another horse in the race so as to be kicked up in such a freakish way that it came in last? It was not Alexander's fault, merely the last in a run of unbelievably bad luck that had plagued him lately. Alexandra had no right to look at him so scornfully. He might not have as much in the cock-loft as his clever twin did, but he was not half-witted.

"Just how unfortunate were you?" his sister probed.

"Oh, nothing serious," he assured her airily. "It's only a question of a few thousand pounds."

"How many thousand?" Alexandra was not going to make this easy for him.

"Well, about ten," he admitted unhappily.

"Ten! You lost ten thousand pounds in a card game!" Even Alexandra's iron self-control deserted her at the mention of a sum that could have kept the household running for several years.

Her brother hunched his shoulder defensively. "There's no need to shout, Alex. Plenty of fellows drop that and more in an evening. I am not so stupid as all that. This was on a horse—a sure thing. I know the owner and the trainer . . ."

"And you thought that with one large bet and an enormous amount of luck you would be able to win back enough to pay off your other debts. I see." And she did see now. That was why he had been more attentive to them all lately, not because he had stopped gambling, but because he had felt sure of winning.

"Please, Alex." He was begging now, smiling in the endearing way he had as a child when people had been unable to deny him anything.

Alexandra steeled herself against the beseeching look in his eyes. If it were only her welfare that were involved she would not have been so hard on him. He couldn't help it, after all. Gambling was in their blood; he just happened to lack the cleverness and the discipline that had won their father a fortune and allowed him to retire to the country and raise a family. However, Alexandra had the others to think about. She hesitated.

"Please, Alex, it's the last thing I'll ever ask. I've already borrowed so much against the estate that those plaguey bankers will not lend me another penny, cheeseparing lot that they are."

"What? You've mortgaged Halewood? Alexander, how *could* you? Do you think of no one but yourself?"

"Now, Alex, calm yourself. Everyone does it. The estate will make it back in no time. Halewood has some of the best farmland in—"

"Alexander"—his sister's voice was dangerously quiet—"you will sell this necklace and the rest of Mother's jewelry, pay back the creditors, and you will *never* risk our livelihood again. Do you hear me?"

This was more than Alexander had hoped. He grasped his twin's hand. "You're a Trojan, Alex! Knew you would stand by me. I shan't ever do it again. I promise."

And she had believed him, fool that she was, Alexandra thought bitterly to herself as she applied another cool compress to his burning forehead. She should have locked him out, refused to feed him, anything to keep them all from the fix they were in now—and there was no doubt about it, they were in dire straits.

Before he had lapsed into unconsciousness, her twin had blurted it all out to her. Things could not have been worse. She should have guessed that disaster had struck when Alexander did not put in an appearance for breakfast two mornings in a row. The Earl of Halewood, no matter how far gone he had been the previous night, no matter at what hour of the morning he tumbled into bed, was never one to miss his rasher of eggs and a hearty slice of beef. But he had not shown himself, nor was his horse in the stables. However, the weather was so bad—an unusually violent storm had swept across the marshes, flattening everything in its path—that they all conjectured he had been forced to put up at whatever house he had gone to gamble away more of his birthright.

It was not until young Andrew, hoping for enough of a change in the weather to ride his pony, had looked out the window at midmorning on the second day and seen his older brother, his head fallen forward on his horse's neck, riding slowly up the long gravel drive, that they realized something was amiss.

"It's Alexander!" Andrew had shouted to no one in particular. "And he looks ever so odd." The boy had gone flying down the steps, closely pursued by his adoring shadow, the seven-year-old Abigail. His shout had reached the morning room, where Alexandra and Althea had repaired to go over the accounts, it being the most comfortable room in the house and possessing one of the few chimneys that did not smoke. They had followed at a more sedate pace along with Mrs. Throckmorton, the housekeeper. Ned Coachman, hearing the restless stamping of the horses in the stables, had appeared around the corner of the house just in time to help his sodden master off his horse.

Alexander's clothes were soaked through and his hair plastered to his head. "Lost my way," he managed to mutter through chattering teeth as Ned supported him up the flagstone steps. He was already coughing by the time Alexandra and Mrs. Throckmorton had gotten him to bed. His breathing was so labored, his face so flushed, that his twin had sent for the doctor immediately.

Trevor Padgett had shaken his head after he had examined his patient. Too much drink, too many long nights at the card table with very little attention paid to exercise or anything else, had made a physical wreck of what had once been a fine young man. He shook his head as he felt for the patient's pulse. "How long were you out like this?" he demanded, exasperation masking the concern in his voice.

"I don't know. Hours, I suppose." The earl gasped. "Blasted difficult to see. Lost my way, you know. Wandered around for an age trying to find it."

"Well, when did you start for home?" asked the doctor, patiently rephrasing the question.

The sick man broke into a fit of coughing and his sister handed him some water. He drank greedily before replying. "I have no id . . . yes, the clock had just struck midnight and I decided I had better go, been gone one day already, you know."

"Midnight! Whatever possessed you? And in such weather!" The doctor shook his head in stunned disbelief.

"I was only at Cranbourne's," Alexander said in defense of himself. "How was I to know I would lose my way? Blasted horse ought to know it well enough by now."

The doctor had looked grave as he motioned Alexandra to

follow him. Closing the door gently behind them, he led her down the hall out of all possible earshot. "I should keep a close eye on him. He was exposed to the elements for what was apparently some time. That and the unhealthy life he has led are likely to bring about a dangerous inflammation of the lungs. Keep him warm, but try to keep the fever down. I shall visit as often as I can." He paused and then smiled kindly. "I do not wish to add to your worries, but I would be remiss in my duties if I were not to warn you that there is cause for concern."

Doctor Padgett had left her reluctantly, wishing he had been able to give a better verdict, for he liked and admired Alexandra and hated to add to the burdens she already bore. That useless brother of hers would continue to cause her anxiety and heartache and there was very little he could do about it.

Trevor Padgett had known Lady Alexandra de Montmorency for years, from the day she had broken her arm attempting to rescue her twin from a scrape he had gotten them into. She'd only been five at the time, but the doctor had known then how it would be with Alexandra, possessed of the intelligence and self-control so noticeably lacking in her brother, eternally saving him from his own recklessness and stupidity.

Back in Alexander's room, Alexandra was thinking much the same thing as her twin, starting up from his restless sleep, grasped her hand in his. He was burning up with fever and the eyes staring up at her were glassy but alert. "Must warn you, Alex, Cranbourne will be calling. Wants you to be his wife."

"What?" His sister was too stunned for the moment to say anything else. She barely knew of Sir Ralph, nor would she ever have acknowledged the slightest acquaintance with a man reputedly blackballed from all the clubs in London and certainly not welcome in any respectable household in Norfolk.

"Come now, Alex," the sick man gasped, "he's not old or decrepit, has a handsome property, and possesses a comfortable fortune. . . ."

"Won in some nefarious way," his sister snapped. "Really, Alexander, you are all about in the head. I would not have anything to do with Sir Ralph Cranbourne if he were the last man on earth."

"Have to." Her twin was overcome with a fit of coughing. "It is either that or I pay him a hundred thousand pounds and I haven't got a hundred thousand pounds. I tell you, I am ruined if you don't."

"*You* are ruined!" Alexandra leapt from the chair to pace furiously around the room, her patience finally at an end. "*You* are ruined. What about us? At least you have enjoyed yourself while you have played mice feet with the future of this family."

"Come now, Alex. You are not getting any younger. No one has asked for your hand, nor are they likely to the way things are going. You're too strong-minded. A man doesn't like a woman to rule him. I know that well enough." Sick as he was, Alexander could not keep himself from getting in a dig at his capable sister, who had always managed to make him feel just the tiniest bit inferior. She rarely said anything, but often he looked into those clear green eyes, so like his own, and felt himself lacking. And then there was the staff, as well as his own brothers and sisters, who always consulted his sister, never him. Alexander de Montmorency might be the Earl of Halewood to the rest of the world, but at home it was Lady Alexandra who commanded the respect. "You'll wind up on the shelf," he warned, coughing more violently than ever.

"Which is a great deal safer, more pleasant, and more respectable than being the wife of Sir Ralph Cranbourne," his sister retorted. "Now go to sleep, Alexander, and let me think."

And she had thought. Alexandra had been racking her brains all night as she sat by the invalid's bedside, but to no avail. She had no one to turn to, nothing she could sell quickly that would raise that sort of sum. When Mrs. Throckmorton herself had brought her her breakfast that morning, she was no closer to any solution than she had been the previous evening.

The wind continued to howl furiously and Alexandra tried to keep her spirits from plummeting into complete despair. She *had* to think of something, not only for herself, but for all the others too—the staff, the rest of the family, all the tenants who depended on Halewood for a livelihood. At last she was forced to the conclusion that the only way to come up with the money her brother owed was to go about recovering it the same way he had lost it. She would have to gamble.

Chapter 2

"Gamble? Alexandra, you must be all about in the head," Lady Althea de Montmorency exclaimed as her older sister broached the plan to her sometime later that morning. "Alexander has spent his entire existence gambling and lost a fortune, yet you, who have never gambled in your life, are planning to win it back the same way? You are my dearest sister and you have done your best to take care of us since Papa died, but it has gotten to you at last, Alex. Your wits have truly gone begging. Althea's large, dark eyes were filled with concern and her ordinarily sunny countenance looked troubled.

Though their faces wore similar expressions of worry, the sisters could not have been less alike in other respects. Where Alexandra was tall and slender, Althea was short, pleasingly plump, and despite being six years younger than her sister, appeared the more matronly of the two. Her features were soft and rounded, her pink-and-white complexion enhanced by the velvety brown of her eyes. Even their demeanors differed. While Althea was gracefully draped against her chair, Alex was perched on hers.

Alexandra glanced over at her sister and smiled. "You should have been the eldest, Ally, you know. You are all reason and calmness the way Mama was, while Alexander and I"—she shrugged—"we are more like Papa. It is only to be hoped that I resemble Papa more closely that poor Alexander does. After all, if it were not for Papa's talent at the gaming tables, we would not have Halewood, which, as you recall, he won at macao."

"However," Althea hastened to point out, "if he had not had such a rackety youth in the first place his family would not have disinherited him and he would not have been forced to seek his fortune at the gaming tables."

"There, you see, you should have been the eldest. You always see things in such a practical way. I must say it would please me no end if I could be so pragmatic now, but we are at the *point non plus* and drastic measures are necessary."

"But, Alex," her sister began.

"I know, I have not frequented every gaming table in Norfolk or every race meeting and mill in three counties as Alexander has done these last years, but Papa *did* tell me I was an angel with cards, and surely no one could have been a better judge than he."

Althea shook her head. Once her sister had made up her mind there was no dissuading her. Undoubtedly Alex would manage to pull it off and save them all, for no one was more resolute, more fearless, or more persistent than she, but indeed, at the moment the odds seemed insurmountable, even for Alex. Althea still remembered the day when her sister had appeared, riding pale but composed up the drive, her right arm dangling limply at her side. In her usual way she had made a bet with Alexander, convinced the stable lad to give her her father's hunter, and had gone galloping off madly on her own. She had broken her arm after urging the horse over an impossibly high fence. Somehow she had remounted and ridden the five miles home again, keeping her mount in check with her left hand.

Resigning herself to the inevitable now, Althea inquired, "But how are you to do this? Playing with Papa every evening is one thing, but you cannot hope to recover a fortune playing penny a point with Lady Challerton and the other ladies who retire to the card rooms at the assemblies, especially as you do not even attend the assemblies." Althea sighed inwardly. It seemed so unfair that Alex, who was old enough to attend these delightful gatherings, condemned them as useless and boring in the extreme while she herself, who would have given anything just to see the lovely gowns, was still too young to go. Not that it would matter what age she was since Alexandra loathed them too much to take her, Alexander was too selfish to escort anybody anywhere, and their brother, Anthony, was off in London with his regiment.

"Of course I shan't play with those tabbies," Alex snorted. "To win a sum such as Alexander whistled down the wind I must go where the play is deep. There is only one place where the stakes are high enough for that. . . . I must go to White's," she declared.

"White's!" Althea gasped. "But, Alex, how?"

"Anthony, of course," Alex responded coolly.

"Anthony?" Althea stared blankly at her sister.

"I shall ask Anthony to introduce me to someone who can vouch for me," Alex explained reasonably.

"But, but . . ." Althea stammered, "but you are a woman."

"I *know* that. I have suffered from that affliction for twenty-three years. Believe me, I am well aware of it, but I shall soon remedy that. As Doctor Padgett does not hold out much hope for Alexander's very immediate recovery, I have some time."

"Time? Time for what?" Althea was even more bewildered.

"Time to become Alexander de Montmorency, Earl of Halewood, of course. I shall put it about here that Alexander has gone to London and that I have left for a long overdue visit to Great Aunt Belinda in Brighton. Then I shall become Alexander. In the meantime, Bessie will nurse him in Mrs. Bates's cottage. I have not found new tenants for it since she died, and now I am rather glad I haven't, for it is quite remote and none of the villagers ever goes there. Of course I shall have to confide in some of the staff, but only Mrs. Throckmorton, Bessie, and Ned need know."

"Alex, do you really think you can fool people into believing you are Alexander?"

"I can only try," was the cheerful reply. "More than once when we were children I pretended I was Alexander when he was not where he was supposed to be. It shouldn't be any more difficult now than it was then." After all, Alex thought to herself, her brother was no more mature now than he had been at ten, when she had easily hoodwinked his tutor and his groom.

"Well," Althea began doubtfully.

"I can see no other alternative. Certainly I cannot marry that toad Cranbourne."

"No." Alex's sister shuddered. "He is the most odious person alive. How Alexander could associate with such a person I cannot conceive. But, Alex, there must be *someone* you can marry. Do you not long for a home and a family all your own? I do." Althea sighed dreamily.

"What, when I have all of you? You are more than enough for anyone." Alexandra quirked one delicate eyebrow. "Besides, I had as lief be alone as at the mercy of some man stupider than I, who, solely by virtue of being a man, would think of me as being his inferior no matter how dull-witted he might be."

"I should not care if I loved him." A delicate flush tinged Althea's softly rounded cheeks. "But you are very different from me, are you not?"

"Yes." It was Alex's turn to sigh. "I wish I had been Alexander's twin brother instead of his sister. Life would have been so much more exciting."

"And so much less comfortable," Althea retorted smiling. Though she could not understand them, she did sympathize with her sister's longings. Alex was too vital, too adventurous to be immured in the country taking care of her brothers and sisters, dwindling into an old maid—though no one as energetic as Alex could ever truly be an old maid.

She, Althea, was content to remain in Norfolk forever, overseeing household tasks and taking care of the children, though she did long for a house and children of her own and a husband who would love her and take her to assemblies now and then. But she knew this would never be enough for Alex. To be sure, Alex kept herself busy managing the estate, doing her best to keep them all fed and clothed, but the routine of sowing and reaping, and listening to tenants' complaints was not enough to keep her amused. Alex read voraciously and sought out intelligent conversation wherever she could find it—usually with either Doctor Padgett or the vicar—but it seemed such a waste somehow. Perhaps this mad scheme to save them from destitution would give her some chance to escape and live the life she longed for. However, Althea was still skeptical about the plan's success. There were so many risks, but Alex was nothing if not someone who loved a risk.

"But how will we go on when you're gone?" Althea wondered.

"Why, you will take care of that."

"I? But I don't know anything about running the estate."

"Don't be silly, Ally. You run most of the household already, and believe me, looking after Andrew and Abigail, which you do so well, is a far greater challenge than seeing that tenants are happy, the sheep are fed, and the field sowed," her sister responded wryly.

As if the mention of their names were enough to summon them, two bedraggled figures appeared in the morning room and made their way quickly over to the fire burning brightly in the grate.

"Abigail, Andrew, what on earth . . ." Althea raised her hand to her mouth in dismay.

"I'm truly sorry, Ally," Andrew began, "I know you told us to play indoors and we did . . ."

"But Andrew threw the ball to me too hard and it went out the nursery window so we raced each other to find it," his younger sister continued.

"However, it was hidden under the bushes beneath the nursery window and it took some searching before you were able to locate it," Alexandra concluded, eyeing the leaves tangled in Abby's golden curls and the mud liberally spattered on their clothes.

"Exactly." Andrew nodded, looking guiltily at Althea. "I know you told me I was to watch out for Abby, Ally, but she was down the stairs and out the door like a shot. I told her not to go out in the rain, but she wouldn't listen."

"Obviously." Althea surveyed the sodden pair ruefully. "Come along. We must get you out of these wet clothes or you'll catch your death of cold." She rose and grasping a grubby little hand firmly in each of her own, she hurried from the room, leaving her sister to continue working out her plans.

Alex gazed out at the leaden sky. Perhaps her sister was right. This time maybe she truly had lost her wits and was embarking on an adventure too outrageous even for her to handle. But what else was there to do? She could not let Alexander's stupidity and selfishness deprive Althea and the children of their home. Their brother Anthony, off with his regiment, was not as dependent as the rest, but he still needed some sort of home and enough money to keep him outfitted as befitted a captain in the First Guards.

Alex was so wrapped up in these disturbing reflections that she did not hear the door open, nor the butler's "A visitor to see you, my lady." When there was no response, Jamison began again, "Sir Ralph Cranbourne . . ."

"I'll announce myself," an impatient voice interrupted, and Sir Ralph Cranbourne strode into the room.

Alex remained seated, fixing her caller with a cool, unwelcoming gaze. She had always disliked Sir Ralph, with his sly smile and impertinent stare that made one feel as though he were trying to undress one or discover one's most private secrets, or both. His flamboyant dress—bottle green coat with enormous padded shoulders and wasp waist, lemon-colored pantaloons and hideously embroidered waistcoat—did nothing to improve the appearance of a man who would always remain short, squat, and ugly, no matter what his tailor did for him.

"You wished to speak to me, sir?" Alex's voice, if possible, was even colder and more distant than her expression.

"Yes I do, Lady Alexandra. I have a most delightful proposition to make." Sir Ralph smiled greedily at her as he pulled a chair next to hers and leaned toward her in the most familiar manner.

Alex's already rigid posture became even more pronounced. "Proceed."

"As you no doubt know, your brother has been most . . . er . . . unfortunate in some of his . . . ah . . . investments as of late. I, naturally wishing to help such a delightful young man, have done my best to extricate him from his financial difficulties, but even I, devoted friend that I am, have my limits. I must now collect the debt he owes me. Loathe as I am to do so, I am forced by some reverses of my own to ask that he repay this rather substantial sum." Sir Ralph reached into his pocket and pulled forth a tattered slip of paper. Dirty and wrinkled though it might be, there was no mistaking either the figure of one hundred thousand pounds or the signature of Alexander de Montmorency scrawled below it.

"However," Sir Ralph continued, licking his fleshy lips and leaning more closely toward Alex, "I should not like to be the cause of any distress to his family, particularly to such a charming lady as yourself, and I believe I have hit upon a way to solve all the difficulties."

Alex held her breath. She refused to do anything that appeared to respond in any way to this toad—not even breathe, much less betray curiosity of any kind.

"Yes." He grinned, rubbing his hands together. Alex could not help the wave of disgust that washed over her at the sight of the dark hair on the back of his fat knuckles. "I have come up with quite a delightful solution. I have promised Alexander to forget these pecuniary matters in return for your hand. He quite agrees with me that it is time you were wed, and I am a wealthy man."

Very carefully Alex let out the breath she had been holding. With an effort, she controlled the shudder of utter loathing that ran through her. "That is not in the least necessary. You shall have your money."

Sir Ralph edged his chair even closer. "Now where would a delightful young lady such as yourself find so much money?" His voice was silky, but underneath the smooth tone there was a hard edge.

He was so close that Alex could smell the brandy on his breath. Fighting nausea, she rose to her full height, noting with satisfaction as her caller also rose that she stood a good head taller than he. "The money need not concern you, sir. I shall have it for you in less than three months' time, you may be sure." Alex gave the bellpull a desperate tug.

Her visitor smirked, refusing to be beaten. "I like women with spirit. They are all the more delightful to tame."

It was all Alex could do not to tell the man how despicable, how utterly loathsome he was, but she would not allow herself to be drawn into any sort of exchange with him beyond what she would accord a perfect stranger. To acknowledge her abhorrence of him would be to admit that he had the power to affect her, and she would rather have died than do that.

"You rang, my lady?"

Alex could have hugged Jamison for responding so promptly. "Jamison, Sir Ralph is just going. Be so kind as to show him out." Alex turned her back on him and walked over to the windows to stare unseeingly out over the lawn, vainly trying to dispel the image of her visitor.

Sir Ralph was left with nothing to do but follow the butler out. As he left the room, he glanced over his shoulder, the look in his eyes so cold and implacable that even Alex had to repress a shudder. "I shall be back," he called as he walked down the hall, "and believe me, Lady Alexandra, you will be glad to see me."

"Never, you miserable insect," Alex muttered under her breath. "Never!"

Chapter 3

~

If Alex had been determined to go ahead with her scheme to save Halewood for her family before, she was even more so now that her freedom was at stake. If she failed to win back Alexander's money, she was certain to end up on the gallows—for she knew she was far more likely to murder Sir Ralph than to marry him. In fact, she might murder him anyway. The thought of watching that repulsive smile fade as she plunged a knife into him was exceedingly attractive at the moment. No, Alex, she admonished herself, think of the children. It would be most upsetting for them to have you hung, even for ridding the world of such a scoundrel as that. You must put your mind to more useful areas of endeavor.

Shaking her head vigorously to rid it of such satisfying fantasies and apply it to the problem at hand, she went off in search of Mrs. Throckmorton and Bessie to see what they could do about altering her brother's clothes to fit her.

She found them both in Alexander's room, where he was sleeping soundly—tossing less, but still breathing heavily and painfully, with an occasional rattle in his chest that did not bode well for the sick man. He did not even stir when Bessie wiped his brow with lavender water.

"I don't like it, my lady." The housekeeper shook her head. "He's breathing too heavylike and he's terrible feverish."

"I know." Alex sighed. "We are doing all that we can, but he was out in that dreadful weather for so long without even a greatcoat. However, I have come to ask your help about another matter."

Alex launched into a description of her brother's many disastrous encounters with the Goddess Chance. The housekeeper and maid gasped in horror when they heard the sums of money that had been whistled down the wind—more money than they knew anyone could possess.

"Oh, my lady, what is to become of us?" Bessie's voice quavered. Orphaned at an early age, she had been taken in by Alexandra's mother as a scullery maid at Halewood and the de Montmorencys were the only home and family she had ever known.

"You can help us all by taking the best possible care of Alexander," Alex smiled reassuringly. "I am afraid we are going to have to practice a slight deception on the world that will involve moving Alex to Mrs. Bates's cottage. I shall need for you to go with him and look after him. It will be rather isolated, I am afraid, but you may take one of the dogs for company. Doctor Padgett will call every day and Mrs. Throckmorton will come occasionally, though we do not want to raise any comment. The rest of the world will think you have gone to Brighton with me to visit Great Aunt Belinda. I shall give you whatever books you wish to read so you do not become too bored. Can you manage that?"

"Oh yes, my lady." In truth, Bessie would have thrown her body in the nearby fens if Lady Alexandra had asked her to, so devoted was she. After the Countess of Halewood had died, Alex, noticing the lost look in the little maid's eyes, had begun to pay attention to her, encouraging her to think of a life beyond the scullery. She had assigned her to one of the under housemaids so the girl could learn enough to advance her position. Noticing how quick Bessie was and how eager to absorb new things, Alex, who was suffering from the boredom of an isolated existence herself, had hit upon the happy notion of teaching the girl to read.

Bessie had been an earnest pupil who picked it all up with the most satisfying speed—so much so that at Alex's suggestion she was now reading to the other servants each evening. Her gratitude toward Lady Alexandra knew no bounds, and she had thought that life could hold no more until Alex had asked her to be her personal maid. The girl had almost expired with joy at being so honored and had been so determined to repay her mistress's kindness that Alex was forever telling her laughingly, "Relax, Bessie, or you will make a helpless idiot out of me. I must do some things for myself or I shall surely die of boredom."

Now the mistress was asking for her to do something truly important and vital to the household where she had been so happy. Bessie's plain face glowed with pleasure and she vowed to carry out her task to perfection or die in the attempt. Then a disturbing thought hit her as she recalled Alex's words. "But however will you go to Brighton alone?"

"I shan't. I shall be going to London and I shall have Ned Coachmen with me, so you see, I shall be perfectly safe."

"London!" The housekeeper and the maid gasped in unison. None of the de Montmorencys, with the exception of Alexander's short-lived career at Oxford before he had been sent down, had traveled further than Norwich, not since Alexandra's father had won Halewood at the gaming table and brought his young bride to settle into a quiet life in rural Norfolk. Even Alexander, rackety though he was, never ventured more than fifty miles from home, preferring to throw away his blunt at local race meetings and gaming tables. In fact, he was quite often heard to say that so much time spent traveling to the metropolis was so much time wasted away from those gaming tables.

"London," Bessie reiterated, "but whatever for?" Mrs. Throckmorton, who was thankful that Bessie's role as Alex's personal servant allowed her to pose questions that her dignity as housekeeper prevented her from asking, awaited her mistress's reply as eagerly as the maid.

"Well, someone must do something to raise such a sum. After all, Papa won this estate at the gaming table. It must be possible to win it back the same way. Towards the end before he died I began to beat him regularly, so I ought to be able to succeed as well as he." The determined note in her voice warned the others that it was useless to remonstrate. Indeed, as Mrs. Throckmorton recalled the many times she had seen just that resolute set to Miss Alexandra's jaw—riding her father's hunter at a tender age, daring Alexander to swim in the lake, rescuing a litter of baby rabbits—she knew that nothing would stop her from accomplishing what she had set out to do.

"But ladies don't gamble, leastways not the way men do," Bessie protested, still unconvinced.

"Ah, but I shan't be a lady. I shall be Alexander de Montmorency, Earl of Halewood," Alex replied reassuringly.

Somehow this failed to comfort her henchwomen, who stared at her in horror. "Come now, do not look so dismayed. Alexander is not known in London and I feel confident enough of my ability to pass myself off as him even in Norwich. All I need is the proper attire and *voilà*!" Alex strode around the room in a perfect imitation of her brother's walk, right down to his air of braggadocio. Then, slumping over, she continued, "Why, I can even be Alexander as we more frequently see him." She swayed perilously, glancing blearily about her as the earl did when he was castaway.

Her audience looked only slightly less anxious after this compelling performance. "Do not worry so," their mistress comforted them. "No one will have the least reason to suspect in the first place that I am not Alexander, and wearing his clothes, padded at the shoulders, I shall be Alexander de Montmorency, Earl of Halewood and hardened gamester." Alex straightened as tall as she could, tilted her head, and leered at them so rakishly that even Mrs. Throckmorton could not suppress a smile.

"But your hair, my lady," Bessie wailed.

"Will have to be cut." Alex dismissed the thick auburn tresses as cavalierly as though they were not her chief glory.

"Oh no!" The maid gasped.

"What is vanity when our livelihood is at stake," Alex exclaimed airily. "Besides, there is no one to admire them anyway and everyone at Halewood can just remember what they used to look like."

More was the pity, the maid thought to herself. It was a crying shame that a lady as striking as her mistress was kept buried in the country when by rights she should have been in London in her own clothes, winning admiration, instead of dressed in her brother's clothes trying to retrieve the money he had lost. While it was true that Lady Alexandra was not what was ordinarily considered beautiful, her attractions being quite out of the common way, she was arresting with her masses of auburn hair, her sea green eyes, and her tall, elegant figure.

Bessie wished her mistress would find a gentleman who would rescue her from the humdrum life at Halewood and take her places where she would have a chance to talk to people about all the many things that interested her, where she would hear the concerts and see the plays she read about in the *Times*. But who was there who could possibly do such a thing?

The gentry around Halewood were not so very different from Alexander, what with their hunting and drinking, though they did not gamble to the extent he did. The only two men clever enough for her mistress were Doctor Padgett, who was too old, and the vicar, who was too mousy. To be sure, whenever either one of them wished for intelligent conversation he would trump up some transparent excuse and ride over to visit Lady Alexandra, but intelligent conversation was all they had to offer and someone like her mistress needed more in a man—much more.

At last a longtime prayer of Bessie's now was being answered, or at least partially so. Her mistress *was* going to London. Unfortunately she was going as a man. Bessie sighed and looked over at the housekeeper, who was also shaking her head. The two exchanged commiserating glances and resigned themselves to the inevitable.

Chapter 4

~

The other person who remained to be convinced in order to insure the success of Alexandra's scheme was the doctor himself. Trevor Padgett presented a far more formidable opponent to such a harebrained idea than either of the two women and he did not bother to mince words, informing Alexandra precisely what he thought of her notion the next day when he came to look in on his patient. "I realize that you have never been the least bit cautious in your entire life, Alexandra. Times out of mind I have known you to court the most ridiculous risk—in fact, one could safely say that despite your quiet existence you always manage to tempt fate in one way or another. But this goes beyond anything you have dreamt up before. Even *you* could not do such a buffle-headed thing."

Alex smiled sweetly at him as she had done so many times before when he had been called upon to remedy the consequences of some outrageous act—the broken arm, a sprained ankle caused by a stranded kitten on a weak branch, the dislocated shoulder which had ensued as she wrested a whip from a vicious tinker—oh yes, Doctor Padgett knew that smile. Apologetic it might be, but there was not a hint of capitulation in it. Like Bessie and Mrs. Throckmorton before him, he sighed and gave himself up to the inevitable. "Very well. You might as well outline what my role is to be in this ridiculous escapade."

"Thank you, Doctor. I know that this is a more serious endeavor than anything I have taken on before, but I truly do not know what else to do and I will not let Althea and the children suffer from Alexander's monumental stupidity and selfishness. If it were just for myself, I should never do such a thing, but . . ."

"Your generous impulses will be the death of you, you know, Alexandra." The doctor shook his head gravely, but he could not help smiling.

Devoted as he was to his work, he had had no time for love and marriage. The family at Halewood had been the only one he had allowed himself to have, and Alexandra, spunky and intelligent, shouldering responsibilities that were far too much for one so young, was his favorite. When the old Earl of Halewood had died, the doctor had done his best to be there for her if she needed it. He would have gladly taken over some of her burdens but she would never accept help, no matter how frequently it was offered. In fact the only weakness she had allowed herself was to confide in him her worries about the dangerously reckless existence Alexander was pursuing. Even then she had not let him assist her in any tangible way, merely thanking him for allowing her to unburden herself every once in a while.

Trevor Padgett shook his head again. "I await your instructions, which I am sure you must have thought out long ago."

Alex had the grace to grin sheepishly. "Well, yes. I was hoping that you would oversee the transportation of Alexander to Mrs. Bates's cottage. No one has gone near there since she died. She was such a tidy housekeeper that it is in excellent condition. I shall send Bessie and Mrs. Throckmorton to air it out and prepare it for Alexander. Bessie has said she will stay with him and we shall give it out that she has accompanied me to visit Great Aunt Belinda in Brighton."

"And why do you not go to visit Great Aunt Belinda in Brighton? Ask her for some assistance instead of throwing yourself into a ridiculous escapade which has far more likelihood of ruining you than of repairing the family finances," the doctor said. Heretofore he had never heard of any relative to whom Alexandra could apply for help of any kind and he seized upon this one eagerly.

"Because for all I know, Great Aunt Belinda never existed, and if she had, I am sure she has been dead this age. Papa only spoke of her occasionally as the only one in the family who would have anything to do with him after his family disowned him."

The doctor frowned. "I still think you should apply to your father's relatives. Surely a family as rich and powerful as his could spare something to save one of its branches from ruin?"

"His family?" Alex's voice was dangerously quiet. "I would rather die than have anything to do with a family that was so desperate to punish Papa that they even broke the entail to deprive him of his birthright. They would never have anything to do with him and they certainly would have nothing to do with us now. Papa would turn over in his grave at the very thought of such a notion. Why, he even took one of the more obscure titles so that he would not appear to be connected with them."

She was her father's daughter, the doctor thought irrelevantly to himself. Standing there, her green eyes blazing, shoulders squared, she did look remarkably like the old earl—as charming a man as one could hope to meet, slow to anger, but the very devil when roused. Alex was as fiercely proud as he had been. However, the doctor would not have counted himself a true friend unless he tried his best to dissuade her from something that could be as dangerous to her person as to her reputation. He girded himself for one last attempt, though he knew it would be useless.

"His family might not have wished to recognize your father as one of them any longer or to offer assistance of any kind to him, but I wager they would give a good deal to keep the name of even a minor branch of the family from being bruited about the *ton* in the manner you propose."

Alexandra's eyes flashed. "I would never stoop to such a stratagem, nor would I lift my little finger to keep their precious name from being smirched! How could you even suggest such a thing?"

The doctor smiled ruefully. She had grown up into a capable, independent young woman, more than able to act as head of the family and direct the running of the estate, but underneath she was still the same little spitfire who had confronted the rascally tinker and who had demanded a horse instead of a pony for her first riding lesson.

"Forgive me, Alexandra," he apologized, "but I had not the least intention of insulting you. However, as the only person in your life who dares offer you advice, I had to make an attempt to stop you. I know it will not do the least bit of good, but I could not live with myself if I had not at least tried. Yes, I shall make certain that Alexander is safely conveyed to Mrs. Bates's cottage, that he is cared for, and that the rest of the countryside believes he has gone to London and you to Brighton. We shall have to move him immediately and conceal the carriage for a while so that it appears he has taken it and then sent it back for your journey."

Alex was mollified by his reluctant though genuine desire to see her through in her plan, and in all fairness, she could not blame him for trying to stop her. After all, lying wide awake in bed the past several nights, even she had begun to doubt her ability to carry it all off.

While it was true that she had never been one to refuse a challenge, she had also never been foolhardy, and there were more than a few moments when she had begun to see the entire idea in just that light. However, it could not be helped. There was no other means of raising the money. Even if they were to strip the house and sell off all the paintings and furnishings, she very much doubted they could raise such a sum in so little time. Besides, then where would they be—living in an empty shell of a house? Desperation could make even as crazy a scheme as hers seem the very essence of practicality.

Watching her closely, the doctor sensed some of the conflict that was raging within her and laid a comforting hand on her shoulder. "Never you mind, Alexandra. I shall see to it that they all muddle along in your absence. If Alexander should improve, which I very much doubt, I shall tie him to the bed so that he cannot make any more trouble for all of you. Never fear, you will do magnificently, as you always do."

Alex smiled gratefully up at him, laying her hand on his. "Thank you. You have always been such a good and true friend to us all. I do not know what I would have done without you."

"You would have been desperate enough for company that you would have gone looking for someone who could offer you true companionship instead of a few paltry moments of useless advice in between patients," he muttered gruffly, avoiding her gaze. Those clear green eyes fixed on him saw entirely too much sometimes, and it would never do for her to know how very much she and the children meant to him. It would ruin her confidence in the objectivity of his opinions if she knew how much he doted on them, how he longed to be a rich man so he could truly smooth away all her cares instead of just sympathizing with them.

"Well, having done my best to encourage you to behave in a rational manner and having met with your usual stubbornness, I can depart with a clear conscience knowing that nothing I can do or say further will persuade you." He shook his head and made his way to the door. "However"—he turned to grin impishly at her—"I shall do my utmost to insure that this mad scheme of yours is no more risky than it need be, and I will keep a jailer's eye on everyone in Mrs. Bates's cottage."

"Doctor Padgett?" He paused, his hand on the doorknob. "Do you think Alexander will pose a problem?" Alex asked. For the first time during his visit she looked unsure of herself. Some of the bravado had slipped away and he saw the worry in her eyes and heard it in her voice. "That is, I mean . . . do you think he will recover?"

Here was a dilemma. The doctor did not wish to upset her any further, nor did he wish to offer her false hope. Alexandra was not the sort of person to thank him for wrapping up an un- pleasant truth in clean linen. He himself was not so sure that they would not be better off without Alexander de Mont- morency, who had done nothing for any of them in the past several years except bring them worry and heartache, not to mention leading them to the brink of disaster. "No," he an- swered slowly, "I do not expect him to recover. He has abused his good health too much. His body does not have the reserves to cope with this last piece of stupidity. But I shall do my very best to keep him alive until you return. That I will promise you."

Alex smiled at him gratefully. "I appreciate all you are try- ing to do for us, all you have always tried to do. Whatever the outcome, we owe you the utmost gratitude for your skill and"—she tilted her head, a teasing gleam in her eyes—"for your advice, even though it is not heeded." Then becoming se- rious again, she continued quietly, "I rather wonder if it would not be better for us if Alexander did not recover. If he does, he will only bring us to ruin again no matter how much he promises to mend his ways."

She shook her head in bewilderment. "I do not know what happened. He used to be the most adventurous, the gayest and best of companions. One could always count on him to stick with one through anything, but something changed when he went to university. After he was sent down, he became reckless instead of adventurous, and without a thought for anything but his own amusement. I hardly knew him anymore and we had been the closest of friends before he went away," she concluded sadly.

That is because you were the best of the pair, the doctor thought to himself. He knew that in truth it had been Alexandra's restless curiosity that had spurred them on in their exploits. It had been her quick mind that had extricated them from most of their difficulties, just as it had been her sense of responsibility that had kept them from doing anything truly destructive. It was she who had been the leader of the two. When Alexander went away long enough to recognize that, he had resented it mightily. Alexander had not really changed. He had always been a heedless lad with no thought for anyone but himself. It was only when he returned and eschewed the companionship and steadying influence of his twin that his monumental selfishness became so evident.

The doctor's heart ached for Alexandra as she stood there, the light from the great leaded windows pouring in around her and beyond, just barely visible through them, the lovely old park she was trying so desperately to save. As quickly as he felt it, he banished the emotion. Repining would get none of them anywhere. Alexandra did not need sympathy from him—she needed help. And she would get it. With a brusque, "Good day," the doctor pulled open the door and hurried out to his waiting carriage, leaving Alex to gaze pensively after him.

Doctor Padgett had been such a good friend to them all. No, he had been more than a friend—almost a father to them after their own father had died, though it was a different sort of fatherliness he had offered. Where the old earl had been ebullient, romping endlessly with Abigail and Andrew, teasing Althea, playing cards with Alex, and riding hell-for-leather across the fields with his oldest son, the doctor had been undemonstrative—almost gruff. But they had known, as children somehow do, that he was fond of them all. While their father had lavished them with presents, Doctor Padgett had listened to their childish troubles, paying as much attention to them and offering advice as seriously as if they had been the most important of his patients.

To Alexandra, he had given the greatest gift—that of encouraging her education. The old earl, though a product of Oxford, had spent the bulk of his time educating himself in games of chance, only availing himself infrequently of any opportunities for informing his mind. Nor, settled happily into the life of a country gentleman, did he see the slightest need for anyone—especially a woman—to learn anything beyond the most rudimentary elements of history, grammar, and mathematics.

The doctor, catching Alexandra one day poring over books left by the estate's previous owner, had recognized a mind which thirsted for knowledge. Being a self-sufficient sort, she had done remarkably well at educating herself. Her gratitude at his explanation of a challenging mathematical equation had led him to suggest that perhaps she might like the vicar to help her with her studies. The look of delight which had illumined the girl's face had sent him straight off to broach the subject with her father.

Though uninterested himself in exploring the rarified realms of intellectual pursuit, the earl had no objection to his daughter's visiting them if she pleased. Thus had begun one of the most pleasurable parts of young Alexandra's life. She was an apt pupil and it had not been too many years before she and the vicar had become fellow travelers in their quest for knowledge rather than master and student.

Alex smiled at the memory of the doctor, holding her small hand firmly in his, bearding her father in his account room. "Alfred, I want you to see that this child is given the education she deserves. I suggest you send for Theodosius right now and see what he can do for her."

Her father had merely smiled benignly at his friend's forcefulness and replied mildly, "Very well, Trevor—that is, if Alex herself agrees to it."

She had been almost too excited to stammer her response. "Oh yes, Papa, if you please, Papa."

And ever since then, the doctor had done his best to make sure that she had everything she needed, battling as pugnaciously and tenaciously as a terrier for her happiness. Indeed, with his beetling dark brows and square jaw, not to mention his fierce loyalty, he did rather resemble a terrier himself. Certainly no dog could have been as devoted to her as he had been for so many years. The very least she could do to repay his kindness and concern was to listen to his advice, even if she did not heed it. The best she could do in this case was to resolve to be as discreet as she could be—if such a thing were possible in the escapade such as she was planning.

Chapter 5

∽

Over the next few days, Alexandra was caught in a flurry of activity and planning, for reliable and devoted as Bessie, Mrs. Throckmorton, and Althea were, there was much to be done, a great many details to be attended to, and all of it with as much secrecy as possible. Alexander was the first and foremost concern, it being imperative that he be moved as quickly and with as little disturbance as possible before he became worse.

Doctor Padgett had left instructions as to how best to transport him most comfortably to Mrs. Bates's cottage and they waited for a moment when he had passed from delirium into exhausted docility before dressing him and carrying him down the entrance hall. From there it was only a few steps to the carriage, the stalwart Ned assisting Alexander's passage in a manner that made it appear to anyone who cared to observe that, despite his being completely castaway, the earl was embarking on a considerable journey.

Later, Bessie made her way surreptitiously to the cottage where Ned had made his master as comfortable as possible. The doctor, stopping to call on Alex after checking in on her brother, was able to report that at least that part of her plan had progressed satisfactorily. The earl was none the worse for his journey, though he was certainly not improved. He remained feverish and restless, tossing and turning, so little aware of his surroundings that it was doubtful he was even conscious of the fact that he was no longer in his own bed at Halewood.

In the meantime, deprived of the invaluable Bessie, Alexandra was forced to rely on Mrs. Throckmorton and Althea to help her prepare for her transformation into the earl. They worked night and day to alter her brother's clothes to fit her, taking them in at the waist, adding padding to the shoulders, and providing a critical audience as she perfected her imitation of Alexander's swagger and strove to pitch her voice to match his. Hers was rather low for a lady, though considerably gentler and more modulated than her brother's, but it took a good deal of practice to get it to her satisfaction. "However, as he is foxed a good deal of the time, all I really need do in order to offer a reasonable approximation of his speech is to mumble and sprinkle it liberally with *damns* and no one will be the wiser," Alex remarked as the three of them sat sewing in the upstairs sitting room, which offered the best light during most of the day.

Althea sighed and laid down the shirt she was stitching. "I do wish you would reconsider, Alexandra, for clever as you are, I do not see how you will be able to pass yourself off as Alexander for such a considerable length of time."

"Never fear," her sister reassured her. "I shall be accompanied by Tony, whom I mean to let do most of the talking. I shall confine myself to the gaming tables; contriving to appear as castaway as possible, which should serve me in well. I shan't be paid close enough attention to put my disguise to a complete test, and I shall not strike anyone as being an opponent worthy of serious consideration."

"But it is all so"—Althea searched in vain for the proper words to express her discomfort with the entire scheme—"so very unladylike. I do not mean to be ungrateful, as you know, Alex, but . . ."

Alex chuckled. "Such a concern would weigh a good deal more with me if I had ever been ladylike in the first place. Now that I have the opportunity to enjoy a masculine existence, I fully intend to do so."

Althea shook her head. "I must say I do not understand you in the least. Why would anyone wish to be a man? Men have to do all the difficult things in life: provide for and protect their wives and children, hunt, go into politics, become soldiers. They cannot have babies or wear lovely clothes or . . ."

Her sister laughed. "That is one way of looking at it, I suppose. But what freedom they have! They can be anything they

wish to be while we, poor creatures, are considered to be fit
only for drawing rooms and tea parties, with no greater ambi-
tion than to be wives and mothers. I know, Ally, dear, that to
you that is the most anyone, male or female, could ask of life,
but I, for one, should like the chance to go into politics or off
to defend my country. Furthermore, a man can go anywhere he
chooses, whenever he chooses. If I even venture into Norwich
without a maid or, at the very least a groom, my reputation is
likely to be shattered. Take Alexander, for example. He has
caroused about the countryside this age, causing no more comment than the odd remark that the young earl is a wild one indeed. I, on the other hand, remain quietly at home and am
considered not a little odd because I do not waste my time
haunting the shops in Norwich in search of gewgaws, or grac-
ing the assemblies—in short, doing all the things that would
procure me a husband and turn me into a respectable person."

Althea sat silent, a thoughtful expression on her face. What
her sister said was true. The gossips in the surrounding countryside were far more likely to comment on her sister's determined spinsterhood than on her brother's reckless disregard
for his person or the family fortunes. Why, not a week ago
Althea had encountered Lady Meacham and her daughters in
the village on one of their never-ending quests for just the
right trimmings for their bonnets. They had inquired most po-
litely after her sister, but Althea had not missed the sly, supe-
rior smile of Susanna, the youngest and prettiest of the
Meachams, who had remarked that it was a great deal too bad
to have missed Lady Alexandra at the latest assembly, but obviously Lady Alexandra had no need of such amusements. The
deceptively sweet tone of commiseration had not been lost on
Althea, who had no trouble in interpreting its implication that
she was unfortunate to be related to someone who was odd
enough to run the risk of becoming an ape-leader.

Though she herself adored the dancing and the sight of
lovely gowns and men in evening attire, Althea did understand
her sister's objection to the petty gossip and tedious conversation to be found at such affairs. She had thought it terribly unfair that Alexandra was thus stigmatized simply for following
her own taste for good company and rational discourse.

Althea had not missed the occasional whispered comment

that it was a sad shame that Lady Alexandra seemed unable to find a husband. She knew how such an attitude on the part of many of their female neighbors must rankle with her sister, who looked to so many things other than marriage for her enjoyment and sense of purpose in life. It was no wonder that Alex found her female status confining, but masquerading as a man? Althea sighed, snipped the thread, and folded the shirt she had just taken in. "Let us hope that no one sees through your disguise and deprives you of your freedom and your reputation."

"Reputation?" Alex snorted. "I do not give a rap for my reputation. Spotless reputations are only of value to women who wish to sell themselves on the marriage market. As I have no intention of doing so, I may acquire the very blackest of reputations with a clear conscience." However, Alex's bravado was not entirely genuine. The risk she was taking was a real one. Anyone finding her out might take advantage of more than her good name, and though her brother Anthony had taught her a good deal of the soldierly arts, she was not at all sure, given a truly determined assault on her person, how capable she was of defending herself, but she would rather have died than let on in any way that she suffered the slightest of qualms.

The ensuing days were so filled with preparation that Alex had no time for second thoughts. There were tenants to be visited and instructions to be left with Mrs. Throckmorton and Jamison, fields to be surveyed one more time to see that all was progressing and that the men were left knowing what they were supposed to do.

Finally, after what was deemed a long enough time for the earl to have journeyed to London and returned the traveling carriage for his sister's use, she had it brought around from Mrs. Bates's cottage via the London road. Bessie, relieved for a moment from her nursing duties by Doctor Padgett, had climbed in with her mistress in order to be seen leaving with her on her supposed journey to Brighton. Laden with trunks and bandboxes, they had rolled down the gravel drive waving good-bye to the forlorn little group on the steps.

Althea, Andrew, and Abigail had done their best to don reassuringly cheerful smiles, but they had been loath to see her go. "Who will take care of us," Abigail had demanded when informed of her eldest sister's departure.

"Why Ally of course. She always reads to you before bed and looks after you when Nurse is busy." Alex turned to smile at her brother. "And I count on you, Andrew, to help keep Abby from falling into any serious scrapes."

Andrew straightened, determined to show he was more than a match for the task entrusted to him. Then, struck by a singularly felicitous thought, he inquired hopefully, "Without you, shall we have no lessons?"

Alex laughed. "It would appear so."

"Horray! Horray!" Both children skipped about in glee as their two sisters exchanged rueful glances.

"However, I could ask the vicar to take my place as Andrew should be under the tutelage of someone else before he goes to school." Alex nodded thoughtfully. "Now would be an excellent time, I think."

Andrew's face fell, then, catching the look that passed between his sisters and the distinct twinkle in the eldest's eyes, he brightened considerably. "You're bamming, Alex, aren't you?" he inquired hopefully.

"Well, it would be a good idea, dear, for you to have to say your lessons to someone other than a family member, for when you go to school you will be dealing with perfect strangers. But yes, I was teasing. I am counting on all of you to help Ally keep things in order while I am gone and lessons would only make your jobs more difficult." She smiled reassuringly, hoping that the promise of no lessons was enough recompense for what must seem to them to be desertion on her part.

They still looked a bit woebegone despite her assurance that she would be back soon, but each and every one of them was determined not to let her down. In fact, Alex was feeling just the slightest bit woebegone herself. Much as she chafed against her humdrum existence, and much as she told Althea that she craved adventure, she was not at all sure how much that was true now that she was actually about to encounter it.

After all, she had never been farther than Norwich in her entire life. She had never slept a night out of her own bed, and had never been without her family for more than a day. She loved them all dearly and would miss them as much, or perhaps more, than they would miss her. They would soon settle back into their daily routine while she would be moving entirely among strangers. It was a rather daunting prospect. Don't be a ninny, Alexandra, she scolded herself. If you do not go off and do this, then we shall all be cast out among strangers.

Strengthened by this thought as well as the memory of the sly smile that had spread over Sir Ralph's repulsive features when he had observed her distaste for her brother's matrimonial arrangements, she straightened her shoulders against the squabs of the carriage seat and resolutely pushed all doubts from her mind.

They stopped first at Mrs. Bates's cottage long enough for Alexandra to change into her brother's clothes and to have her long auburn curls clipped by a tearful Bessie.

"I know 'tis the only way, my lady, but oh, your beautiful hair!" The maid had moaned in distress as one thick lock after another fell to the floor.

"There is naught else to be done. I hope that I am not such a vain creature that I cannot survive the loss of a bit of hair," Alex responded in a rallying tone. She refused to admit, even to herself, that each snip of the scissors was depriving her of something of which she had secretly been rather proud. Alex had known she was not the beauty her mother had been, nor had she aspired to be. Although the masses of dark red hair had been rather distinctive, her head did feel a good deal lighter now, and the curls that now brushed against her ears made her feel delightfully airy and free after the weight of the severe coils, which had been wound smoothly at the back of her head.

Cautiously she peeked into the looking glass that Bessie held up for her inspection. Much to her surprise, Alex rather liked what she saw. The curls gave her a slightly raffish air that softened the effect of her aquiline nose and determined chin, making her appear younger and less serious. More reassuringly, she was the image of her twin, or at least a younger, healthier, less dissipated Earl of Halewood than the one who lay delirious in the bedchamber at the back of the cottage.

Emerging from that very bedchamber and catching sight of the false earl, Doctor Padgett marveled that Alex was the image of what her twin had been, and was struck again by the unfortunate effects a ruinous life had had on his patient's health, which, as he unhappily informed Alex, was not the least improved. "I very much fear that no matter what remedies I try, and despite any experience or skill I may have gained over the years, I can do very little for him." The doctor shook his head sadly.

"I know." Alex waved aside his apologies. "He has brought it all on himself, and now on us. I just hope you will not have to bury him before I return from London, which you may be sure I shall do as quickly as possible.

"But now"—she swaggered forward clapping a beaver at a rakish angle on her auburn curls—"do I not look my part?" She paused, hand on her hip, one leg thrust forward, a challenging sparkle in her eyes.

Loath as he was to give what seemed like any sort of sanction to this dangerous escapade, the doctor was forced to admit that aside from her brother's family, only Alexander's closest companions might have noticed the difference. As they were foxed more often than not, there seemed very little likelihood of anyone's penetrating her disguise. He shook his head, smiling ruefully. "You are the very picture of your brother before he turned to gaming and drink. See that you do not follow in his footsteps, my fine young man." He wagged a stern finger at her, but his eyes were twinkling. "Now off with you so you may reach Cambridge by nightfall."

Alex laughed and turned toward the open door of the cottage through which she could see the carriage waiting patiently. Now that she was actually on her way, she was forced to admit that she was assailed by doubts, not the least of which was leaving such good friends and protectors as Bessie and the doctor behind. All of them in their own ways had dedicated much of their lives and themselves to making her existence easier. Not only would she miss their advice and support, she would miss the sense of having people who cared as much about her welfare as these two did.

Hurriedly blinking back unexpected tears, she shook hands with the doctor, gave the equally tearful Bessie a quick hug, and hurried out, forestalling Ned, who had secured the reins and hurried to help her into the carriage. "Now, Ned, none of that. If this venture is to be a success, you must begin to think of me as a great strapping man and not the tiresome young lady you threw on her first horse."

"Yes, er, *my lord*, very good, *my lord*." With a diligent frown Ned laid heavy emphasis on the words as he climbed back on the box and took the reins. Lady Alexandra was a clever one all right—touched in the upper story, what with going through with this scheme of hers—but obviously keeping her wits about her by making sure of such tiny details. Perhaps, just perhaps, she might succeed. He fervently hoped so. Ned was devoted to Lady Alex, as he had been to her father before her, and he had no intention of serving anyone else, God be willing. If Ned had had his way, he would have had that useless brother of hers horsewhipped for putting their future in such jeopardy. Failing that, the least he could do was crack the whip over the leaders and set them on the road to London and the recovery of their fortunes.

Chapter 6

〜

Exhausted after the emotional turmoil of the past weeks, the sleepless nights spent planning her course of action, the hours of practice dedicated to capturing Alexander's mannerisms to perfection, Alexandra ought to have relaxed against the cushions of the carriage with a sigh of relief that the first part of her scheme had been successfully carried out, but she was far too excited by the prospect of what lay ahead to do such a thing.

There was so much that was unknown awaiting her in London, so much risk involved that she could hardly envision what to expect. Being of a practical nature, she tried to put vain speculations and worries out of her mind in order to calm down and clear her thoughts for the challenges to come. No matter how much she told herself to lie back and get a moment of repose, she could not. The idea of leaving behind the all-too familiar lanes and cottages and journeying into countryside that was completely foreign to her was far too intriguing to miss the least little bit of the trip by something so mundane as resting. Even while they were traveling roads she knew as well as Halewood's own graveled drive, she sat on the edge of her seat, observing it all again with the new perspective of someone who was leaving it all behind.

Would she soon long for the sight of neatly tended cottages among the great houses of London? Or would the countryside in her special part of Norfolk come to seem endless and boring in the extreme after the constant activity and the magnificent edifices of the metropolis?

After what seemed an age, Alex was rewarded by a gradual

change in the scenery as the treeless fens and vast stretches of fields gave way to the more solid ground and gentle undulations of Cambridgeshire. Thatched roofed cottages were replaced by tile and slate and she leaned forward eagerly to absorb each new detail. How lucky men were that they might hop in a carriage or mount a horse without much ado, unencumbered by the need for companions to maintain the spotlessness of their reputations, and see all these new things, even if it were merely to observe the tiny differences in geography between one county and another.

At last they arrived in Cambridge, but the hour was so advanced that Alex was unable to see much beyond the crowded streets. Ned, having conferred with other neighboring coachmen before they left, had been assured of excellent accommodations to be had for both man and beast at the Rose and Crown in Market Square. Before she knew it, Alexandra was being ushered into a private parlor by a most gracious host. She was assured that the punch soon to be sent up would be much to her liking and that the missus was known for being an excellent cook of anything that his lordship could possibly desire.

Alex thanked him, wondering how on earth she could dispose of the punch he seemed determined to press on her. She ordered a fowl, simply dressed, for her supper, but in truth, she was far too excited to eat more than a few bites. Accustomed to practicing the strictest economies because of her brother's ruinous propensities, she wrapped up the remainder of the generous meal in the hopes that it would sustain her and Ned and save them the expense of having to order another meal on the road.

As for the punch, after a tentative taste, which quite burned her throat and stung her eyes with the strength of its fumes, she waited until all was silent in the innyard and quietly poured it out of the window. To be sure, it was a most effective way to preserve both her manly reputation and her clear head, but it also brought to mind the difficulties she was likely to encounter among the choice spirits at White's. How was she to keep from consuming voluminous quantities of port without arousing comment?

Alex shook her head. As with so many things, she would

have to deal with these problems when they arose. She would just have to cope with life in much the manner her father had taught her to play cards; looking at each hand as she was dealt it while remaining calm and collected, allowing her mind to stay clear and her face impassive, and emptying her thoughts of needless anxieties and speculation, concentrating instead on extracting the most advantage from any given situation. "You will always do well, Alexandra," the old Earl of Halewood had told her one evening not long before he had died, "to look at the distribution of the cards while the others are worrying about how much money they will win or lose. Remain unaffected by such emotions and you will always come away a winner—maybe not a big winner, but a steady one, and that is what counts. I eventually learned to do that and it is that attitude that brought me Halewood and all of you."

It was the memory of the warm smile and utter confidence accompanying those words that was sustaining Alex now. She settled into the soft pillows, so welcoming after the hours spent jolting over the country roads. Ned had assured her that the turnpikes would be better as they got closer to London and she admitted ruefully that she was looking forward to it. For the moment, though, she was enjoying the luxury of being able to stretch out her weary limbs.

Alex awoke early the next morning. Even had it not been her custom to rise at daybreak, the noise in the innyard would have made it impossible to sleep. She had never heard such a racket—ostlers shouting, horses stomping, and wagons and carriages lumbering in and out. She thought regretfully of the bird songs which usually awakened her at home and realized that it was going to be some time before she could enjoy such quiet again.

Still, all the activity and the prospect of the continued journey were exciting and Alex was more than ready for the breakfast the chambermaid brought up for her. She bolted it eagerly and hurried to the yard where Ned, having paid the shot, was waiting for her. "Good morning," she greeted him as she climbed into the carriage.

"And a good morning to you, my *lord*," he greeted her carefully. Though Lady Alexandra looked the spitting image of her brother, her eager observant air and attention to those around

her was all her own. It was going to be difficult to think of her
as anything but his mistress, who commanded all the love and
respect that he, Ned Brimblecombe, would never accord to
that loose fish of a brother of hers. He climbed onto the box,
grabbed the reins from the lad who had been holding them,
and they were off, rattling through the streets of Cambridge
past black-gowned students burdened under piles of books,
laughing and teasing each other as they hurried off to meet
with their masters.

Peering eagerly out of the carriage, Alex could not help
thinking what a delightful life theirs looked to be with nothing
to do but study and pass their time among scholars. How
Alexander had detested university life and how she would
have loved it! But there was no time for reflection. Soon the
cloisters and colleges of the city were behind them and the
gently rolling countryside surrounded them once more.

It was again late in the day when they reached London at
last. As they reached the crest of Highgate Hill, Alex could see
the glow of the great city laid out below her. It seemed as
though she had but a moment to catch her breath at the sight of
the vast metropolis before they were immersed in a maze of
streets that were filled with more shops and more people than
she had ever imagined.

How Ned made his way through the press of traffic, she
could not fathom, but at last they drew up in front of the
Clarendon. It was an elegant hotel and a trifle dear. Alex,
though willing to play the part of a riotous lord, had chosen it
despite the expense because she was not ready for the rough
and tumble of a place such as Limmer's, and she felt certain
that someone of Alexander's stamp would be out of place
among the clerical clientele at Ibbotson's. Besides, she was
unsure of where she would be dining, and it seemed best to
choose an hotel where she could procure a good meal, though
news of the shocking price of the Clarendon's meals had even
reached places as far away as Norfolk.

She was soon settled in the first style of luxury. The thought
of the price did give her some pause, but there was nothing for
it. One must incur some expense to make a fortune, she told
herself. After all, no one is going to gamble high stakes against
someone whose pockets do not appear to be well lined.

Having eaten a supper that fulfilled all the promise of the Clarendon's reputation for fine French cooking, Alex dispatched a note to her brother Anthony at the Guards' quarters in Portman Square. She then fell into bed where, despite her exhaustion, she tossed uneasily, her mind too full of plans and too distracted by the unaccustomed noise outside to fall into the oblivion she so desperately needed.

It was thus with great surprise that she was awakened by the clanking of andirons when the chambermaid came to lay the fire the next morning. Apparently she had slept better than she had thought.

Alex was just finishing off the remains of her breakfast when there was a scratch on the door and a footman on the other side announced, "Gentleman to see you, my lord."

The door opened to admit a tall, blond young man magnificent in his regimentals. Ordinarily Captain Anthony de Montmorency's handsome, open coutenance wore a sunny expression for, the best of good fellows, he liked and was liked by one and all. Today, however, the green eyes were cold as a winter sea and the mobile mouth was set in a hard line.

Unable to do anything to curb the follies and excesses of his older brother's way of life, and resenting the hardship they brought on the rest of his family, Anthony had sought escape in military service. Now, inexplicably, Alexander was here in London and Captain de Montmorency was forced to confront all the unpleasantness he had done his best to put out of his mind.

"You summoned me, Alexander? It had better be good and it had better be quick for I am due on guard duty at St. James in an hour's time." Under no illusions about his elder brother, Anthony knew that if Alexander had sent for him it was because he wanted something from him. The Earl of Halewood, always in pursuit of his own pleasures, had no time for a fellow unless he could use him and Anthony was not about to be taken advantage of as he had been so many times in the past.

Alex rose and laid a conciliatory hand on her brother's shoulder. "Now don't fly up in the boughs, old fellow. I happened to be in town and, naturally, family ties being what they are, I wished to see my dashing brother."

"Well I haven't any money, and even if I did, you could not

have it. I shall send it to Alex and the children," was the curt rejoinder. Anthony broke away from the hand on his shoulder and began to pace the room angrily.

"Tony, I am disappointed in you. Are you not even glad to see your eldest brother after so long? You have so little faith. Not that I couldn't use a bit of the ready. Hit a spot of bad luck at Newmarket and . . ."

"Forgive me, brother," Tony broke in savagely, "but duty calls and I have no time for this litany that has been trotted out for me so many times before. It won't fadge, Alexander, and you know it." With that he strode across the room, grabbed the door handle, and was about to fling himself out when another voice protested softly, "And here I thought you would be glad, or at least surprised, to see me."

Anthony paused midflight and turned around. "Alex? You, here?" he began incredulously. But she was not there, only Alexander slightly inebriated as usual and smiling his foolish smile.

At the expression on her brother's face Alex burst out laughing. "My disguise is better than I had hoped if I can put you in such a temper, Tony."

Captain de Montmorency sank into a nearby chair, staring blankly at the figure before him. "Alex?" he said at last in accents of disbelief.

"In the flesh, brother dear." She pirouetted in front of him. "Well, what do you think?"

A reluctant grin spread over his face. "You should have been on stage. You are dashed good, Alex. You are Alexander to the life." His face darkened. "And speaking of our dear brother, I assume that he must really be under the hatches this time. Something is mightily amiss or you would not be here. See here, Alex, I may be younger and I may not have as much in the brain-box as you do, but I do know enough to understand what you are risking by coming to town like this. I won't let you ruin your reputation to pull that blackguard out of yet another of his fixes."

Alex smiled fondly. "That is very sweet of you, Tony, but at the point we have reached, such sentiments are not only a luxury, they are useless." She quickly described for him the latest disaster, then outlined her plans for averting it.

Her brother's face became increasingly grim as she spoke, and the knuckles of his hands gripping the chair became whiter and whiter until at last he sprang up and began to pace the room again. "That scoundrel!" he gasped. "I could wring his neck. Alexander has no right to play mice feet with the family's inheritance. He is the most selfish—" Tony broke off as he searched for words black enough to describe his older brother.

"Self-centered man alive. I know." His sister sighed. "And I suppose he always was, only we were such good playmates, he and I, that I didn't really notice it until recently."

"But, Alex, one hundred thousand pounds! How can you possibly win that? To win such a sum one has to wager a good deal and we don't have a feather to fly with. Besides," he broke off bitterly, "I should be raising the wind, not you, and I cannot lay my hands on that much."

"I know, Tony. You would if you could, but you cannot, for you don't gamble as well as I. Very few do, and I am counting on that. But you can do something that I am unable to do."

"What is that?" he broke in, anxious to do anything that would be of the least assistance. It was so unfair that Alex, who had devoted much of her life to raising all of them, should have to continue looking after them. She should now be enjoying an establishment and a family of her own.

"You can introduce me to someone who will vouch for me at White's."

"White's? Alex, you must be all about in the head!"

Chapter 7

"You must be all about in the head." These very same words were on the lips of Christopher, Lord Wrotham, as somewhat later that morning he sat in the cavernous drawing room of the Earl of Claverdon's townhouse in Grosvenor Square. The recipient of these sentiments, a diminutive lady of uncertain years who was swathed in a pale pink gauze morning dress more appropriate to a young miss in her first Season than to the mother of a grown man, was taken aback. "How can you say such a thing about your own mother, Christopher? *All about in the head!* I am sure I am no such thing. Lord Grainger is devoted to me." The blue eyes opened wide and the lips, penciled into the shape of a perfect rosebud, pouted prettily.

"Mother," her son interjected, unable to suppress a sigh of pure exasperation, "the man is only a few years older than I. He cannot wish to become leg-shackled to a woman old enough to be his mother and someone who can give him no heirs. After all, think what *his* mother would say to such a match."

Dorothea, Dowager Countess of Claverdon sniffed tearfully, "You are too cruel, Christopher. If you could but see how he dances attendance on me you would agree. But you never go anywhere except to White's or Tattersall's even when you do come home from your horrid wars, so how could you possibly know?"

"And what does Hugh have to say about all of this?" Lord Wrotham inquired, obviously exerting a good deal of restraint to remain calm.

"Oh, Hugh," the countess dabbed her eyes with a scrap of lace, "you know him, he never had the least sensibility." The countess dismissed Lord Wrotham's stepbrother with a disparaging wave of her hand. "I never even broached the subject with him. After all, how could one possibly discuss such a delicate topic with someone who wears as much brown as he does. Which"—she paused to gaze with pride at her handsome son—"I am glad to say you do not. And I must say you look excessively fine. I do wish Hugh would consult your tailor, his clothes are always so ill-fitting. Is it Weston?"

"Stultz," was the short reply. "But really, Mama." Lord Wrotham strove to return to the matter at hand only to be interrupted by his unrepentant parent.

"Christopher, you know I must have gaiety. I was not made to dress in black and sit in the corner with the town tabbies."

"I know, Mama, I know." His sigh was the sigh of a man who had taken part in this particular discussion times out of mind. "But you also were not meant to play the fool. Lord Grainger is half your age if he is a day."

"And people say that *I* look half my age, so there you have it, perfectly unexceptionable," his mother concluded brightly. Then, a sly sparkle in her eyes, she continued, "However, if you were to escort me to these affairs, for example to Lady Derwent's rout, why then I should be able to attend it without requiring Lord Grainger's escort. Not even those who are most jealous of my youthful appearance—and I must say there are more than a few—could make the least comment, except, of course, that you look far too old to be my son." She leaned over to stroke her son's bronzed cheek. "Of course, it is all the fault of this silly war which you feel you must fight. It has aged you, you know, and if I do say so, I think it excessively selfish of you to leave your mother at home with nothing to do but fret and worry about you."

Lord Wrotham snorted. In truth, his mother's unblemished countenance had far fewer lines than his swarthy one. Years in the hot sun of the Peninsula living in primitive quarters had hardened him into a battle-weary veteran who stood out conspicuously among the rest of his peers, who had whiled away the past few years in the clubs and drawing rooms of London with nothing more upsetting to consider than the cut of their coats or the loss of a few pounds at the gaming table.

"Please, Christopher," the countess begged, "you so rarely go to these things, and once we are there I shall not lack for partners, so you have no need to dance attendance on me. Besides, the Carstairs will be there and I do so want you to meet their eldest daughter, Lavinia. She has become all the rage this Season, though I can not imagine how someone as ordinary-looking as Amelia Carstairs could produce an incomparable."

A gleam of understanding lit up her son's dark blue eyes. Lord Wrotham smiled grimly. Now it all became clear. His mother, ordinarily the most flighty of mortals, could become exceedingly single-minded when pursuing her own particular interests. Unable on her own to stop her only son from deserting her by playing on his sympathies for her helpless widowhood, she was now trying to entice him with the attractions of another of her sex. She must be getting desperate, he thought cynically to himself, if she was willing to relinquish to another female what little attention she was able to demand from him. Heretofore, even the slightest references she made to other women had been, if not derogatory, then certainly not complimentary, for in his mother's opinion, no other woman of any age could ever be as fascinating as herself. That she could even suggest her son might acknowledge the presence of another woman spoke volumes.

Until now it had never occurred to the Countess of Claverdon that anyone else could be of the least interest to her son. Supremely selfish and possessed of a delicate, fragile beauty that belied an indomitable will where her own wishes were concerned, she had taken her son's devotion to her as her due from the moment he had been born. Not content with reducing Christopher's father to abject slavery as he rushed to fulfill her every whim, she soon discovered that his son was equally susceptible to her smiles and her tears—until, that was, Lord Wrotham had been so disobliging as to break his neck on the hunting field and deprive her of her most constant source of masculine attention. Unable to support life without an ever-present adoring male, she had remarried, becoming Countess of Claverdon within the minimum amount of time that it was respectable to do so, and disabusing her son of the notion that his father—or any other man—meant anything more to her than a never-ending source of admiration.

This rather cynical view of his lovely mother had only intensified over the years. As a young man about town, Christopher had been able to witness firsthand her flirtatious behavior. To do the countess justice, she was always a charming and beautiful companion, continually exerting herself to cultivate masculine attention, even if it was only her son's. However, after her second husband had fallen victim to pneumonia, leaving her again bereft of guaranteed devotion, she had become rather tiresome in the demands she made on Christopher. Always gay and coquettish, she had treated him more as an escort than a son, an awkward and embarrassing role for one making his own entrance into society. Her stepson, Hugh, now Earl of Claverdon, had been most disappointing in that regard, as he had resolutely refused to worship her in the proper way. Possessed of a retiring nature, he remained happily at his principal country seat the entire year, never participating in the giddy social world in which his exalted rank would easily have established him as a leader. That he very generously gave over his entire house and staff in Grosvenor Square to his stepmother was quite beside the point when compared to his boorish insistence on staying in the country when she required his escort in town.

In a short while Christopher, bright, adventurous, and restless as a child, had grown bored with the endless empty rounds of the *ton*. Unable to derive enough amusement from courting risk at the gaming tables or in curricle races, he had cast about for something to make his life both more interesting and more meaningful.

Unlike his friends, who sought passion and romance in pursuit of the incomparables of the *ton* or the beauties on the stage, he was left entirely unmoved by the scores of females who did their best to ignite even the tiniest spark of response in such an eligible bachelor. A deadening familiarity with all the stratagems employed by beautiful women left him completely immune to the charms of the most lovely and talented females the capital had to offer.

In short, the only person possessed of enough spirit and intelligence to interest and challenge the young Lord Wrotham had been that upstart genius, Napoleon Bonaparte, and, in some smaller part, the general's unflagging adversary, Sir Arthur Wellesley.

Convinced that the conflict raging on the Continent was the only place likely to offer him an opportunity to do something with his life besides waste it consulting with his tailor or whiling away the hours at White's, Christopher had purchased a commission in the First Hussars. Deaf to his mother's tears and her dire predictions of his immediate demise, he had headed for the Peninsula.

For one brief moment, he had considered remaining in England and taking an interest in the substantial estates left him by his father, but beyond ensuring that they were run smoothly and profitably, he found little to challenge him there. Besides, if he were to remain at home, he did run the risk of his frivolous parent descending upon him with a large house party determined on amusement that he would be expected to provide.

In fact, desperate to keep at least one captive male within a day's journey, his mother had suggested this very thing to him. Fortunately, when Christopher, firm in his resolve to follow the military life, had called upon her to bid her farewell, he had looked so handsome in his regimentals and had brought with him two brother officers whose appearances were so dashing, that he was able to convince the countess of the appropriateness of his choice.

The felicity of his decision was soon apparent to all, for Major Lord Wrotham had quickly distinguished himself as an officer whose good sense and cool courage could be relied upon in the most desperate of situations.

At Talavera he had even caught the eye of Wellesley himself as the First Hussars valiantly attempted to leap an unexpected and treacherous ravine right before engaging in furious fighting with the French. His own magnificent horsemanship and enthusiasm had urged others across when they might have hesitated and caused more confusion and disaster than there already was. At Ciudad Rodrigo he had again been conspicuous in the Hussars' repeated charges against the French cavalry as they strove to break through Picton's lines.

Eventually, courage and quick thinking had distinguished Major Lord Wrotham, even among men renowned for such things. He had begun to become well known—enough so that Wellesley, now Marquess of Wellington, in search of men he could trust to go into the fiercest parts of the battle and return unscathed with reliable information, had made him an aide. This hazardous position precisely suited Major Lord Wrotham, whose taste for excitement and risk had only increased since his arrival in the Peninsula.

But it was more than the test of his bravery and resourcefulness that made his experience there so gratifying. It was the chance to do something with his life, to contribute his own particular skills to a cause he believed in, that Christopher found particularly satisfying after years escorting a mother who measured her success in life by the tributes she received.

Thus it was with mixed emotions that Christopher had received the news of the Treaty of Paris. On the one hand, all that he had fought for had come to pass; on the other, where was he now to find any life as vital and challenging as the one he had been leading?

Fortunately for him, Wellington still had need of clever, observant assistants who were sympathetic to his particular concerns and accustomed to his way of doing things. Major Lord Wrotham was requested to accompany Wellington to Vienna, where the rivalries—political, social, and romantic—were so intense as to make his new duties only slightly less hazardous than they had been on the Peninsula. If he was not dodging the eager embraces of amorous ladies determined to win the heart of a handsome, battle-hardened hero, he was avoiding jealous lovers, foreign politicians who mistrusted the motives of the British delegation, or spies who were suspicious of everybody. Still, it had been a heady experience made only headier by the escape of Napoleon from Elba.

It was the Corsican monster's renewed threat that was responsible for Lord Wrotham's present unwilling appearance in London. Naturally, he had been flattered when the Duke of Wellington himself had pulled him aside one evening and requested that he return home to drum up support in Parliament for the creation of an army that would be equal to the battle that was sure to come. "To tell you the truth, Wrotham," he had declared, "I am not very pleased with what I have now got—inexperienced, ill-equipped, and not enough of them.

And," he added regretfully, "many of them are strangers to me. What with so many fine lads from the Peninsula away in America, we shall have to ask Parliament to call out the militia in order to raise enough troops. I shall feel your absence here sorely, but you will be of more use to me in London."

So here he was, once again forced to grace his mother's drawing room and show at least some semblance of interest in her, for it would have been impossible to avoid doing so. Even had he not called upon her directly after he arrived in the metropolis, she was so well-informed of the least little *on-dit* that she would have learned of his whereabouts within a day of his arrival. At least he had had the presence of mind to procure chambers for himself and his batman at Stephens's hotel in Bond Street before presenting himself in Grosvenor Square. This had secured for him some measure of privacy and peace of mind.

Unfortunately, to accomplish his task, Lord Wrotham was forced to go where men of rank and influence were, and he thus had more than ample opportunity to witness his parent disporting herself with the worshipful Lord Grainger. If it had been someone even a decade older than the besotted lord, Christopher would have been delighted to relinquish the role of escort, but even he, inured as he was to his mother's propensity for enslaving hapless males, was taken aback at the state of affairs, hence his presence in Grosvenor Square.

"Very well, Mama," he said with a sigh. "I shall take you to Lady Derwent's rout, but I am pledged to meet with Farrington at White's later in the evening, so you will not be able to dance until dawn as you usually do."

"Oh, Christopher"—his mother pulled a face at him—"I am not such a flighty creature as all that. Why, Nevill—that is Lord Grainger—always bring me home at a most respectable hour."

Chapter 8

❧

All in all, the rout had not been all that bad. Lord Wrotham had been able to snatch moments of private conversation with two of Parliament's more influential members and had even borne up during a quadrille with his mother's protégé, who had turned out to be as vain as she was beautiful. But, buoyed by thoughts of his imminent departure to the Continent the minute his mission was accomplished, Christopher had been able to respond to her inanities with more than his usual patience.

However, it was with considerable relief that after seeing his mother safely home, he strolled leisurely to White's. Not that the sight of men wasting their minds and their inheritances on the turn of a card was any more enlightening than partnering women who could do nothing but call attention to themselves, but it did at least offer some sort of a mental challenge if one were alert enough to take it.

"Wrotham." A giant of a man waved cheerfully to him the moment the major crossed the threshold.

"Hello, Teddy, old fellow. How are you?" Christopher sustained a buffet on the shoulder that would have felled the average man.

"Devilish bored, I'll tell you," the giant responded with a woebegone air. "I tell you, this head-of-the-family bit is a plaguey business, it is. Nothing but people nattering at you all day long about one thing or another. If I could, I would give it all up for that miserably wet tent we shared in the mud at Ciudad Rodrigo." The new Marquess of Lindale dismissed the renowned Palladian villa and an exceedingly fine old Tudor pile he had recently inherited, not to mention a hunting box near Melton Mowbry, with a disparaging wave of the hand.

"But come, tell me what you are up to and what news you have of the lads in the regiment. What of Charlie Welbeck? Was he forced to return to that dragon of a mother of his or did he marry that cosy little armful he was smitten with in Oporto?" And laughing and reminiscing about old times, he led his former comrade-at-arms into the gaming room.

It was as though Christopher had never left. To be sure, the bow window in front was new since he had last been there and the proprietor was different, but the faces gathered around the gaming tables had not changed, nor had the bored and slightly vacant look in their eyes. Wrotham sighed. He never should have come here. It was no different from the rest of London in its empty pursuit of pleasure. Better to have returned to his chambers at Stephens's and pored over the latest dispatches. He glanced lazily about the room. No wonder Teddy was bored among this company of useless fribbles throwing away the fortunes they had been born with.

His gaze stopped at one table, arrested by the sight of regimentals on a tall blond lad observing the play. At least here was a fellow officer, and by the look of his bronzed and weathered skin and the lines crinkling at the corners of the eyes of an otherwise young man, he was a soldier who had seen action somewhere in some sunny clime. He looked to be as out of place as Christopher was, but now Teddy was pulling him toward another table, where they were waiting for him to make a fourth at whist, and Christopher soon forgot the kindred spirit at the table in the corner as he put his mind to work on the cards in front of him.

Meanwhile, the younger man in uniform, Captain de Montmorency, was keeping an eagle eye on the play in front of him. Having at last capitulated to his sister's request that he provide her with an entrée to White's, he had sought out General Scott, who not only had his consistent and tremendous winnings to recommend him as a mentor, but also had been a crony of their father's as well.

"How do you do," he welcomed Alex in his blunt way. "Knew your father in his wilder days, damn fine card player. If you're anything like him, you'll be more than a match for the

fellows here. Why, I beat 'em regularly, almost as regularly as
your father bested me. We missed Alfred sorely when he left
us." And with no more ado, he had seen to it that Alex was admitted to that venerable temple of chance, the gaming room at
White's.

Alex had strutted into the crowded gaming room with a confidence she was far from feeling. However, a covert glance at
those lolling around the green baize-covered tables reassured
her that many of the players were much the worse for wear, if
the number of empty bottles around were any indication, while
others bore the dazed look of those who had been staring at the
cards too long to make much sense out of them anymore. She
had taken her seat at a table where the general had waved to
several acquaintances and introduced her to Sir Gerard Chum-
leigh as a partner who would not fail him. Alex had settled in
nicely and was soon experiencing gratifying success that she
took pains to keep moderate at first.

Having adopted her sponsor's well-known rule for success
at the gaming table, Alex had eaten only boiled chicken and
toast, and had drunk water so her mind would be clear when
she took her place at the table. It was unlikely, given the raffish crowd that her twin ordinarily consorted with, that anyone
in town would be at all familiar with his reputation. But just to
be on the safe side, she always had a bottle of port beside her,
which Tony, whose job it was to ensure the proper setting for
their charade, would consume or dispose of while Alex ad-
justed her speech and movements accordingly, allowing her
eyes to glaze over, her words to slur, and her motions to become more erratic as the evening wore on.

Even she was not able to capture the full extent of Alexander's bluster and braggadoccio, but it seemed unlikely that the
types of characters her brother was friendly with would wan-
der into White's. They were more inclined to frequent the less
savory companionship of the gaming halls. Besides, if she
were to adopt his offensively loud manner, it would attract attention to herself and perhaps also call attention to the fact that
she rose from the table each evening a winner—a situation
better left unnoticed if she were to continue her scheme.

There was one, however, who did notice. Lord Wrotham,
bored with beating partners too foxed or too stupid to offer

much challenge, soon left his table and strolled over to the one where Tony stood guard. "I'm Wrotham of the First Hussars," he introduced himself, appraising Tony with the eye of an experienced commander. He liked what he saw. Fair-haired and boyish though he might be, Captain de Montmorency possessed the steady gaze and self-confident bearing of someone who had been tested often, and who'd met each test with success. The green eyes were alert, observant, and vivid in a face weathered by constant exposure to the elements.

"Captain de Montmorency, First Guards," Tony responded in friendly fashion, taking the proffered hand.

"One of those fellows that crossed the Adour with us, were you?" Christopher inquired, eager to discuss something besides his tailor or the latest incomparable.

"Yes, beastly weather wasn't it? Though you cavalry fellows aren't ever so close to it as we are, slogging along in the mud as we do," Tony replied, his eyes lighting up at the chance to trade stories of more exciting times and places with someone who could appreciate them.

Soon both of them were immersed in life on the Peninsula—the dust, the heat, the unforgiving terrain. The card room and its members receded, to be replaced by foraging parties and battalions on the march.

But Christopher was not too immersed in the memories to observe that Captain de Montmorency's companion appeared to be defeating his opponents with stunning regularity. His curiosity piqued at the sight of any member of the *ton* putting his mind to anything, even gaming, he began to watch more closely.

Slowly, he edged inconspicuously to the right in order to catch a glimpse of the cards the man was holding. They were not at all promising, but the young man sprawled in his chair, feet out-thrust, a blank look on his face as he waited for his opponents to make a move, did not appear in the least dismayed.

"He's done it again, damn me if I know how," one of the young man's opponents sighed.

"If you paid the least attention to your hand or to the game, Ceddie, you would," his partner snorted in disgust. "Though how he divined that I held those kings, I shall never understand."

"Eh, what?" The young man who was the subject of all this discussion shook his head, peering blearily at his partner. "Finished, have we?" He smiled muzzily. "I've had it for tonight, lads. What do you say, Tony, shall we toddle along in search of some amusement that isn't so taxing on the brain-box?" He rose unsteadily from his chair and turned around to clap a hand on Captain de Montmorency's shoulder. "And who is this, Tony?" he inquired curiously, eyeing the man who had been sharing military reminiscences.

"This is Major Lord Wrotham of the First Hussars. He was in the Peninsula as well. While you have been wasting your time on a pack of cards we have been discussing the crossing of the Adour. My brother, Alexander," Tony continued, turning back toward his new acquaintance.

"How d' do." Alex fixed a vacuous grin on her face and nodded in a friendly fashion before heading unsteadily toward the door with Tony, who, after smiling apologetically at Christopher, hurried forward in order to put a steadying hand under Alex's elbow.

Now that he had been apprised of their relationship, Christopher could detect a resemblance between Captain de Montmorency and his brother. While Tony's hair was burnished gold, his brother's was deep auburn, but the green eyes and aquiline features were the same. However, something that he could not quite identify puzzled Lord Wrotham. To all intents and purposes, Tony appeared to be here keeping an eye on his brother who, from the implication of the captain's remarks and the edge to his voice, must spend a good deal of time at the gaming tables. But it seemed from the reactions of the other card players that Alexander de Montmorency had been so consistently successful that there was little enough cause for worry. Furthermore, such concern in an establishment where fortunes were won, and more often lost, every day of the week, seemed incongruous. Christopher did not remember ever having encountered a de Montmorency before and though not a regular, especially in the more recent years, he felt certain he would not have forgotten a player such as Alexander de Montmorency.

Besides all that, there was something different about the man—something that did not quite ring true. Christopher, accustomed to sizing up men in an instant, had been struck by a sense of inconsistency. Alexander's movements were those of a man who was more than a little disguised, yet the look he had initially directed at Christopher before being introduced by his brother had nothing of the blank stare that bespoke a fogged brain. On the contrary, it had been extremely acute and speculative, as though he were taking the measure of Major Lord Wrotham in a way that few people bothered to do. He had quickly hastened to dispel this impression of alertness by staring stupidly at Christopher during the actual introduction, but not before Christopher had noticed the difference in the two looks. This seeming contradiction had aroused Christopher's curiosity and thus made him extremely sensitive to impressions, such as the lack of the smell of spirits on the breath of a man who had enough empty bottles at his elbow to have befuddled several men.

Lord Wrotham had spent enough time among soldiers to be able to detect the signs of those who had consorted too freely with Bacchus. He had also seen more men than he cared to count insist that they were sober enough to take on any task, men who had learned to sober up enough to walk steadily and look lively, but they had never been able to disguise the pungent aroma of spirits that they exuded. Alexander de Montmorency had not exuded any such aroma.

Then he must have been at great pains to convince the rest of the table that he was foxed, Christopher realized. Such a deception could only have been employed for one reason—he wished to lull the minds of his opponents into dullness and complacency in order to win more easily. He was a man intent upon winning, there was little doubt of that. Wrotham did not think for one minute that the young man had employed nefarious methods, for he had observed him closely enough to see every play and to be assured that it was pure skill and not marked cards that had won him over a thousand pounds that evening.

The major's blue eyes narrowed. Yes, Alexander de Montmorency was definitely a man to bear watching—not that Christopher distrusted the man, for he did not appear to be dishonest except in his misrepresentation of the befuddled state of his mind—but because the man was so obviously determined to win consistently and even more determined that no one realize that he was doing this. Why? He did not betray the wild gleam in the eye of the hardened gamester, nor were his bets anything out of the ordinary. In fact, they were so paltry that those devoted to the Goddess Fortune were likely to scoff, but their very modest nature was unusual in itself.

Every indication pointed to a man working toward some goal. A military man himself, the major knew enough to appreciate a well-developed strategy when he saw one, and Christopher felt sure that he was seeing one now. The idea intrigued him. That any member of the *ton* should systematically set out to earn money was highly irregular and made Christopher exceedingly curious about the character of the man behind such an endeavor.

Surely someone bent on winning money steadily, a little at a time, would undoubtedly return the next day, and the next day he, Wrotham, would be there to watch him. It was bound to be more rewarding to observe this man relieve foolish, wealthy players of their money than trying to get an overly cautious Parliament to commit to sending Wellington the crack troops he had commanded in the Peninsula or calling out the militia. Yes, it would be most interesting. We shall see how well your plan proceeds on the morrow, sirrah, Christopher muttered to himself as he too headed toward the door.

Chapter 9

~

Alex wove along St. James Street for some distance, her pace as uneven as it had been when she quitted White's. At last, certain that they were beyond sight and sound of anyone who had been at the club, she straightened and let out a sigh of relief. "Whew! At least the initial bit is over. I don't think I did it too shabbily. They were all too foxed to pay much attention to me in the first place, but still I don't think anyone suspected anything in the least bit havey-cavey, do you? Just think of it, a thousand pounds in a few short hours," she crowed gleefully, "and I hardly had to wager any of the money Mama left me at all."

"You used the money Mama left you?" Tony was aghast. "She only left you and Ally two thousand pounds apiece, and the way Alexander is going, you will need every penny of it to take care of yourselves. I only wish soldiers shared in prizes they way naval officers do. I should be out there in the thick of it winning it all to take care of you and the children, and Alexander could go to the devil with my blessing," he continued fiercely. "He is the most selfish—"

"I know, I know, Tony," his sister broke in soothingly, "but there is so little we can do about it now and I'd as lief have you around as constantly risking your neck in battle for prize money. Though I daresay"—Alex could not suppress the tiny sigh that escaped her—"you will be in thick of it somewhere over there soon enough."

"Yes indeed. Wrotham is here for that very purpose. He is actually on Wellington's staff, you know. Lucky dog. He's bound to be taking part in the coming dustup." Tony's eyes gleamed with excitement, and there was no mistaking the enthusiasm in his voice.

"How bloodthirsty you young fellows are," Alex drawled in perfect imitation of her twin. "There's nothing like a little saber rattling to win your attention."

Tony grinned sheepishly. "Well, it is a great deal more exciting than mounting guard—or wasting one's time at White's, for that matter." He shot a quizzing glance as his sister.

"Now, Tony," she began indignantly, "you cannot say that I am *wasting* my time when I won over one thousand pounds in less than three hours and it was as easy as rolling down a hill."

"Have care, Alex"—Tony wagged a cautionary finger at her—"lest you become another victim. Many men with more town bronze than you have fallen into that trap. Dame Fortune can be most alluring."

"Of all the—" Alex gasped, outraged. Then she saw the twinkle in her brother's eyes. "Really, Tony, I ought to call you out. I am not so green as all that. Besides, luck has very little to do with it all and well you know it. It is not that I think I am so very clever; it is just that most of the others are either disguised or cork-brained, or both. The moment I have the one hundred thousand pounds, I shall retire in good order and probably never set foot out of Norfolk again." She fell silent a moment, pondering a future spent taking care of the hall for Alexander, should he live, or for Tony. For the first time in her life, the future she'd planned for herself looked depressingly bleak, especially when compared to jauntering about the country and rubbing shoulders with the best of them at White's. Shaking off her sudden sadness, she turned to Tony with a bright smile. "So you see, I shall have to make the most of my visit here."

"Oh?" Knowing full well his sister's taste for adventure, Tony eyed her with considerable misgiving.

Alex laughed. "You needn't look so Friday-faced, Tony. I shan't do anything truly outrageous. I merely mean to enjoy myself while I am here."

"That is just what I am afraid of." Her brother shook his head, sighing lugubriously.

Alex chuckled. "Now, Tony, you know I never come to any harm. All I mean to do is see the sights, attend a few plays, and gawk at the nobs like any other rustic. And, of course, win a great deal of money."

By now they had reached the Clarendon and she turned to lay a reassuring hand on his arm. "Never fear, I shan't do anything bacon-brained, or at least not any more bacon-brained than I already am doing."

"Ah, I shall rest easy then," was the sarcastic reply. Knowing the strength of his sister's will, Tony was forced to be content with that. He was well-enough acquainted with Alex to know that whatever risks she might incur, she was nobody's fool, and more than well able to take care of herself. He just had to hope she was as capable of coping with the challenges the city had to offer as she was of coping with those in Norfolk. Tony had infinite faith in her, but all the same, he resolved to purchase for her the very next day an elegant but serviceable walking stick suitable for self-defense.

Left alone in her room, Alex sat down to consider the evening. She longed to order a glass of warm milk to calm her nerves and soothe the headache that was creeping across her temples, but decided the staff would think it to missish. She was forced instead to content herself with throwing open the windows and taking several deep gulps of the crisp night air before pulling off her clothes and falling into bed.

Once in bed, however, she found she could not fall asleep. Images of the evening kept crowing in her brain: the glare of the lamp over the table, Sir Gerard's amiable but foolish smile, and then, faintly at the back of it all, a pair of bright blue eyes in a deeply tanned face that appeared to be taking it all in, and far more of it than she would have wished—Major Lord Wrotham. His height, his broad shoulders, and his air of command immediately set him apart from the other devotees of White's, but there was more to it than that. He was observant while the others, if they looked up from their cards or dice at all, merely stared blankly off into space.

The major's watchful eyes had missed nothing and Alex had had the uncomfortable feeling that they had seen through her bluster and assumed inebriation. As she had turned to meet him, she had caught his look—penetrating and questioning— and had suddenly felt convinced that he knew her secret. The question was, just how much of it did he know and what would he do?

Somehow she didn't think he would expose her. He didn't look that sort of man. For some strange reason Alex was disposed to trust him—as much as she was disposed to trust anybody, that was. There was something in the directness of his gaze, with its air of quiet confidence, and the self-assured way he carried himself that made one feel he was a man of his word, a man to be relied upon. However, the view that such a man would take of a person bent on deceiving the entire *ton* was another matter altogether.

Well, there was nothing Alex could do about it now except brazen it out and hope for the best. Perhaps he would not be at White's in the ensuing evenings. Gaming must be pretty tame sport to someone who had spent the better part of the year on Wellington's staff and the ones prior to that in the Peninsula. She could see how her brother was chafing under the forced inactivity after so many years spent fighting the French and how boring he considered life in the metropolis. The major must feel the same way, if not more so.

Enough wool-gathering, my girl, she admonished herself strongly. If you are to win more tomorrow you must be at your sharpest, and for that you need rest. With an effort she concentrated on thinking up all the things she would like to see in the metropolis besides the gaming room at White's. Slowly soothed by the prospect of more diverting, less challenging activities to pursue on the morrow, she fell into a deep sleep and was only awakened by the sound of the maid bringing in her hot water and laying the fire.

After dressing, perusing the *Times*, and fortifying herself with a hearty breakfast, Alex sauntered out of the hotel, curious as to what the city had to offer for amusement besides games of chance.

Her first destination was Hatchard's, where she spent two blissful hours examining all that the bookseller had to offer. After lingering over *Travels in South Africa* by the Reverend J. Campbell, and Major General Lord Blayney's account of his years as a prisoner of war in Spain, she at last settled on the three volumes of *Guy Mannering*, happily anticipating the joy with which Althea would greet her selection.

What a luxury it was to be able to arise in the morning with nothing more on one's mind than the prospect of new sights and experiences—no housework to oversee, no tenants' cottages to be visited, no account books to be worried over. Alex could barely remember a time when these and a hundred other tasks had not awaited her attention every day.

She thought briefly of Ally and the children. How they would love to see the elegant carriages crowding Piccadilly and the splendid horses that drew them, and how Ally would sigh at the exquisite walking dresses worn by the women Alex had passed in Bond Street. Truly, it seemed a shame that she, who cared little for such things was here in London while Althea was not. But there was no help for it, Alex was the only one who could procure them the money to continue to live as they had. However, she resolved to observe it all very closely and record it as best she could for those waiting eagerly to hear from her back home. A particularly dashing phaeton drove by and Alex sighed enviously at the handsome team pulling it. How she would love to go to Tattersall's and look over the prime bits of blood on display there!

Then with a start she realized that there was nothing in the world to stop her from doing so. As Alexander de Montmorency she was free to go anywhere and do anything without running the least risk of causing comment. The full significance of the freedom conferred upon her began to sink in and she almost laughed aloud.

As Lady Alexandra de Montmorency there was so little she was permitted to do by society, and none of it by herself. Why, even her solitary rides through her own fields were looked upon as something approaching the scandalous. As Alexander she had the world at her feet, waiting to be explored. She grinned, set her beaver at an even more rakish angle on her head, and strolled along toward Tattersall's, marveling at the delightfulness of life accorded to the male sex.

She could have happily spent the rest of the day at the auctioneer's admiring the magnificent animals being paraded back and forth, listening to bits of sporting conversation, and observing the improbable mixture of customers—from Corinthians seeking out perfectly matched pairs to sporting clerics looking for a good hunter to cavalrymen selecting an animal who could be trusted to carry them in the direst of circumstances. From grooms to lords, all were united by their common preoccupation with these splendid animals.

How she missed Trajan, the powerful gray that had been her father's last gift to her before he died. "I never let on that I was buying it for a woman," he had confided with a grin, "lest the man refuse to sell him to me." Most of the county would have agreed that such a horse was no mount for a lady, but the magnificent animal had consistently demonstrated only the best of manners with her and he had become nearly as close a companion for Alex as Ally and the children.

But keeping Trajan in London would have been an enormous expense, so Alex had left him behind with instructions for everyone in the household to look after him, from Cook, who was to set aside a regular supply of carrots and apples, to Andrew, who was to feed him these choice morsels, to Jem the stable boy, who was responsible for cleaning out his stall and rubbing him down.

Standing there with the smell of horses and hay all around reminded Alex so strongly of home that it brought a sudden pang of longing to be back where everything was safe and familiar. It was a pang she quickly stifled with thoughts of the job she had come to London to do and the sights that were still left to see. After all, she could not very well go home and face the children without having been to the Tower, the Egyptian Hall, or Madame Tussaud's famed waxwork exhibition.

There was no time like the present to see these things and write them down while she could still view these wonders with the freshness and curiosity of a visitor. Judging from the faces passing by her on the street, it either did not take one long to become inured to all that the metropolis had to offer, or it was fashionable to appear so. Well, she for one, was not going to be dictated to. To Alexandra, boredom, despite its cultivation by the *ton*, was the indication of an empty mind, and if to be curious was to be too rustic to be *à la mode*, then so be it.

This air of inquisitiveness and curiosity did set her apart from the crowd, at least for one interested observer—Major Lord Wrotham, who was among the military men in search of new mounts. Dearly as he loved Brutus, the horse that had carried him with such steadiness and dependability through so many battles was showing signs of age. His wind was not what it had once been and lately he had been favoring the right fore-leg for no reason that the major, his batman, Radlett, or any groom had been able to fathom. Now, with the possibility of a crucial conflict looming in the future, was not particularly the time Christopher wished to become acquainted with a new mount, but Brutus deserved a peaceful old age on one of the major's estates, and he would get it. Christopher was deter-mined on that score.

It was just as he was listening to the auctioneer enumerating the finer points of a rather splendid-looking bay that Lord Wrotham caught sight of Alex, and he immediately lost inter-est in the horse. The major's first impulse was to greet the mysterious gambler of the previous evening, but on second thought, he decided that he would learn far more by quietly watching him.

After some minutes of close observation he was amply re-warded. Close scrutiny confirmed his original impression of the man. There was something unusual about him, something that set him apart from the rest of the crowd, any crowd, whether it be the players at White's or the fanciers of horse-flesh. What was it? The major frowned, puzzling it out. It was not his physical presence. De Montmorency was a well-enough-looking man, but nothing out of the ordinary, except for the rich auburn hair. Otherwise, he was somewhat taller than most, of a slender build, but nothing to cause one to take a second look. What was it then?

After some minutes of consideration Christopher decided that it was the air of alertness and inquiry that made him stand out. Somehow, looking at the man, one was struck by a sense of purposefulness about him, whether he was sprawled at the gaming table or watching an auction. True, he did his best to appear as accustomed to it all as the rest of the *ton*, but his air of casualness was a studied one, calculated to dispel any possi-ble interest in him. Why was that?

Even more intrigued than before, Christopher looked for-ward with eagerness to stopping in at White's that evening. In the meantime, however, it was time to call on a few of the more conservative members of Parliament in order to convince them that it would be in their best interests, as well as those of the country in general, if Wellington were to be given what he needed to secure peace for Europe and markets for English goods. The major had just received some recent figures concerning the size of Bonaparte's ever-increasing military strength that were sufficiently threatening to alarm even the most recalcitrant members.

Sighing at the prospect of hours of niggling argument ahead of him, and convinced that at least today there was no prospect of a replacement for Brutus, he left the enclosure and headed off to track down the first of his quarry.

Chapter 10

Alex's interest and curiosity, which had so intrigued the major, was causing a good deal of consternation in other quarters. Captain de Montmorency, calling on his peripatetic sibling that evening, was aghast to hear of her exploits. "On your own around London?" Tony clapped a hand to his brow and sank into the nearest chair.

"But, Tony, you can hardly expect a budding Corinthian who is hoping to attract gaming partners to remain invisible except at the gaming table," his sister pointed out reasonably. "That sort of behavior would very likely arouse suspicion."

"I suppose, you are in the right of it," her brother conceded reluctantly. "Hatchard's is unexceptionable enough, but Tatt's?"

"But, Tony, people who throw away their blunt at White's are far more likely to frequent Tattersall's than a bookseller's. I went to Hatchard's for my own amusement. The other was, er, in the way of business, you might say."

Tony grimaced. "You don't fool me for a minute, Alex. I know you were equally as amused, if not more so, casting an eye over the prime bits of blood as you were poring over the most recent offerings from the printers. And here I thought that storming the fortifications at Nivelle would be the death of me. You are far more a threat to my health than Soult ever was."

His sister grinned. "Relax, brother dear. I was most circumspect. I merely sauntered along, not calling the slightest bit of attention to myself, but mingling enough to be accepted as one of the crowd."

"I suppose I should be grateful for that at least," he retorted.

"So you should. I was most tempted to try my luck in the subscription rooms, but . . ."

"You what?" Tony leapt out of his chair.

"Never fear, I know I do not have your knack for picking a winning horse"—Alex looked thoughtful for a moment—"but I might give you some of my winnings to place on a particularly sweet goer."

"Never mind," her brother interrupted hastily, "I shall let you stick to the games of chance. I prefer to risk life and limb against something much more predictable—like gunfire."

"Very well, Tony, but don't say you weren't given a chance to save the family fortune," she teased.

"I consider shepherding you to White's and drinking your port contribution enough to the family fortune," he retorted, shaking his head at her. "Now come along, you have a fortune to win and the evening is wasting away."

And so, bantering all the way, they made their way to St. James Street. Their arrival being considerably earlier than the night before, the company was thinner and Alex felt rather more conspicuous, but a welcoming nod from General Scott, who happened to look up from his hand at the moment they entered the gaming room, reassured her.

For a time they both stood watching, then a corpulent young man laid down his cards in disgust, exclaiming, "I'll be damned if I'm going to continue playing with you, Reggie. You're in too rare a form tonight for me. I might as well just fork over my blunt to you and save you the effort of playing. Let someone else who can offer you a run for your money take you on." Catching sight of Alex as he waddled away from the table, he continued, "Here is a likely-looking player. How about you, sirrah?"

"I . . ." Alex was groping for a reply when the young man spoke.

"Here, Nigel won't mind you as a partner. You could hardly have worse luck that I did. What do you say, Nigel?"

Thus appealed to, his former partner could only confirm that Colin had had the devil's own luck that evening and he invited Alex to join him.

Not having her partner selected for her as she had had before, Alex was rather uneasy, but she was soon able to read him. By leading her own cards well, she was able to coach him into helping them do quite well for themselves. Well enough, at least, for Nigel to crow sometime later, "It only takes some new blood to make the Goddess of Chance desert you, Reggie."

"That is because the stakes are so blessed low. Raise 'em to a level that makes a man think and then you'll see what we are made of," his friend replied.

"Very well, then, one hundred pounds a point, winner take all." Nigel was not about to be shown up by his opponent.

Alex had a good job of it concealing her dismay, but she managed a laconic nod. Come, my girl, she encouraged herself, this is precisely what you wished to do, challenge your opponents enough to rake in some real winnings. Relax, it is perfect. You already know your opponents; the only thing changed is the stakes, which only works to your advantage. Keeping this little monologue in mind, she was able to accept the cards dealt her with a degree of equanimity. Once she began to examine her hand, she forgot everything as she planned her strategy.

So intent was she on playing, though she did her best to mask this by lounging in her chair and drooping her eyelids, that she was completely unconscious of the little crowd that, attracted by the rise in stakes, had slowly formed around them. It was not until Nigel laid down his last cards with a bewildered shake of his head, pronouncing disgustedly, "Damn me if I can see how this happened, why I had a hand . . . Dame Fortune is kind to you young rustics. But just wait until you have been on the town awhile, sirrah, she'll be as hard on you as she is on the rest of us," that Alex looked up and saw that they had an audience.

And there among them, his gaze fixed intently on her, was Major Lord Wrotham. He smiled and greeted Alex pleasantly enough, but that did nothing to allay the uncomfortable suspicion that he had been observing her very carefully for quite some time.

Though it was not quite her place to invite him, Alex decided to seize the bull by the horns. If he suspected her of cheating, or whatever he suspected her of, it was time to prove him wrong. "Will you not join us, Major?" She indicated the place vacated by the disillusioned Nigel.

An appreciative smile tugged at the corners of Christopher's mouth. So the lad knew he was being watched, did he? He was as clever as the major was beginning to think he was, and bold too, to challenge him so quickly. De Montmorency must be very sure of his card-playing skills—either that, or he was very cleverly employing marked cards. But Christopher's innate sense of character told him that the young man with the auburn hair, bright green eyes, and determined chin, who was now regarding him with just a hint of wariness, was not the sort to profit by dishonest means. No, if the major knew his man, and he usually did, this one was confident of himself and his abilities, and he was set on proving them in the most demanding of situations. "Why, thank you, I shall, if the others agree." There was a general nod. The major sat down and the cards were dealt.

Almost the moment the play began, Wrotham knew he was up against an opponent who was very good indeed. The lad never seemed to give an obvious lead, but that was the very skill of it. Even though Christopher was alerted to this, he was still surprised when the game ended in de Montmorency's favor. The second game the major and his partner most definitely lost because Wrotham was more intent on studying his opponent's play than on his own.

The man seemed less intent on taking the individual tricks than on winning the entire game. Something of a veteran, both of the Peninsula and the card table, Christopher could recognize and appreciate a master plan. A connoisseur of strategy, he knew he was witness to one unfolding right under his nose, though he still remained uncertain as to its final objective. The more he saw of Alexander de Montmorency and his brother, the more curious he became as to just what that goal might be. Consequently, when their partners lost interest in whist and drifted away to enjoy the riskier but less intellectually taxing rattle of the dice box, he challenged Alex to a game of piquet.

By now quite aware that the hussar with the watchful eyes was more than a little interested in her, Alex was hesitant to take him on in a game that did not provide the distraction of other players. However, it would never do to reveal any sort of reaction at all so she merely nodded as though whatever she did was of supreme indifference to her.

Christopher called for another pack of cards while Alex, seeing that for once his eyes were not fixed on her, took advantage of the opportunity to switch her full glass of port for Anthony's empty one sitting next to it. Her brother looked down at her, grinned, and after making a discreet show for her benefit of mopping his brow, downed it in one gulp.

Once the waiter had brought the cards and another bottle of port, the play began. Afraid that she had appeared too alert and had thus revealed that she was aware of Christopher's speculative observation, Alex sank lower in her chair and allowed herself to make a few very small blunders, but not so many as to put her opponent on his guard, before she began playing in earnest.

Eventually, ever so slowly, it became apparent to the major that Alex was as formidable an adversary at piquet as at whist. The youth's memory and skills at calculating the cards that had been played or were in his hand made the major feel as though he were sitting with his own hand in full view. Every once in a while he shot a curious glance at de Montmorency over his cards but the young man continued to lounge in his chair, his face devoid of any expression, seemingly totally uninterested in the drama that was unfolding on the table in front of him as the mound of vowels piled up at his elbow. There was no doubt in the major's mind that Alexander de Montmorency was a cool customer, a very cool customer indeed.

He straightened in his chair, eyes alight with the exhilaration of pitting his own intelligence against a worthy adversary. It had been such a very long time since he had truly matched wits with anyone and he was enjoying it immensely, despite the fact that he seemed to be coming off much the worse in the encounter. Aha, he looked at his hand. Surely the cards remaining made him invincible now. "Quart," he called out triumphantly.

"Ah . . . equal," Alex responded, trying to keep from laughing at the dumbfounded look on Wrotham's face. The major was an excellent card player who had a better grasp of strategy than most, but he did not possess her phenomenal memory and the sixth sense for the cards that her father had assured her made her virtually unbeatable. "Alex, my girl," he would often remark, "it is the greatest shame I cannot take you to White's. I have foresworn the place, but I would go back once more just to see you take them all on." Well, here she was, and not doing too badly either. Even Tony had begun to relax and chat, secure in the knowledge that his sister was more than a match for most of the players here. Certainly Lord Wrotham had looked to be no mean opponent and she had managed to trounce him.

Exhausted by hours of concentration and forcing a tense body into a languid pose, Alex yawned and peered blankly around the room. "Well, I am done for this evening. Shall we toddle along?"

Rising unsteadily, she grasped the back of her chair and smiled blearily at Lord Wrotham. "Fine game, sir, very fine game." She swept up the vowels, crumpled them together, and thrust them in her pocket, then headed for the door with Tony and the major following in her slightly erratic wake.

The cool night air felt delicious on Alex's cheeks. The breeze smelled fresh after the stuffiness of White's and the headache, which had started as a tightness in her shoulders and moved up the back of her neck to form a tight, throbbing band around her forehead, vanished as if by magic. She took a deep, gulping breath, straightened her shoulders, and heaved a sigh of relief at having successfully survived another evening.

Alex's relief was short-lived, however, as Wrotham, catching up with the two of them, invited them back to his hotel. "For the night is yet young and I would prefer to hear of someone else's encounter with the French on the Peninsula than the latest *on-dits* at Lady Hadlington's masquerade, and just at present there is nothing to tempt me at either the theater or the opera.

"Well, I . . . we," Tony began awkwardly, rolling a frantic eye at his sister.

"Don't deny me," the major begged. "I am like to expire of boredom if I have to explain one more time that Bonaparte is not a monster, but an exceedingly clever strategist, and that it will take seasoned troops and not some act of God to save us all from him—that is, if anyone is concerned at all about events on the Continent. In the main, they remain totally ignorant of the impending crisis, preferring to worry instead that there is an unsightly wrinkle across the backs of their coats, or that the way they tie their cravat is not as intricate or as original as the next person's."

There was no help for it. With the most imperceptible of shrugs for her brother's benefit, Alex responded, "Why, thank you. It is flattering to be considered worthy of rational conversation." Doing her best to recall what she had recently read of the Corsican's latest movements, she strolled along with the two military men who, without further ado, had plunged into a discussion of supply lines and troop movements. They compared the swift travel and flexibility of the French troops who lived off the country to the better-fed English, whose speed was hampered by the vast train of carts and animals that followed behind them.

In short order they reached Bond Street and Stephens's hotel. Making their way among the throngs of military men, they followed the major to a spacious suite of rooms that the invaluable Radlett had managed to secure for them after much greasing of palms.

Chapter 11

That intrepid batman was waiting to welcome them when they arrived, but promptly disappeared in search of the ingredients for making his famous punch. "Radlett is known throughout the regiment for his punch, and many's the time it has kept us all warm even though we lacked any sort of blankets or a place out of the cold and wet to lie down," Christopher remarked as he closed the door behind them. "But I am sure you had such a person in your regiment as well." He smiled at Tony. "Someone who could be counted upon to produce food from a barren countryside and kindling from what everyone saw only as a rocky wastleland."

"Ah yes. It was Major Neal's Finchin who took care of us. And I must say he had much the look of your Radlett—a sharpish sort of fellow who could barter in any language and seemed to get the best of them, whether it was a Portuguese innkeeper, a Spanish peasant, or upon occasion, a Frenchie with something to trade."

The major nodded. "It is the generals and commanders of regiments who are mentioned in the dispatches, but it is people like Radlett looking after the men following the generals into the breach who are truly responsible for our victories in the Peninsula. What, after all, is a colonel without men to command, and how many of our bold young officers who came over to Spain for the sport of it would have lasted a minute without the care and advice of some grizzled old batman?"

"Do you object, as I have heard that Wellington does, to the lack of training we give our officers? If they are so ill-prepared, then throwing them against men who have attended schools on military strategy is putting them at the greatest of disadvantages, is it not?" Alex inquired, forgetting for a moment that she had intended to play least in sight during this particular gathering.

"Why, yes I do, I suppose, though nothing teaches one so well as experience." Christopher directed a sharp glance at her. It was as he had expected, behind that foolish look that Alexander de Montmorency so carefully maintained, a clever mind indeed was at work.

"But then you must also feel that Britain should maintain an army—an attitude that goes strongly against the grain of the independent-minded citizenry. Too often such a standing army becomes an instrument of oppression for a tyrant."

"Yes . . ."—Lord Wrotham frowned, considering for a moment—"but if we had even a small army composed of professionals—veterans who had seen action, who were kept in readiness at all times—we would not now be in the position of having to beg for troops, and raw recruits at that." A sardonic note crept in his voice. "And I would not be here kicking my heels in this blessed place and having to go hat in hand from one oblivious peer to another begging for support in Parliament. Nor would Tony be wasting his time on guard duty."

"Too right," Tony joined in. "It is a crying shame too, to see all those splendid fellows who carried the day at Salamanca and Badajoz, who endured all sorts of hardships for their country, tossed back on the land without so much as a thank you."

"And," Alex added, "with very little chance of supporting themselves or their families, times being what they are."

Wrotham nodded grimly before turning to accept a glass of punch from Radlett. "Ah, excellent as always, Radlett. Now if you could by another stroke of your magic return us to real scenes of action where we might truly accomplish something, all would be well."

"Ah, that's asking, isn't it, sir? You know I would if I could," the batman commiserated. "All these dandified gentlemen one sees in London are like to make a decent fellow sick, they are." Shaking his head, he proceeded to hand glasses of punch to Tony and then to Alex, who accepted hers cautiously, knowing there was no escaping drinking it this time. She only prayed that the batman's recipe was famous for its taste rather than its strength. Seated on the other side of the fire, Tony was too far away to exchange glasses. She hoped she would not disgrace herself by choking on it. Best to lead these two into a distracting discussion and deal with it as well as she could.

"Then you must be less than pleased with the motion against the renewal of war with France that it is rumored Whitbread is bringing." There, that was a topic sufficiently incendiary to direct their minds toward other matters.

"That fool," the major muttered. "I find his reasoning that a warlike response on our parts to the latest development will cause Napoleon to arm further to be entirely unsound. As if a show of force incites Bonaparte rather than his own unbounded greed for glory. It was not a show of force on our part that inspired him to escape from Elba, after all."

"Aye," Tony agreed. "That is the thinking of a man who has never faced Boney's troops or his generals. Given the chance to win back their fame and honor, they reckon not with the world's reaction. I say that if we do not arm ourselves, and quickly, it will be a very near thing."

"Precisely!" Leaning forward eagerly, Wrotham set down his glass with a snap and Alex seized the opportunity to toss down the fiery liquid all in one gulp. Ugh! It tasted as bad as any medicine Trevor Padgett had ever given her and it burned all the way down. However, she managed to swallow it without gasping and without betraying any visible signs of discomfort beyond a slight watering of the eyes. "We cannot let people like Whitbread gain the upper hand in this country, which I very much fear they will do," the major continued. "Wellington fears the same thing, and that is why I have come back over here."

"But Whitbread is only one small voice, albeit a powerful one," Alex broke in. "I am sure that resistance in Parliament is more a result of inertia than anything else. People are so overjoyed at the thought of peace and a return to prosperity after all these years, that the idea of rearming and incurring new taxes is a dismaying one. I am certain that in the end, the general tenor of opinion will be in your favor. Why, even the recent article in the *Edinburgh Review* on Bonaparte's campaign in Russia, much as it deplores the horror of war and recognizes the exhaustion of all the peoples who have spent so many years opposing him, acknowledges the necessity of responding to this new crisis with military measures."

"Does it so?" Christopher looked thoughtful. "I did notice such an article, but I confess I did not read it as it looked to be merely a description of the disasters of his foray into Russia."

"In the main it is, but at the very end it addresses the problems of war in a more general way and demonstrates how an appetite for glory can corrupt people, from a leader on down to the humbler citizens of a nation. All of them eventually forget the reasons that made them go to such desperate lengths in the first place in their thrill over valorous deeds and great conquests. It suggests that this sort of blood lust will reanimate the French to the degree that they will flock to Napoleon again if he offers them a chance to recapture their glories. The author takes a most pessimistic view of the possibilities of peace and advocates England's immediate response to the threat."

"Would that it were immediate." The major looked grave. "People here have no notion of how inspiring the man can be, how he can make citizens and soldiers alike do his bidding—and very quickly and efficiently too."

"Yes," Tony chimed in. "Even though we never encountered the Emperor himself in the Peninsula, we felt the force of his personality in his generals. And his enormous capacity for instantly marshaling forces and moving them about all over the map was reflected in his armies in Spain. The British would do well to heed the past. It will never do to underestimate the man. After all, who could be more familiar with his tactics than Wellington and"—he nodded toward the major—"if your presence here is any indication, Wellington is taking his reappearance very seriously indeed."

"Very," Wrotham agreed solemnly. "This will be the first time the Iron Duke has actually faced Napoleon himself and I very much fear that given the circumstances, he is at a great disadvantage, for Napoleon thrives on concentrating his troops and moving them swiftly. Wellington, though a sound tactician, has his strength in defense and solid lines of supply. For that sort of warfare to prevail, one needs time and troops, neither of which he has. His communications in the Peninsula were always better than those of the French. Now he does not have that advantage, and the terrain between France and Belgium, unlike those beastly tracks in Spain, is such that it favors easy communication and advance for the French armies."

"Too right. Such hostile countryside as Spain and Portugal made it impossible for the French to requisition supplies the way they had counted on, but now what with a sympathetic population and fertile farmlands it will be the merest romp compared to all those miles slogging in the mud or the dust. I daresay we shall be called up soon, at least I hope we are. This kicking one's heels on guard duty while the whole world is amassing for war on the continent is the very devil!" Tony pounded his fist on the arm of his chair emphatically.

"Isn't it though." The major smiled sympathetically. "Were you at Vitoria, by the way?"

And with this, the two officers plunged into reminiscences of the heroic exploits, glaring blunders, and privations shared by all of those who took part in the Peninsular Campaign. Alex leaned back in her chair and listened to them, reflecting on how very different their lives were from hers. How pleasant it was to sit here while her brother spoke of hunting in the Pyrenees or the gallantry of a brother officer who, despite his colonel's orders to retreat, had grabbed the colors, stormed a wall single-handed, and stood there waving the troops on. How much more interesting were men's lives and conversations than women's. Why, she was lucky if she could lead a female conversation off the topics of household tasks or fashion on to anything as serious as the poor laws or the income taxes put into effect to finance the war. These were things that truly concerned her and engaged her attention, but if she were to bring them up in any company except that of Trevor Padgett, she would invariably meet with blank stares, derisive smiles, or worse.

This being a man had a good deal going for it, Alex was beginning to realize. Men had freedom, the possibility of participation in events beyond the realm of household or parish, and a wider variety of amusements to pursue. In short, the existence of Alexander de Montmorency was infinitely more varied and stimulating than that of Alexandra de Montmorency. If her twin survived, he would be lucky if she relinquished his identity to him, now that she had had the opportunity to enjoy it.

Across the room, Tony, interrupted briefly by the reappearance of Radlett with more punch, suddenly became conscious of his sister's presence. What was he thinking bringing her here to a gentleman's chambers? He must be all about in the head, though the quick glance he stole at Alexandra revealed her to be enjoying herself hugely. However, there were fine lines of strain around her eyes and the slump of her shoulders betrayed her exhaustion. It was high time she was home in bed. In the first place, Alex was unaccustomed to town hours; in the second place, it was extremely wearing to have to assume a role as she had done for such an extended period of time; and in the third place, the worries that had plagued her even before she arrived in London would have sapped the energy of anyone, even his redoubtable sister. Tony waved Radlett away with a regretful sigh. "Thank you, no. I must be off. I have guard duty early in the morning and must be up betimes. It is time I was in bed."

As Alex arose from her chair, half relieved, half regretful, her brother continued, "Of course there is no need for Alexander here to leave such excellent company."

"No, no." Alex managed a huge yawn. "Rustic that I am, I am as yet unaccustomed to these town hours, but I thank you for a pleasant evening and look forward to drubbing you again, sir." She cocked a quizzical eyebrow in the major's direction.

"To be sure." Wrotham grinned. "But I shall be ready for you, I warn you. You have defeated me for the last time."

"A challenge I shall most assuredly take you up on." Alex bowed low before heading out the door.

It said a great deal for her self-control that she was able to contain herself until they had strolled some distance down Bond Street. "Ten thousand pounds, Tony!" she exclaimed with glee. "Just think of it."

"I am thinking of it," her brother replied grimly, "and also about Major Lord Wrotham's marked interest in you. It was no accident, I'll wager, that he played with you this evening or invited us back to his chambers. The man was watching you like a hawk. He suspects something, I feel sure of it."

"Pooh, don't be silly, Tony." Alex dismissed her brother's worries with a wave of her hand. "He is merely watching to see whether or not I am cheating. He asked for new cards and was most observant of my every move while we were playing, but after that he let down his guard. I am but a new player come on the town who has enjoyed some success. Naturally he is suspicious, and it is a very good thing too, for now that he sees I am not a Captain Sharp, he will set the opinion for the others and they will take me on. Mark my words."

Chapter 12

Meanwhile, back in his chambers, Lord Wrotham was berating himself for just that letting down of his guard which Alex had been so quick to notice. At least you are not a flat, he muttered to himself as he relived their entire encounter at the gaming tables, but you may be all sorts of a fool. If he is not cheating, then what is his game? For game there is, I am certain of it.

The major stared absently into his glass of punch as he tried to recall every particular of his two evenings with the de Montmorencys. Certainly the younger, Anthony, was the genuine article. He was too ingenuous to be anything else but the honorable soldier he seemed. His reminiscences so nearly matched the major's and in such minute detail that Christopher had no questions regarding him. However, there had been moments when Captain de Montmorency had seemed as unsure of his brother as Lord Wrotham was. Alexander de Montmorency was a puzzle, there was no question about it. There was no doubt also that a keen intelligence lay behind the slightly bosky exterior that he was at such pains to present to the world. The comments he had made on the recent events were too thoughtful and articulate for someone who spent as much time with the bottle at the gaming table as he apparently wished everyone to think.

In fact, Christopher had quite enjoyed the evening. It was rare to meet anyone whose eyes did not glaze over at the mention of anything more serious than the ankles of the latest opera dancer or the recent transactions at Tattersall's. Even rarer still was to come across someone who was not only aware of what was happening in the world outside the *ton*, but who actually reflected on it or had anything of substance to say about it.

Come to think of it, he himself had not seen the article in the *Edinburgh Review* to which Alexander had alluded. It must be in the pile of papers on the escritoire. He rose to rummage through them. Ah, there it was, under the stack of gilt-edged invitations and the latest reports from his bailiff. Christopher pulled it out. Yes, it looked most interesting—not at all the sort of thing a man like the one Alexander pretended to be would pay the least attention to. In the major's experience, such types, if they could be persuaded to read anything at all, made sure it was nothing more taxing than the racing form at Newmarket.

Intrigued, Wrotham returned to his place before the fire and plunged into reading the article, telling himself that there was no use tackling the question of Alexander de Montmorency until he had been able to glean more information about the man—but where best to start? Of course, the first place to check was *Debrett's*, but after that, what? If he was but newly arrived in town no one knew him well enough to offer any sort of perspective. Close observation still appeared to be the only way. The major resolved to watch him like a hawk.

Snuggling under the bedclothes at the Clarendon some time later, Alex too was reviewing the evening with mixed reactions. There was a certain measure of satisfaction, but also a certain amount of trepidation. She was delighted with her winnings. Not only was she making steady progress toward the amount needed to rid herself of the odious Sir Ralph, she was also establishing herself as a player to be reckoned with, both in her own mind, and in those of prospective opponents.

She had always felt reasonably confident of her skill, but it was most reassuring to have this consistently borne out. Her mind, freed of worries on that score, was then able to concentrate on other things, such as why she had insisted on participating so vocally in the conversation in Wrotham's chambers. She should have pretended to be three parts foxed and sat there completely silent, a bleary, vacant smile on her face. Certainly that would have been more in keeping with Alexander's character.

But the conversation had been so intriguing that she had been unable to keep herself from joining in. For so long she had wished to discuss those sorts of issues but had lacked the opportunity. Of course there had been Doctor Padgett, thank goodness, who could be convinced to talk about something besides the weather or the transgressions of his neighbors, but by now Alexandra knew his mind as well as she knew her own and could guess his reply even before she posed the question. It was exciting to hear the stories of life in the Peninsula, a life filled with so much more adventure and meaning than hers.

How she had longed to join the army with Tony, to see the world and really do something. Listening to it all was, she supposed, the next best thing to being there. But that's what she should have done—listened. Instead, she had been unable to keep from posing questions that had nagged at her for sometime, and, as a result, she'd seen the curious looks the major had given her and known that such active participation in the conversation had been a mistake.

Lord Wrotham was nobody's fool and he had already evinced a rather disquieting interest in her. As she thought back over her two evenings at White's, Alex realized that subconsciously she had been aware of his scrutiny the entire time, both when he was talking to Tony that first evening, and the next, when he had challenged her to piquet.

Of course it was natural to suspect a newcomer who did so well at the tables. Alex had limited her bets to small ones and had kept her play unobtrusive, but to an observant man such as the major, this did noting to obscure the fact that she was consistently beating all comers. Lord Wrotham was no mean card-player himself, and she had thoroughly enjoyed pitting her wits against his. With an opponent of his caliber it truly was a game and a test of skill, while with the others it had been the merest exercise, the leading of lambs to the slaughter.

Alex hoped it was only her incredible winning streak and not her person that had raised the major's suspicions, but she had her doubts. Even after the game was over and she had felt his eyes upon her. Certainly the invitation to return to his chambers had been no casual one. Despite her awareness of that, she had gone ahead and stepped out of her role as the foolish drunken sot.

There's no use crying over spilt milk, she scolded herself. Just see that it does not happen in the future and avoid Major Lord Wrotham at all costs.

This was easier said than done, for not only did her brother enjoy the man's company, so did she. Brief though the acquaintance had been, Alex found herself liking Lord Wrotham very much. There was something about him that made one feel almost from the start that one could trust him.

Whether it was the direct gaze that seemed to take in everything, or the proud, almost aloof air that showed a lack of concern for the opinion of others—a quality notably lacking in most of the self-important members of the *ton*—she could not say, but Alex had instinctively felt at ease with him despite the occasional speculative glances he cast in her direction.

Then too, there often appeared a glint of humor in his eyes, as though he did not take himself or the rest of the world too seriously. This in a man who was obviously extremely competent and highly trusted by his superiors made him all the more unusual and attractive.

Remember that you came to London to make a fortune, not friends, Alex reminded herself severely. But she was unable to suppress a wistful sigh. It was so rare that she came across anyone interesting or intelligent enough to converse with in the manner she most enjoyed. Now here was someone not only capable of carrying on a decent conversation, but who had so many exciting experiences to relate besides. And of all the luck, he seemed to be the person least likely to be hoodwinked by her charade.

Alex had seen him glancing around the gaming room at White's. The sardonic curl of his lip and the cynical glint in his eyes were all the evidence she needed that Christopher, Lord Wrotham, saw quite clearly through the foibles and pretenses of most of his fellow creatures. She had better have care lest she become the object of even greater scrutiny, though somehow she had the oddest feeling that even if he were to discover her secret in its entirety he would not be shocked.

His sense of honor, apparent even from their brief acquaintance, might be offended by the fact that she was deceiving people, but Alex still sensed that someone who had sacrificed as much as he had for his country could sympathize with her for doing the same for her family.

Prey to these disquieting thoughts, Alex tossed and turned, finding the welcome oblivion of sleep unusually evasive. To distract herself, she forced herself to recall every hand she had played that evening and to examine the possible consequences of alternative plays she might have made. It was not necessarily a calming exercise, but it did take her mind off her more uncomfortable thoughts, and she was finally able to relax sufficiently to feel confident about what the next evenings at the gaming table might bring.

Soon she was playing out entire games in her mind, keeping a running score of the points. Totting up the numbers in her mind was rather like counting sheep and eventually it had the desired effect. Slowly she drifted off, with visions of aces, jacks, queens, and kings whirling around in her head.

It was with great surprise then that Alex awoke to bright sunlight and a knock on the door. "Gentleman to see you, sir," said a voice on the other side.

Who on earth? Alex had only a moment to panic before she threw on Alexander's old dressing gown, and grabbed a razor from the shaving things lying on the dressing table so as to appear interrupted in the midst of her morning ablutions. She opened the door and barely contained the sigh of relief when she saw her brother shaking his head and grinning at her.

"What a slug-a-bed! Why anyone would think you had been on the town for years instead of days with the hours you keep. Come on, finish dressing." Tony ambled into the room and directed an amused glance at the razor still clutched in his sister's hand. "I've something to show you that will clear the cobwebs from that foggy brain of yours."

"I won't be a minute," Alex promised, hurrying into the dressing room. She pulled on biscuit-colored pantaloons and a fresh shirt, struggling with the cravat that still presented a challenge to her each morning, but she comforted herself that no matter how poorly tied it was, it still looked better than her twin's mangled results always did. Shrugging into a bottle green jacket she reappeared. "There. Ready." She declared with pride.

"And without even a valet to make you presentable. You are a marvel, Alex." Tony smiled at her as he reached over to give one more tweak to the cravat. "Though I fear all this dressing may be for naught when you see what I have brought."

"Whatever?" Alex was mystified, but her brother only looked the more secretive as he led her downstairs.

They reached the pavement and Alex, her eyes adjusting to the brilliant sunlight, at first could see nothing. Then a lad holding two horses appeared. Alex recognized Tony's faithful Caesar flicking his ears with interest as he surveyed the passersby, but her eyes were immediately drawn to the magnificent black stallion next to him. "What a splendid animal!" she burst out. Then, realizing the infelicitous nature of this remark, she amended it. "Of course no one could be more faithful or better than Caesar."

"But he does suffer by comparison," Tony continued. "My feelings, and I am sure his, are not hurt, for Nero is an unusually fine specimen. Got him off Rokeby. He's in the regiment, devil of a fellow. Most bruising rider you can imagine and keeps a regular string of horses—family breeds them on their estates in Ireland. Wouldn't mind doing that myself one day when I'm too old for soldiering." Tony broke off, momentarily distracted with a blissful contemplation of a future surrounded by the finest of horseflesh.

"He knew you were in town for a short while," her brother continued, "and he wasn't using Nero. The animal was getting no exercise and eating his head off so he offered him to me after I assured him you were almost as good a rider as I." He grinned wickedly at his sister, who took instant exception to his assessment of her prowess.

"How can you say that when I have never had my horse refuse the hedge to Squire Edgecumbe's fields, nor have I ever failed to clear the ditch that Welham Beck runs through— never even had a horse wet his hooves in it—while *some* people have had to empty it out of their boots!"

Tony laughed. "Still the same old Alex—never could stand to have anyone ahead of you on the hunt, and the merest hint of criticism sends you into the boughs. But seriously, I thought you might enjoy a little more vigorous form of exercise than strolling down Bond Street. Having Nero here as a companion should keep you away from Tatt's."

"Of all the unjust . . ." Alex began furiously, then catching sight of the wicked sparkle in her brother's eyes, she stopped. Grimacing in disgust, she retorted, "And you're still the same old Tony. A worse tease than you, my fine lad, has never existed; of that I am quite certain." The exasperated expression quickly softened as she laid a hand on his arm. "Nor has a kinder brother ever existed. Thank you so much."

"Now that is much more the thing. Why don't you go change and let us put him through his paces. I fancy he must be as eager for a gallop through the park as you."

And that is another advantage to being Alexander instead of his twin, Alex thought to herself as she was pulling on her boots a few minutes later. If I were Alexandra, I should never be allowed to ride at anything but the most sedate pace. Even then it would have to be at the most fashionable hour when the park is so crowded that it is virtually impossible to do anything except a slow crawl.

Chapter 13

~

It was good to get out-of-doors and to exercise something
besides her brain, Alex decided as they made their way
down Piccadilly. Maneuvering a highly strung animal
through such a press of traffic was new for her, but she felt
equal to the task despite the exception Nero took to a cart
horse who, resenting the existence of all those animals not
hauling heavy burdens, delighted in nipping any creature in his
vicinity. A passing curricle had forced Nero within the horse's
range, and it was only the quickness of horse and rider which
saved him from having a nasty bite taken out of his flank.

Things were a good deal better once they had gained the
park. Cantering across the expanse of green, Alex at last admitted to herself how much she missed the freedom and the
fresh open spaces of the country. While it was true that becoming Alexander had given her an independence of movement and a variety of activities not previously allowed even to
the eccentric Lady Alexandra de Montmorency, in coming to
London Alex had sacrificed the sense of liberty only to be experienced away from the confines of civilization. Narrow
streets and crowds of people were fascinating, but they were
limiting at times. She longed for the vast green vistas of the
Norfolk landscape more than she had realized. Here in the
park, empty, as yet, of those wishing to see and be seen, the
view was broken only by the presence of a few solitary riders,
and a peacefulness descended on her that Alex had not felt
since leaving the country.

Brother and sister slowed down and rode some time in silence until Tony broke it. "By Jove, now there is a beautiful

girl!" And indeed she was. From the tip of her pert little hat to the toes of her dainty boots she was perfection, with golden curls escaping from under the brim of her hat, and her slender figure straight in the saddle as she trotted sedately with her groom. Her mount, though not of the caliber of Nero and Caesar, was a neat little bay—certainly a very fine lady's horse and sufficiently well bred to win Tony's approval.

Alex grinned. As far as she knew, her brother was entirely unaware of the female sex. Even now she had her doubts as to whether it was the girl herself or her horse that was attracting Tony's attention. Certainly it was no frivolous rider who appeared in the park at this hour when no one was around to see and be seen.

Tony urged Caesar forward so he could get a better look while Alex followed closely behind. Certainly the initial impression improved with proximity. The young lady's eyes were of the deepest blue and her mouth a delicate bow that curved into a shy smile as, under the watchful eyes of her groom, she acknowledged their passing nods.

"And that is all I shall know of her unless her horse bolts or casts a shoe at the precise minute I happen by," Tony groaned. "Why do you have to be my brother at this particular moment when I need a sister to discover her name and strike up an acquaintance?"

"Do not despair." Alex could not help chuckling at her brother's woebegone expression. "We shall contrive something. I only wish I had not sent Ned home with the carriage, for he could have entered into a casual conversation with the groom. Perhaps you should send your batman out tomorrow morning to exercise Caesar and he can become friendly with the man."

Tony was much struck. " 'Tis a clever idea." Then gloom again descended. "But knowing someone's name does not equal an introduction. Besides, someone as lovely as that is sure to have hundreds of fellows around her."

"Don't be such a pudding-heart, Tony," his sister scoffed. "If I had not seen some of your battle scars with my own eyes, I should think you a very poor creature. Where is the man who led his comrades against Soult's charges at Nive? Does the concern over a certain woman's favorable impression unman you more than hails of bullets or cannon fire? Why—" Alex broke off at the sight of another rider approaching them, a rider whose significant height and proud bearing looked vaguely familiar. Surely it was not . . . but, with a sinking heart, she realized that it was all-too likely that Lord Wrotham would be exercising his mount at such an hour, when the lack of people afforded ample room for truly strenuous activity.

Unfortunately, he seemed to recognize them too. He waved and there was no help for it but to make the best of the situation. Alex was thankful now for the amount of time she had spent at home at Halewood riding astride. All the remonstrances she had suffered at the hands of her mother and other despairing nurses were worth it because she felt confident of performing her part creditably now. Still, she had been hoping for a few moments of peace when she did not need to be on her guard. Now that chance was gone.

What was an opportunity lost for Alex was, however, an opportunity gained for Christopher and he had seized upon it immediately. Here was an occasion to observe the de Montmorencys in an environment free from the distracting presence of other gamesters. As he had decided late last night after much thought on the matter, the best way to solve the riddle of Alexander de Montmorency was to question the man directly—and he was determined to gain some answers. Christopher greeted them cheerfully and then turned to Alex. "I should expect to encounter a military man like Tony at such an hour, but for one who is not accustomed to camp life it is another matter indeed."

With difficulty Alex restrained the defensive retort that rose to her lips as she tried desperately to picture Alexander's probable reaction to such a remark. In truth, Alexander would have been in bed at this hour sleeping off the excesses of the previous evening. "Oh tolloll. 'Tis nothing. Such a fine day . . ." She waved an airy hand.

"But the concentration you exerted last night in order to rise a winner from the tables must have been rather wearing, to say the least." Wrotham continued to press her.

Alex decided that her best defense against this probing was to adopt a vague smile, which she did, grinning like an idiot as she replied, "Yes, it was a rather amusing evening was it not?"

"Most amusing," was the sardonic reply. "As was the one before it. You seem never to lose as even the best of us occasionally do."

"Winning streak, you know," Alex confided.

The major's eyes narrowed. "In my life I have observed night after night of gaming and I do not ever remember Dame Fortune smiling so consistently on one particular person as she does on you."

Alex continued to look unconcerned, but all the while her mind was racing furiously. Was the man accusing her of cheating? If he were, what was she to do? Surely she would have to call him out. Even Tony, a little ahead of them, his mind still occupied with the vision he had just seen in the park, slowed his pace and was now listening intently to their exchange, though he tried not to give the appearance of doing so. Alex shrugged. "Very lucky fellow."

"I should say that luck had nothing to do with it." The major's voice was ominously quiet.

Alex remained silent, hardly daring to breathe.

"I should say that it was extraordinary skill."

She let out her breath as imperceptibly as possible. At least he did not think her a Captain Sharp, but there still was a dangerous note of suspicion in his voice. Laughing foolishly, she turned to look at him incredulously.

"Yes"—the blue eyes bored into her—"I should say that a great deal of skill and concentration is being applied to your games and that you do not particularly wish for the rest of the world to be aware of that. Now why on earth would that be?"

"Why indeed?" Though she longed to intone the phrase with accents of utmost dignity, Alex was forced by the role she played to adopt a whimsical air, smiling vacuously at her interrogator, who continued to scrutinize her with the most alarming look of comprehension in his eyes.

"I shall tell you why." He addressed her as crisply as he would any fractious and recalcitrant subaltern. "It is my belief that somehow you, or someone near and dear to you, owes a great deal of money and you have taken it upon yourself to win it back." It was the luckiest of guesses, thought up on the spur of the moment, Lord Wrotham admitted to himself, but he saw the green eyes widen for a fraction of a second before the fatuous expression returned. So, he had not mistaken his man after all. No one who played as expertly as Alexander de Montmorency, no one who took such a lively and intelligent interest in national affairs could truly be as much a buffoon as the Earl of Halewood was making himself out to be. "And," Wrotham continued silkily, "though I have the highest respect for your brother, who is obviously a valiant soldier, I do not see that Captain de Montmorency has the ability to be certain of winning a fortune at the gaming table."

The barely imperceptible look of consternation that passed between the two brothers confirmed what had only been the merest of suspicions, but for some inexplicable reason, Christopher hastened to reassure them. "Believe me, your secret—whatever it is—is safe with me. I know it is none of my concern, but I have come to enjoy your acquaintance and if I may be of any assistance in helping you toward the successful completion of your scheme, I should be honored, if you would allow me to be."

Lord, he sounded a prosy prig, but for some reason he could not fathom, the major was determined to help these two. Perhaps it was because they, unlike many of the *ton*, had a goal they seemed to be working toward, or perhaps it was because he had almost been fooled and he respected anyone clever enough to do that and to beat him at cards as well. Perhaps it was that he admired the pluck behind their plan.

Tony and his sister sat silently, each trying desperately to concoct some plausible tale that would keep the major from probing further.

"How much are you trying to win?" Christopher probed gently.

"A hundred thousand pounds." Alex was the first to speak. "However you must not blame Tony. He is the merest pawn in all this. I was forced to put him up to it because I know no one in London, save for General Scott, and he I know only through my father's reminiscences."

Having said this much, there was nothing to do but continue. Drawing a deep breath, Alex took the plunge, praying that she would sound convincing, that Tony would not say anything untoward, and that the major would understand. "It was the pater you see," she began tentatively. Then, warming

to her story, she hurried on. "In the last years of his life he became convinced he was not leaving enough to provide for us
so he bought shares in a joint stock venture. Unfortunately, he
was far more fortunate at risking his blunt at the card table
than he was in business. The entire scheme collapsed and we
were left with nothing. The shock of it killed the old fellow.
There was naught I could do to raise the wind quickly so I
mortgaged the estate, hoping that with some economy and improved agricultural practice I could rescue our finances."

Alex laughed mirthlessly. "However, it was not enough, so
here I am. The pater was an old rip in his time—spent his days
with the likes of Fox, among others. He lost so much money
then that his family disowned him, but at last he learned a
thing or two about games of chance and eventually won back
his fortune and more and settled down. He stopped gambling
entirely, but he taught me all he knew—said I was better than
he ever was, even in his prime. Knowing all the dangers of it, I
have avoided games of chance until now. But now, well, what
else was I to do?"

"What else indeed?" the major murmured. "A hundred thousand pounds is no paltry sum. From what I can tell, you have a
good start, but it will take you some time to amass all that, and
every day you stay in London cuts into your profits."

"I know." A worried frown wrinkled Alex's forehead.

"It appears to me that you need some management in this
affair—no offense to Tony, of course. But my youth was undoubtedly more misspent than his or yours, and I can arrange
it so you play only with those who risk stakes worth your
while. Your strategy of winning slowly and unobtrusively has
stood you in good stead thus far, but now it is time to take
proper advantage of the situation."

Alex looked doubtful. "I don't know, I mean, I have only
just arrived and I am not all sure I am equal to a contest with
the likes of those you propose."

"Oh, come now, man," Wrotham scoffed. "You may lack
town bronze, but you do not lack skill. I am accounted more
than a fair card player and you bested me. All you need is
someone to bring you to the attention of those who might otherwise not waste their time on a green lad just down from the
country."

"That is most kind," Alex began cautiously. She stole a glance at Tony, who nodded imperceptibly. "Thank you, I think," she concluded lamely.

Christopher grinned. "Naturally you suspect my motives, but I assure you they are of the purest and they are completely self-interested. I am suffering from intolerable ennui here. Boredom, pure and simple, has driven me to it."

An answering gleam appeared in Alex's eye. "When you put it that way, what can I do but accept your help? Having suffered that malady often enough myself I feel compelled to relieve someone else of such an enervating emotion."

"It is agreed then?"

"Agreed."

"Very well. We start this evening. I look forward to seeing you at White's." And with that the major touched his heels to his horse's flank and cantered off, leaving Alex and Tony to stare after him.

Chapter 14

It was Tony who recovered first. "No need to fret, Alex, Wrotham is a right one. I am convinced of it. He is too much a gentleman and a soldier not to be a man of his word, and he does seem to be on the best of terms with numerous people who could prove most useful."

"Yeeeees," Alex agreed, but her tone lacked conviction. "I always did sense that he looked upon us with some degree of suspicion from the very start. However, I suppose it is a good deal better to have that sort of person for, rather than against one."

"Too right. I fancy it would be rather uncomfortable to get on the wrong side of someone like the major. I have seen his sort in the Peninsula, the kind of fellow who would lead you into the mouth of hell, looking after you all the way, but if you were to behave badly, he would be as implacable with you, if not more so, than with the enemy. You don't want to upset a man like Wrotham. He would be the very devil to deal with if he believed you to be anything but honorable."

"Well, that's encouraging," his sister responded gloomily. "With any luck he will only think of me as an ivory turner instead of a woman of ill repute." Why his opinion of her should matter in the least, Alex could not say, but it did matter.

"Surely you are not going to fall into a fit of the dismals now when we are fully committed to this charade. You should have done that back in Norfolk. It is too late now to entertain any missish notions such as that," her brother scolded.

"Missish! I am not in the least missish," Alex protested furiously.

"Delighted to hear it. I thought for a moment there that you were going to cry off just when the opportunity to play deep was presenting itself. Oh I know you have been winning steadily, but this one thousand or five thousand pounds a night will not do. My nerves won't stand for it. I say go for thirty or forty thousand and be done with it in a few nights."

"Thirty or forty thousand pounds!" His sister was aghast. "I could never . . ."

"Of course you can. Why, the pater won Halewood in three sittings and you are a better player than he ever was." Tony paused for a moment, reflecting. "Don't drink so much."

"Don't drink at all, you mean," Alex responded dryly. However, her brother's bracing tones were having the desired effect and she seriously began to consider the odds. Was it safer, after all, to play moderately over a long period and run the risk of being discovered, perhaps even before she had reached her goal, or was it better to put her faith in her own abilities as Tony and Lord Wrotham seemed to and get the whole thing over as quickly as possible. After all, Bonaparte was amassing his forces with unbelievable speed. Who knew how long it would be before Tony's regiment was called upon to fight. Without Tony, Alex shuddered, the whole business was dangerous indeed. Such an eventuality did not bear thinking of.

"Very well then, I shall play deep, but mind you, the first time I lose . . ."

"You won't lose," her brother scoffed. "Why, you're far more likely to lose your disguise and your reputation gallivanting all over London as you seen to feel compelled to do, than you are to lose your blunt at a card game."

"I will not!" Alex was offended. "I think I make a better man than Alexander did."

"You won't get any argument from me there. Now come along. I must get back to the barracks. They're almost ready to change the guard."

They rode back to the Clarendon, each reflecting on the morning's events—Alex mulling over the major's surprising offer and Tony trying desperately to concoct a scheme for introducing himself to the beautiful young rider in the park.

Alex spent the rest of the day writing to those she had left behind, regaling them with every detail she could think of—

relaying to Ally the latest style in bonnets and the cuts of pelisses she saw on the fashionable ladies on Bond Street, describing the fine points of her new mount to Andrew, and telling Abigail about the wealth of street vendors and the wonders of the great buildings. Finished with the letter, she caught up on the news, reading through a stack of the *Times* that had piled up on the chair. And lastly, mindful of the evening ahead of her, she lay down on the bed and did her best to fortify herself for the challenges to come.

She dozed fitfully, with visions of hands and particular plays straggling in and out of her consciousness. At last she rose, and after consuming a light supper of boiled fowl, strolled off to Tony's barracks in an attempt to clear her head before settling to a night of play.

Tony was ready when she arrived and more than eager to discover what the evening held in store. "Don't be in such a pucker," he reassured his sister. "Wrotham would never steer you wrong. Mark my words, you're bound to leave White's a good deal more plump in the pocket tonight than when you came in."

"I hope so, Tony. I hope so." Alex sighed.

The major was as good as his word. Though he was already seated at a table when they arrived, he was obviously keeping a watch out for them. The moment the de Montmorencys entered the gaming room he nodded and beckoned them over. "Ah, Hughes," he addressed the man across the table from him, "here is a partner worthy of your skill." He turned to Alex. "Let me introduce you to Ball Hughes, who is such an habitué of games of chance that nothing surprises him. I feel certain that you can offer him and Thanet and Granville here an evening enlivening enough to catch their attention."

With that, Alex found herself seated at the table with the three gentlemen. Though they nodded amiably enough at her, there was a gleam in their eyes and a distracted air of the dedicated gambler, someone for whom nothing held any interest except the next toss of the dice or turn of the card. However, these signs were somewhat reassuring to Alex, who had been convinced by her father's countless stories that those in the grip of such a fever could not begin to compete against a coldly rational opponent.

This indeed proved to be true and Alex, at first unsure of her ability when faced by such noted gamesters, was soon confident that she was more than equal to them. The more successful she was, the more determined they were to continue playing, and the amounts placed as bets grew larger and larger. These astronomical figures were increased in response to the comments that Wrotham so deftly interjected. His "Why that is a paltry bet, Hughes. Surely you have more faith in Dame Fortune than that"; or "Granville, I never knew you to be so clutch-fisted. Surely you are not going to let Hughes outshine you . . ." only encouraged the players to risk higher and higher stakes.

The rest of the evening, and a good many of the morning hours as well, were a blur to Alex. Nothing existed for her beyond the green-covered table, the figures on the cards, and the white blur of the faces of the other players. All was darkness beyond the pool of light washing over them and nothing outside of that golden circle was of the slightest importance. Her head ached from the concentration, and her face was numb for maintaining a properly bored and impassive expression. As for her limbs, with the exception of the hands which held her cards, they had lost all feeling hours ago.

At last Lord Granville surveyed his cards and shook his head in disgust. "I have lost enough for one evening, gentlemen. I had better seek out less expensive company so that I may live to bet another day." And winking broadly, he rose from the table and headed for the door.

"I'm with him," Thanet declared. "I have proven beyond the shadow of a doubt that the Goddess of Chance does not smile upon me this evening. I shall stop and give her some time to reconsider." And flinging an arm over his friend's shoulder, he too staggered out.

Alex looked at her partner and shrugged. "I daresay that means we must call it a night. Thank you, sir." And as casually as if she won fifty thousand pounds at every sitting, she rose and turned to her brother. "What do you say to a little fresh air, eh, Tony? I'm all for a stroll before retiring."

"Eh?" Not a little dizzy from having surreptitiously consumed Alex's constantly filled glass, Tony came to with a start. "Ah, er, yes, do me good. Just a quick one before duty calls."

Off observing the play at another table, Christopher saw them begin to make their way out. For once at a loss as to what to do, he stood rooted to the spot. On the one hand, he wanted to join them and review the evening's enormous success. On the other, he knew that the more he remained in the background, and the less connection he appeared to have with the de Montmorencys, the better.

Alex solved his dilemma for him as, wavering slightly on feet that were unsteady after hours of immobility, she managed to pass by his table on her way to the door. "Appreciate your giving up your place, old fellow—damned fine play it was, damned fine." She nodded owlishly. "Capital fellows, all of them." And clapping a hand on his shoulder she winked almost imperceptibly before continuing on her erratic path.

It was a gesture of a moment, the true significance of it cleverly hidden from all the rest, but the major had read the gratitude in de Montmorency's eyes and knew that his efforts on the lad's behalf had not been wasted.

It was so rare that anyone acknowledge his efforts or thanked him that Wrotham was surprised at how much the simple act of appreciation meant to him. In truth he had done very little, for it was the lad's extraordinary skill that had earned him a place at that particular table and kept him there long enough to win what must have been a sizeable amount, if the bulge in his pocket were any indication of his success.

Christopher wanted to follow after them and assure them that the pleasure was his, that the gratification of helping someone help himself was reward enough, but he was forced to contain himself until such time as he could meet up with them privately.

Meanwhile, as she stepped outside, Alex heaved a sigh of relief and grabbed her brother's arm exultantly. "Fifty thousand, Tony!" She breathed. "Can you believe it? All in one sitting?"

"Told you so, Alex. A few more nights like this and I shall be free to do something restful like shipping off to the Continent to fight Boney." Tony grinned.

"Really, Anthony, you are the most provoking thing," his

sister retorted. "But you are the best of brothers to help me, and I can't thank you enough."

"Don't thank me. Thank Wrotham. He's the one who is really going to help you repair our fortunes and free yourself from the clutches of Cranbourne."

"Yes." Alex fell silent, thinking again how quickly the major had sensed she had some sort of mission in London and then, having wormed it out of her, had immediately proceeded to offer his most valuable assistance. He was a man of both sympathy and action—a very rare combination indeed. She only knew of one other such person, Trevor Padgett, and certainly the major was a good deal more attractive than the doctor.

Good heavens, where had such an absurd thought come from? She never paid the least attention to anyone's physical appearance. Now here she was recalling the expression in Wrotham's eyes and the energy radiating from him that made one even more aware of his height and the breadth of his shoulders. She never noticed such things and yet here she was remarking to herself that Major Lord Wrotham was a very striking-looking person indeed. Alex blinked. It was most definitely time to seek out her bed. Her wits, worn out by an evening of intense concentration, had obviously gone wandering.

Fortunately, brother and sister had been walking at a respectable pace and reached the Clarendon just as Alex recognized the complete deterioration of her faculties. She bade Tony good night and hurried up to her chamber. As she entered, she caught a glimpse of herself in the looking glass—a slim, straight figure, long-limbed and moving with a certain pride, her hair glinting red in the candlelight. Come to think of it, she made a fine figure of a man herself. On that thought, she tumbled into bed fully clothed. The last thought in her mind, disturbingly enough, was of Lord Wrotham and whether or not she would continue to prove worthy of his interest and assistance.

Chapter 15

In truth, the next time Alex encountered the major it was in rather unexpected circumstances. The sun was alarmingly high when she awoke, fully dressed, to a room so bright that she knew it must be close to noon. Drat! She had missed her opportunity for a ride in the park while it was still uncrowded. Soon it would be filling up with elegant carriages and splendidly mounted riders all vying for attention. A ride at that hour, under such conditions, was not so much fresh air and exercise as it was a social affair fraught with as much gossip and slander as any ball or assembly. Strolling along Bond Street would be hardly less of a crush, but at least she could make mental notes of everything she saw and send it along in a letter to Ally.

Less than an hour later, exquisitely attired in buff-colored pantaloons and a dark blue coat of Bath superfine, cravat carefully tied in a Mathematical that she had mastered at last, Alex was sauntering along Bond Street, swinging the gold-headed cane which Tony had given her, and trying to unobtrusively study the delicious gewgaws on display.

Pausing to examine the decoration on an elegant bonnet, she nearly stumbled over Lord Wrotham, who was just emerging from a shop, a woman on his arm. Somehow Alex had never thought him to be much in the petticoat line, why she could not precisely say. She rather hoped he would be so absorbed in his companion so as not to notice Alex and thus afford her time to take a better look at the woman with him. It was the vain hope of a minute, for they were upon her before she could move or turn away.

The major halted and nodded at Alex. "Hello, de Montmorency," he exclaimed in friendly fashion. "As you are new to town, I should warn you that if you have anything at all to do with females"—the major glanced sardonically in the direction of his companion—"it is a far greater risk of your blunt to walk along here than it is to bet it at White's."

The woman at his side, a vision in an elegant pale blue walking dress that matched her eyes, smiled coquettishly at Alex and then turned to the major. "But, Christopher, you are keeping me in suspense. Who *is* this handsome acquaintance of yours? I do not believe I know him."

Much to her annoyance, Alex blushed to the roots of her hair—something her twin would never have done. He abhorred anything female, especially one of as indeterminate an age as this one, who wore a decidedly predatory expression.

A look of resignation settled across the major's tanned countenance. "Very well. Allow me to present you to my mother, Lady Linwood, Countess of Claverdon. Alexander de Montmorency."

The flirtatious smile broadened as the lady peeked at Alex from under the brim of a very youthful bonnet. "Why, I believe I knew your father Alfred. You have the look of him. What a scamp *he* was, ripe for any mischief, that is, until he met your mother. *Then* he became a pattern card of perfection." She sighed romantically. "What a beautiful couple they made. It was so sad they proceeded to bury themselves in Norfolk or whatever outlandish place it was."

"Norfolk." Alex could not help grinning. How uncomfortable the major was. Why, he was frowning like a veritable thundercloud. Undoubtedly he was escorting her under duress and he looked to be a man who had suffered through this scene on numerous occasions.

"You must call on me," Lady Linwood cooed. "I do so adore the younger set. Everyone of my age has gone to take the waters or is a doting grandmama—horridly dull."

As there seemed no chance of his mother's doing so, Alex decided to put the major out of his misery. "That is very kind of you, ma'am. I certainly hope to do so, but now I must be off as I have . . . ah . . . an appointment that must not be kept waiting." Alex tried to look as self-conscious as possible, hoping to convey the impression that the appointment was with another female and thus dash any designs Lady Linwood might have on Alexander de Montmorency.

Wrotham's mother wagged a gloved finger at Alex. "Naughty boy. There is no doubt you are your father's son."

Alex made good her escape and hurried along as quickly as possible, trying all the while to appear as though searching the street for a certain carriage. Arriving at Piccadilly, she heaved a sigh of relief and stopped to consider her next step. Hatchard's presented an alluring prospect and so she proceeded in a leisurely manner in that general direction, chuckling to herself as she did so.

No wonder the major had joined the Hussars. Alex could tell from the firm clutch that Lady Linwood had kept on her son's arm that she was not the sort to let him out of her sight unless she was provided with a more attractive male escort. Alex had seen her type before, even in the backwater of Norfolk—a clinger if there ever was one, and a woman to whom male attention and admiration were the very breath of her existence. Her son did not appear to relish the role she had cut out for him.

Women seemed to be the order of the day, for when Alex returned to her rooms sometime later, she was greeted by a jubilant Tony. He was fairly bursting with his news. "It's happened, Alex," Tony exclaimed joyfully. "I have met her!"

"Her?" Alex's mind could bring up nothing but a complete blank.

"Yes, you know." Tony glanced at his sister curiously. Ordinarily she was most clever, but now she was staring at him as vacantly as though she had not even been present when he'd first seen the most beautiful girl in the world. What other *her* could he possibly mean? "The girl on the horse." He sighed ecstatically. "The girl we saw riding in the park."

Alex was quick to recover from her momentary lapse. "How wonderful! Tell me what happened."

That was all the urging her brother needed and he launched into his tale. He, being far more accustomed to riotous living than his sister, had been up betimes this morning as usual and went out for a ride before duty. It was then he saw her again and he cursed himself for a fool for not having followed up on his sister's suggestion and sending his batman out to exercise Caesar and strike up a conversation with her groom. However, fate seemed to have taken a particular shine to Captain de Montmorency that day, for while he sat there cursing his lack of forethought, a pug that had been straining at a leash held by a thoroughly bored footman broke free and dashed in the girl's direction yapping excitedly. The young lady's horse had taken instant exception to the nasty animal and bolted.

"And naturally you rushed to her aid," his sister concluded. "What could be more likely to win a girl's heart than to be rescued by a dashing captain of the Guards?"

"Her name"—Tony sighed reverently—"her name is Lucinda Addington and she is here to make her come-out, though in general she much prefers the country to the town. She is the sweetest . . . well that is to say I think you and Ally would quite like her. She has younger brothers of her own whom she misses as much as she does her country rides." Tony was silent for a moment, lost in blissful contemplation of this stroke of good fortune. Then, struck by a sudden thought, he turned to his sister.

"She asked if I might perhaps be going to the Carstairs' ball. Lord, I don't know. I never attend those things, but when I said that I might possibly do so, she asked, very modestly mind you, if it would put me out to escort her and her mama. Apparently her papa has been called back to Berkshire on some urgent problem at home. You might have knocked me over with a feather when she asked, for I feel certain that an incomparable such as she must have the fellows falling all over themselves to do the least little thing for her." Tony beamed happily.

His sister smiled. "Perhaps, but I know no one could be as kind or as gentlemanly an escort as you, Tony. Of that I am certain."

A cloud descended over her brother's beatific countenance. "But what about you, Alex? As we left White's last evening I heard Knightley mention something to someone about taking you on. Now *there's* a pigeon worth plucking. They say he never plays if the stakes are less than ten thousand, and no one except General Scott ever beats him. You'll need me there if he approaches you tonight."

"Don't be so old womanish, brother dear, I shall ask Wrotham to accompany me. He knows what to do well enough, having observed us so carefully from the moment we began our campaign." Alex spoke with more confidence than she felt, but she was determined to give her brother his chance with the woman of his dreams. Tony was a dear and he deserved all the happiness he could get. If it had not been for his support and the little bit of money he had been able to send them at Halewood from time to time, she did not know how she would have managed. Besides, it looked as though Halewood would soon be requiring a new master and an estate as vast as theirs would need a mistress.

Of course, she could continue managing Halewood as she had for Alexander, but Bonaparte could not last forever and faced by inaction, Tony would undoubtedly sell out and come home. He had spoken more than once, rather wistfully, of raising horses as his friend Rokeby did. From the little Alex had seen and heard of Lucinda Addington, the girl seemed to be far more the sort of person to help Tony run the estate than any other young miss he was likely to meet in London. A teasing smile quirked the corners of Alex's mouth. "You escort Lucinda and her mother. Any woman who can convince you to attend a ball must be a rare woman indeed."

Tony grinned. "Oh she most certainly is, but you are more important at the moment and I . . ."

Alex raised an admonitory hand. "Hush. I shall hear no more of it. It will look better if I go on my own every once in a while, else people might begin to wonder what we are about if we are always seen together."

Though she put a brave front on it for her brother's sake, Alex was more than a little nervous when she entered the crowded gaming room at White's all on her own that evening. However, General Scott, on his way to a table, greeted her with a, "Hello my lad. Hear you have not been putting your father to shame"; and several other members nodded to her in a reassuringly friendly fashion. Alex acknowledged their greetings and then, trying not to appear as anxious as she felt, scanned the room, desperately trying to catch a glimpse of Wrotham's familiar broad-shouldered figure.

The major, idly watching a group hazarding their fortunes

on the cast of the dice, had been aware of Alex's presence the moment the youth appeared. There was something about de Montmorency, Christopher decided as he strolled over to meet Alex, that set him apart from others, at least when he was not playing at the role of careless gamester. It was not physical presence, for though he was a little above-average height, he was slender. Nor did he have any other outstanding features. It was more a matter of the way he carried himself. There was an energy about him, and the self-possessed air of a man who knew what he was about, a man accustomed to thinking and acting for himself instead of slavishly following the whim of fashion.

"Hello," he greeted Alex, smiling. "What have you done with your shadow?"

"Tony? He is accompanying a certain lady and her mother to the Carstairs' ball."

A gleam of amusement lit the dark blue eyes. "Then I say, prepare yourself for his absence in the future, for in my experience, when a lad like Tony even notices something besides pistols, sabers, or horses, he is more than halfway to being caught in the parson's mousetrap. But come along. I want to introduce you to someone who can help you attain your goal." With an encouraging wink, he led Alex to a table where a tall, rather cadaverous man sat languidly riffling a pack of cards and trading witticisms with a group of young bucks who seemed to hang on his every word.

"Hello, Knightley." Wrotham laid a hand on the man's shoulder. "I have someone here you might like to meet. You may have seen de Montmorency cleaning out the pockets of his opponents. Knowing you as a man who likes a challenge and him as a man who can offer one, I thought you two should become acquainted."

Surveying Alex with glittering dark eyes, the thin man nodded ever-so slightly and gestured to a chair. "So you think you can beat me, do you?" The languid air had disappeared entirely and the long fingers which had been idly playing with the cards suddenly clenched around the pack.

"No, sir." Alex struggled to mask the hesitancy in her voice. She took a deep breath. "I am merely looking for a decent game." She broadened her casual drawl. "It is rather more dull here than I had hoped. Somehow I had expected that here in London . . ." she allowed herself to trail off as she pulled out the chair indicated and sat down.

"Then you have come to the right place. Mind you, the first time I play with someone, I only play one partie and the stakes are ten thousand. After that, I shall see."

Alex swallowed hard and nodded in as offhand a way as she could muster. Having listened to her father's stories countless times, she was able to recognize a hardened gamester when she saw one. Everything about Sir Derek Knightley, from the pale, hollow cheeks, to the intense gaze and the nervous fingers all indicated a man who lived for games of chance.

Well, Alex comforted herself, after all, you took on one of the world's most confirmed gamblers night after night after night at Halewood so this should be nothing new or different. Surely Knightley can be no worse than Papa was at one time. Once you convince him that you are worth the trouble you will have your pick of players, so go to it. Without further ado she accepted the cards being dealt her.

Just at that moment, Alex felt the back of her chair shift ever so slightly. Without even turning around, she knew that Wrotham had laid a hand on it and was gripping it as tensely as she was twisting her ankles around each other under the table. Somehow just knowing that he was there was infinitely comforting to her and it gave her courage to look at the cards in her hand.

Once she had seen them, she was able to concentrate on the matter at hand and push all her other fears into the background. Fortunately for her nerves, she was able to win the first deal, but, she cautioned herself, that was to be expected, the dealer always being at a slight disadvantage. Still, it was better than having lost. Courage, Alex, she muttered to herself as she took her turn dealing. There was a reassuring creak from the back of her chair and she knew that she was not alone in her anticipation of the next deal.

From then on, absolute silence reigned except for an occasional "Good" or "Tierce." To both Alex and the silent observer behind her, the game seemed endless, but slowly, ever-so slowly Alex gained the advantage until at last, unbelievably, the man opposite laid down his cards with a curt nod remarking, "Fine match, de Montmorency. I believe I shall be willing to consider you as an opponent or as a partner." And with that, he was gone, leaving Alex to sag limply in her chair.

"Had enough, or are you now ready to take on the entire club, you young fire-eater?" a voice inquired behind her. Wrotham! In the concentration of the last deal Alex had completely forgotten him. She turned now to see the blue eyes twinkling down at her. But there was something else there as well—an expression that Alex could not fathom at first. Then she realized that it was respect, a most novel reaction to her and an exceedingly gratifying one. To think that men, even those less worthy of respect than she was, received such recognition as a matter of course while she, as a woman, had never experienced such a thing made her envy her brother—not that Alexander would ever have earned it or even wanted something that she had longed for.

Alex shook her head. "Actually, I think I have had enough for one night. I believe I shall toddle along. The fresh air will do me good." She made for the door and the major followed. Drat! The man seemed disposed to accompany her. How very awkward, but there was nothing for it except to let him.

Chapter 16

The door had barely shut behind them when the major clapped Alex on the back. "Good show, de Montmorency! Devilish good show. Knightley does not take kindly to being beaten, but it will only serve to whet his appetite the more. Why, next time you ought to be able to demand fifty thousand a game."

"Surely not," Alex demurred. "Besides, I can't risk that much, nor can I be assured of walking away a winner. Tonight was a very near thing."

"Nonsense, you had him from the moment the cards were dealt."

"Perhaps," she conceded. "But still, it was a good deal nearer a thing than I am comfortable with."

"Stuff and nonsense. You are far too modest. But come, join me in my chambers. Radlett will make us some punch and you will tell me how the devil you managed it. There were several deals when I could not see how you knew to proceed."

"Ah." Alex grinned. "That would be telling, wouldn't it. And what if I wish to beat you again sometime?" The major chuckled and they strolled along for some time in companionable silence.

As they rounded the corner onto Piccadilly, three dark shapes detached themselves from the shadows. The ruffians lying in wait for dandies flush with wine and winnings from the table had not counted on their quarry appearing so early in the evening. Grinning at each other, the two largest pounced on their unwary prey while the third remained out of sight until his assistance was needed.

Taken completely unawares, Wrotham was momentarily thrown off balance by the attack and it took him some minutes to recover. As it was his assailant who had led the offense, Alex had a moment's warning before hers was upon her and was able to grab her walking stick and lay it about. The heavy gold head applied energetically to her attacker's knees, though not very good science, was effective.

In the meantime, the major had managed to assume a more advantageous stance and delivered a bruising right to his opponent's jaw. The fellow staggered a moment, shook his head, and came charging like a wounded bull at Christopher. He was a brute of a man, taller than the major by several inches and outweighing him by at least two or three stone, but Wrotham, known throughout his regiment for his pugilistic skill, stepped lightly aside, throwing the man off balance, which allowed him to deliver another punishing blow. The thief was stopped dead in his tracks. A look of astonishment came over his face and he toppled over like a brick wall.

The major turned quickly to see how his companion was doing. Alex, who had been coached by Tony in many of the manly arts, but not boxing, was at somewhat of a disadvantage. Had the contest been with swords or pistols, she would have been able to hold her own, but as it was, she was forced to adopt rather rough-and-ready methods, which consisted of dancing around her aggressor and landing a blow with her stick wherever possible, making sure all along that his punches never touched her.

She was doing well, but tiring, and in a desperate attempt to end it all, she most inelegantly butted her attacker in the stomach with her head. It was not a move she was particularly proud of, but it worked beautifully. The fellow gasped, clutched his ample midsection, and doubled over onto the pavement.

Unfortunately, Alex, transfixed with astonishment by the efficacy of her maneuver, neglected to step out of the way and, caught by her opponent's bulky shoulder as he fell, hit the cobbles at the same time he did. She had only a moment to curse herself for her stupidity before the world went black.

The third would-be thief, having witnessed the effectiveness of the major's fists, took to his heels, leaving the victor surrounded by prostrate bodies. It was no more than a few steps to his hotel and Wrotham, accustomed to bearing far more seriously wounded comrades over infinitely worse terrain, decided to support his inert companion back to his chambers rather than trying to obtain transport.

Bending down, he hoisted Alex up with astonishing ease. The major was somewhat surprised that such a tall fellow of an average build should weigh so little, but as it made his task all the easier, he thought no more of it beyond being grateful for the lightness of his burden. Dumping Alex unceremoniously over his shoulder, he carried her within sight of the hotel, where he deftly slid her off. Then, draping her limp arm over his shoulder, he grasped the slender waist and made his way into the hotel, weaving slightly so as to give the impression that both of them were slightly the worse for wear.

Once in his chambers, the major dropped his burden into a chair and grabbed a bottle of brandy. Gently he undid Alex's cravat, opened the neck of the shirt, and was just about to tip the brandy down her throat when he noticed a curious thing. De Montmorency's chest was tightly wrapped with bandages. Was it a wound, perhaps, from some duel? Not a little surprised, Christopher looked again, a little closer this time, and it was then he saw the gentle swellings above the bandages. The brandy bottle slipped from his nerveless grasp and crashed to the floor, spilling its contents all over the carpet.

A woman! Alexander de Montmorency, Earl of Halewood, was a woman? Wrotham sat down heavily, his mind in a whirl. Surely not! No woman would dare pose as a man, much less enter the holy of holies, White's, and then proceed to trounce them all at cards as well. He looked again. No, there was no mistaking the roundness above the bandages, the smooth whiteness of the skin. No wonder his burden had been so light! The major rose and gingerly eased off Alex's coat and felt the shoulders—padding. He grinned and shook his head in astonishment.

Then with a start he came back to the immediate problem. Brandy, he must have brandy. Radlett was out, having been given the evening off, but after rummaging around Christopher was able to unearth another bottle. Gently he parted the lips which, come to think of it, had always seemed rather delicate for a man. Slowly the major tipped the bottle allowing some of the liquid to slide down her throat.

There was a gasp, a choke, and the thick dark lashes fluttered open. The green eyes stared blankly for a minute and then, focusing on the major, regained their customary alertness. "Wrotham?"

"In the flesh," he asserted. "But who are you?"

There was not a moment's hesitation. "De Montmorency, of course."

Clever girl, the major applauded her silently. "There weren't many who could sustain such a blow to their heads and keep their wits about them.

"You may be a de Montmorency, but Alexander, you surely are not."

One slender hand, traveling to rub the rising bump on the side of her head encountered the open collar of the shirt. Realization dawned. "Oh."

"Just so. And if you are not Alexander, who are you? Was there ever an Alexander, and if so, where is he?" the major inquired pleasantly enough, but the blue eyes were looking at her most intently.

"You ask a good deal of questions, sir," Alex retorted, an angry flush rising to her cheeks.

"Can you blame me? I assure you, it is only out of the idlest curiosity. I have known you long enough to be sure that this masquerade is being perpetrated for only the best of motives."

Alex shot a quick suspicious glance at him, but her interlocutor was not jesting. Instead, he was regarding her with a mixture of perplexity, sympathy, and what appeared to be admiration.

"Why is Alexander not out repairing the family fortune?" he prompted gently.

"Because he was the one who lost it." Try as she would, Alex could not hide the indignation in her voice. "Besides, he hasn't the slightest head for cards."

"Whereas you play them like an angel."

"Papa always said so," she responded simply.

Wrotham glanced at her curiously, taking in the auburn hair, green eyes under delicate brows, and the determined chin. His lips twitched. "No doubt the hapless Tony had not the least idea of all this until you appeared at his quarters."

Alex nodded, an answering gleam in her eyes. "Tony is the dearest brother imaginable, and he is doing his best to help provide for us, but . . ."

"He draws the line at his older sister's ruining her reputation," the major finished for her.

"Reputation, pooh." Alex dismissed a young lady's most precious commodity with a wave of her hand. "A reputation is useful only if one intends to be married."

"Which you do not?"

"Good heavens, no! After all, even if Alexander does survive, he needs someone after him constantly to keep him from bringing us all to complete destruction."

"So I gather it was he and not your father who made the, er, unfortunate investments."

"Yes." The green eyes kindled. "A more cork-brained, selfish—" Alex broke off. "Well, never mind. Let us just say that he got us into dun territory."

"From which his sister—you are his sister, are you not?—is doing her level best to rescue him."

"Not him!" Even Alex was taken aback at the vehemence in her tone. "He may hang. It is Ally and the children. Yes, I am Alexander's twin sister, Alexandra. And I *won't* let him ruin their chances at happiness. I can take care of myself, but Ally would like desperately to have a Season and a family of her own. Andrew, if it were up to him, would eschew a proper education, but he is going to have one, nevertheless. Then there's Abigail. For the moment, she just needs a home."

"Alexander, Alexandra, Anthony, Althea, Andrew, and Abigail?"

"Papa said he would never be sure which child was which so if he chose names beginning with an *A* no matter what name he called he was bound to get one of us to answer."

"I see. Very sensible of him. And you have taken it upon yourself to provide all these things they need?" The major shook his head in disbelief, but it was a disbelief that had more than a touch of admiration in it. "Was there no one else, no other way?"

"No. Papa's family disowned him years ago and Mama's

are all dead. Alexander's solution was to marry me off to"—the thought of Sir Ralph Cranbourne was so disgusting that Alex could not even bring herself to pronounce his name—"to the man who holds all the vowels for his debts."

"You know," Wrotham began, "I am beginning to dislike this Alexander more and more, but even he could not be so lost to all decency as to let you do this."

An impish twinkle glistened in her eyes. "Perhaps not, but he was unconscious at the time."

The major gave a shout of laughter. "You certainly are determined. But what is to say he will not come pursuing you when he regains consciousness?"

"He is so very ill, I doubt he will recover," was the sober reply. "And, in truth, that might be the very best thing for us all. I tried to help him mend his ways. I truly did try."

"I am sure you did, but it has been my experience that when a man is bent on the path of self-destruction it is worse than useless to try to stop him. Those who do, only bring themselves to grief. Now," he added in a bracing tone, "just how much do you need to win in order to free yourself of the odious Sir Ralph and recoup the family fortunes?"

"About thirty or forty thousand pounds more," Alex responded listlessly.

"Well, I shall see to it that Knightley does not forget that he wishes to win back his losses, and that others are inspired to take you on. I shall bring you your opponents and you will relieve them of their money."

"You mean you will help me?" Alex could not believe her ears.

"Of course I shall help you."

The astonishment on her face was so patent that he could not help asking indignantly, "What did you think I would do, expose you? A pretty sort of fellow I should be."

Alex jumped up and seized the major's hand. "Oh, thank you, thank you. You are so very kind."

"Kindness has nothing to do with it. How could I possibly sit idly by when I have a chance to help someone who has faced life's problems with as much courage and, er, ingenuity as you have? But now I do believe you should go home to bed. You received quite a blow on the head and it won't do to have those brains of yours the least bit muddled. Come, I shall escort you home." He held out his arm.

"There is not the least need to do that," Alex replied, unaccountably flustered by the gesture and the warm admiration in his eyes.

"Have you forgotten why you are here in the first place?" The major was incredulous.

"No . . ."

"Well, then."

"But who will escort *you* back? For after all, you will appear on your return what I would appear now, a man alone in the streets."

The major grinned and shook his head. "You are quite a handful, you know. Almost, I begin to pity the unknown Alexander. What you say is perfectly true, but though you make a most excellent figure of a man, you lack the experience in battle that I have. Let us just say letting me watch over you is the price I shall exact in return for my silence on the entire matter."

"Why, that is blackmail!" Alex was indignant, but she took the proffered arm and was glad of it, for the room swam unpleasantly when she rose from her chair. However, the dizziness subsided in an instant and she found herself, though tired, perfectly capable of walking to her hotel. Along the way she could not help reflecting that though it was entirely unnecessary, there was something very comforting about having the major's arm supporting her.

Chapter 17

No sooner had she undressed than Alex, utterly worn out by the events of the evening, fell into exhausted slumber. The strain of the game would have been enough to ensure a deep sleep, but that, coupled with the attack and the subsequent discovery of her disguise, had utterly fatigued her.

The same could not be said of Christopher. His brain a jumble of confused thoughts, he replayed the entire evening in his mind as he sauntered back to his lodgings. Once in his chambers, he tore off his coat, poured himself a generous glass of brandy, and flung himself into a chair in front of the fire to sort things out.

Who could have guessed that a woman, genteel and accustomed only to a quiet life in the country, would attempt such a thing? He did not know many *men* who would have exhibited the iron nerve and determination that Alex had. Yet here was a woman, hardly more than a girl actually, who had taken on the entire membership of White's as coolly as if she were taking tea with her neighbors. Any female of Christopher's acquaintance, if she had done anything at all, would have railed mightily at her unfortunate fate, sought out the wealthiest man in sight, and done her utmost to catch him in the parson's mousetrap.

Not only had Alex confronted her problem with quiet dignity and efficiency, she had responded with equal presence of mind to his discovery of the secret of her identity. Christopher tried to picture his mother in such a situation and failed. It was simply too mind-boggling. Casting back in his memory from his first love, who had thrown him over for the chance to become a duchess, to his next-to-last opera dancer, who had left him for the protection of someone of greater *ton*, Christopher decided that if there was one thing the women in his life had cared for more than wealth, it was reputation—position in society. Yet Alex, faced with the total destruction of hers, had been entirely unconcerned. All her energies were directed toward helping her family, to the total disregard of the possible effects her efforts might have on her own life.

It was a revelation to Lord Wrotham. He knew far too many men, let alone women, who thought of nothing more than their own immediate comfort. This was largely the reason he had been so glad to go to the Peninsula. Though one could not escape much of the vanity and selfishness prevalent in the *ton*, at least in war, one was forced to prove oneself in more concrete and valuable ways.

The major stared into the fire as he conjured up all the mental pictures of Alexandra. He could not help grinning to himself as he thought of the first time he had seen her, lounging in her chair, looking for all the world as though she were completely castaway. Her imitation had been so well done that he could only assume she had seen her brother in such a state more times than she cared to remember. Next came the image of her, intent and earnest, as she discussed the state of Europe and the attitude in Parliament toward the emergency there. Not the least of these memories was the glimpse he had caught of her out of the corner of his eye as she laid her walking stick about the knees and shoulders of her recent attacker. But mostly he envisioned her, green eyes dark with concentration, the slim, white hands steady, and the otherwise mobile features devoid of all expression as she sat at the gaming table night after night, calmly and methodically beating one opponent after another.

What an incredible woman she was! No, Christopher amended, what an incredible person she was. Any man who had done such a thing would have instantly won his admiration. That it was a woman who had taken on such a task was almost incomprehensible to him.

The major found himself looking forward to the next day with unaccustomed anticipation. What would Alex do next? In fact, the more he thought about it, the more he realized that the

de Montmorencys, first as stimulating acquaintances, and then
as two people with a mission, had been responsible for the zest
in his otherwise dull sojourn in London. Alexandra's disguise
only added piquancy to it all, and he could not wait to see her
again, to learn more about this astounding person. What kind
of woman would even dream up such a scheme, much less
carry it out?

Lord Wrotham was not the only one eagerly awaiting the
next morning. Back in his quarters in Portman Square, Anthony too was having difficulty falling asleep. Lucinda
Addington, attired in the demure costume of a young miss in
her first Season, was even more bewitching than Lucinda
Addington in a riding habit, and just as enchanting. She had
been all that was charming to every one of the young bucks
who crowded around her, neither flirting with nor favoring one
over another. And while her exquisite loveliness made Captain
de Montmorency's heart beat a good deal faster, she hadn't
made him feel tongue-tied.

Not for Miss Addington the gossip of the *ton*—she could
not have cared less about such things, especially when accompanied by a gentleman who had spent the last years in Spain
and Portugal fighting the armies of the Corsican monster. She
wanted to know all about army life. Was it as dreadful as they
said? Had he ever actually killed a man? What was going to
happen now that Bonaparte had escaped?

Anthony felt as easy with her as with his two sisters, though
in truth, Lucinda fell somewhere in between. She asked questions with the air of wide-eyed innocence so much like Ally's,
yet delved after the truth regardless of unpleasant details in a
way that reminded him very much of Alexandra. And she had
looked so very enchanting as she listened eagerly to his Peninsular exploits. Looking down into the blue eyes fixed so admiringly on him, Tony was suddenly less impatient than he
had been to return to the Continent and the inevitable struggle
with Boney.

In truth, it was not the supposed glory of war that had made
him join up, but rather boredom with the life of a second son,
an existence that was so dull and unproductive compared to
life in the army. Tony sighed. Life could be most confusing at

times. He could not wait to talk to Alex about it all. She had a knack for seeing right to the heart of a matter that made even the stickiest of problems seem manageable.

Good old Alex. She had been mother, father, and elder brother to him. His mother, sweet as she was, had been involved with the younger children. His father, in addition to looking after the estate, had had more than enough on his plate with Alexander, a constant source of irritation. It had been Alex, so very clever in her own right and so eager to learn, who had helped Tony with his lessons. When Alexander had refused to let the younger Tony tag along on the twins' explorations and adventures, Alexandra had always sought out Tony afterward and shared with him everything she had seen or learned.

Tony had been very grateful for this attention and had repaid her as best he could by teaching her swordplay or marksmanship when Alexander refused to do so. Now she was the equal to any man at both these skills. He had written her long letters from London and the Peninsula, sharing with her as much as he could of the wider world he was experiencing. However, deep down inside, Tony knew that try as he would, he could never completely erase the loneliness and isolation his sister suffered.

Of course Alex would rather have died than let on that she found her life the least bit dull. "Complaints of boredom or solitude are merely the reflections of an empty mind," she always declared. Still, it did seem a pity that someone as clever, curious, and adventurous as his sister had no one to share this with. Captain de Montmorency was more than ready to admit that he possessed far less in the cock-loft than his sister. In fact, most people did. He could never have kept up with her in a discussion as Wrotham had, for example. Tony was as ripe for a lark of any sort as his sister, but he was never around to accompany her, and her twin refused to do anything for anyone but himself, so Alex was left without a comrade to share in any adventures. Althea, though devoted to Alex, was far too timid to attempt anything more spirited than a ride around the fields of Halewood on a docile mare.

Thinking about the environs of Halewood, Tony concluded that the de Montmorencys were more interesting and adventurous than anyone else in the vicinity. This left little chance for Alex to meet a proper companion for her outside of her family. If only some of the fellows in his regiment were the right sort he would have brought them home to visit, but though Tony would have trusted any one of them with his life, none of them were up to his sister's weight. Alex would have made mice feet of them the moment they began to discuss anything besides horses or fighting.

Poor Alex. She seemed destined to live out her days immured at Halewood, doing her utmost to ensure that all of them were happy and comfortable. Tony wished he could think of something clever to keep this gloomy prospect from occurring, but it was his elder sister, not him, who always came up with the intelligent ideas.

Having taxed his brain with more philosophical musings than it was used to, Tony did at last fall asleep. However, he was up betimes the next morning and off at the earliest hour he felt he could count on his sister's being up.

Despite the rigors of the previous evening, Alex had arisen and was finishing a hearty breakfast which she had ordered in her bedchamber when Tony arrived. One look at her brother's beatific countenance and she was satisfied as to the success of his evening. "No need to ask whether you enjoyed yourself at the Carstairs' ball," she teased.

Tony flushed scarlet. Alex relented and laid a reassuring hand on his arm. "I am delighted that the young lady is all that you had hoped for. Come, sit down and tell me all about it while I ring for more coffee."

Alex could not remember when she had seen her brother so excited except on his first furlough after joining his regiment. She was happy for him, but at the same time could not help feeling the tiniest bit sad—or was it lonely—she could not be certain. For Tony, despite his prolonged absences, had been the closest to her in the family. Oh, Ally was all that was sweet and loving, but Alex's drive and thirst for adventure made the more traditional Ally highly uncomfortable. Tony, on the other hand, had not only understood, but also had done his level best to give her what he could, providing her with that sort of companionship when he was at home and sharing it with her in his letters when he was away.

Now he had found someone that any idiot could clearly see he wished to make his life's companion, and it made Alex realize for the first time just exactly how much he meant to her. Enough of such churlish thoughts, she chided herself as she settled down in her chair to listen to the catalog of Lucinda Addington's many charms.

At last, having praised his lady love sufficiently enough even for a besotted suitor, Tony paused. "But what of your evening, Alex? How did you fare with Knightley?"

"Ah, well you may ask." Alex grinned and proceeded to regale her brother with her own adventures.

"Oh, Alex, I should have been there!" Tony exclaimed, overcome with remorse. "I knew you would come a cropper if I left you to your own devices."

Unable to decide which was worse, allaying her brother's guilt by reassuring him that his protection had been unnecessary, or acknowledging that he had been correct in thinking she needed his escort, thus making him feel even more remorseful, Alex did her best to minimize the incidents of the evening. "Pooh, Tony. All's well that ends well. I was never in any real danger. All the training you have lavished on me insured that. And now Wrotham knows all, for which, given his very reasonable reaction, I am glad. I did not like deceiving him."

Alex could not have said exactly why, when she was so thoroughly enjoying pulling the wool over the rest of the world's eyes, that she did not relish doing so where the major was concerned, but Tony, too wrapped up in an agony of self-reproach at not being there when his sister needed him, was too preoccupied even to notice this odd remark.

Chapter 18

The appearance of a boy with another pot of coffee broke the reflective moment that both brother and sister had fallen into and recalled Tony to the original purpose of his visit. "I say, Alex, it is a lovely morning and I thought we might go for a ride in the park before it becomes crowded. It will clear the cobwebs from our brains."

"And we can see who else might be there," his sister amended slyly.

"Now, Alex"—Tony laughed, his tanned cheeks flushing—"I was merely thinking of the exercise. Besides, after being out so late last night, Miss Addington will undoubtedly need to recover."

This pronouncement did not, of course, keep him from looking hopefully around the minute they entered the park, but his assessment was correct. There were just a few military men, one of whom looked vaguely familiar, exercising their mounts.

Alex was surprised at how easily she spied him, but somehow, even at a distance and surrounded by fellow officers, the broad shoulders and erect posture of Lord Wrotham were distinctive. "Oh look, there is Chri . . . er, Lord Wrotham."

Squinting against the morning sun, Tony surveyed the group of riders. "Eh? Where? I don't see him," he remarked, making Alex realize that this sensitivity to the major's presence was only confined to certain interested parties. It was Alex's turn to blush, which was most odd, because she hardly ever blushed. Perhaps the warmth she felt spreading over her face was merely from the sun that was just appearing over the treetops.

"By Jove, so it is Wrotham," Tony remarked as the group of riders approached.

By now they were close enough for the major to recognize the de Montmorencys and he broke away from his companions and came trotting over.

Christopher too had been quick to identify Alex and her brother. Somehow, he would have wagered a considerable sum that he would find her out at this hour clearing her mind after the rigors of the previous evening. But even if he had not been half expecting her, he would have recognized the slender figure anywhere. Then a ray of sun had touched the copper curls, confirming his hopeful impression, and he had headed eagerly in their direction.

"Good morning. What a magnificent animal! Did you find him that day you were at Tatt's?" The major quirked a teasing eyebrow at Alex.

"Good God!" Tony exploded. "You saw Alex at Tattersall's? Now we *are* in the basket."

"Don't fly into the boughs, Tony. I fail to understand why being seen at Tattersall's is any more ruinous to my nonexistent reputation than spending my evenings in the gaming room at White's," his sister remarked calmly. "Good morning, Major. Yours is a rather impressive mount itself."

"Yes. Well, at least he once was, but poor old Brutus is in need of a rest. He has been a faithful companion through more skirmishes than I care to remember, and it is high time he retires to a well-deserved quiet pasture in the country. I simply could not ask him to accompany me into this next battle, so I must find a replacement soon—not an easy task, I assure you."

"So you expect to be returning to the Continent. Have you then been successful in persuading Parliament to raise more troops?" Alex asked.

Christopher smiled to himself. No doubt about it, Alex was awake on every suit. He wagered that there was not much those clear green eyes missed, or that the delicately shaped ears did not pick up. "Napoleon has been able to arm and supply his troops more quickly than even those accustomed to dealing with him would have expected. Our spies inform us that every tailor in Paris has been set to making uniforms and every blacksmith in France pressed into service making guns for his soldiers. The man's command of resources is incredible. The government here is still reluctant to move, but I expect that soon the evidence of Boney's intentions and the force he has built to carry them out will be so overwhelming that even Whitbread will be unable to deny us reinforcements."

Tony, listening to this interchange, realized he was not as excited as he once would have been by news of an impending engagement. Not that he was not as anxious as he had ever been to whip the Corsican, but the attractions that England had to offer were more compelling now that Lucinda Addington was among them.

Nor did his sister look forward to the coming clash between the two armies with any more eagerness than her brother. Not only would Tony once again be risking life and limb, the major would as well. There was no doubt of the risk—a thin scar over the major's eyebrow attested to that. When questioned, he had attributed it to a lack of strength and speed on the part of a French cavalryman, coupled with the skill of an excellent surgeon, but Alex also knew that only very deep cuts made with very sharp blades could be patched together so cleanly. She shuddered to think how close a call it must have been, and she did not care much for the idea that there were likely to be even more close calls in the near future.

Despite the strain of playing a part and constantly keeping on her toes at the gaming table, Alex could not remember when she had enjoyed herself more, or when she had shared such a close companionship. Much of that was owed to the presence of a certain major. Although she knew their friendship had to come to an end, she realized with a sudden pang that she did not like to think about it.

Regarding her curiously, Christopher wondered what on earth Alex could be thinking about to bring such a serious expression to her face and a sadness to her eyes. Then he recalled his last words and cursed himself for a fool. Of course she would be worried to death over her brother's imminent departure. It was not as though the poor girl didn't already have enough on her plate.

Casting about in his mind for some distraction, the major recalled an announcement he had seen in the *Times* and blurted out, "*King Henry the Fourth* is playing at the Drury Lane. I'm of a mind to go—would you both care to join me?"

It was not the most felicitous of subjects for a play, what with its intimations of war, but it did the trick. A brilliant smile dispelled Alex's pensive expression. "Oh I should love to," she replied eagerly. "I have never seen a play, at least not a real one with real professional actors. Should you like to go, Tony?"

Shakespeare was not Captain de Montmorency's idea of a jolly evening, but his sister looked so excited he had not the heart to demur. Then the happy thought struck him that Lucinda Addington might just possibly be attending as well. Certainly she was more likely to appear at Drury Lane than the gaming room at White's, which was his alternative. He was therefore able to conjure up enough real enthusiasm to acquiesce with becoming alacrity.

"How delightful. I do look forward to it. Thank you ever so much," Alex continued, fairly bubbling over with enthusiasm.

Christopher couldn't help thinking that she wore the look of a little girl who has just been given a new doll. No, Christopher amended the thought, a woman such as Alex would have scorned such a thing—a new pony, then. He was oddly touched. So many women in his life had demanded so many things from him—constant attention, flattery, jewelry, trinkets of every sort—and here was someone thrilled by his invitation to see a play.

How very dull Alex's life must have been until now, if such a prospect excited her so, and how little opportunity she must have had to set aside her responsibilities and enjoy herself. Considering it, Christopher realized that for all the intelligence and humor in those eyes that observed the world so closely, her face more often hinted at somber thoughts—she was clearly someone who had been forced to deal with a great many difficult things.

Heretofore, the major had always wished that the women he encountered were a little more serious, a little less inclined to inconsequential chatter. Now, all of a sudden, he was desperate to think up ways to bring a little frivolity into this particular woman's life.

These were the reflections of a moment, but Alex, sensing

she was the object of Lord Wrotham's scrutiny, glanced over at him to find him studying her closely, an unreadable expression in his dark blue eyes. Somewhat taken aback at being the subject of such intense observation, she cocked her head and raised one inquisitive eyebrow.

The major chuckled. "I beg your pardon. I was wool-gathering, and now the horses are getting restless. Shall we let them stretch their legs?" In truth, Wrotham's proposal was motivated less by concern for his mount than frank curiosity, for he was dying to see Alex galloping across the park. It was early enough in the morning and sufficiently deserted for them to give the animals their heads.

Christopher was not disappointed. Lady Alexandra de Montmorency rode the way she played cards—like an angel. She sat the huge animal with effortless ease, as though they had been born together—so well, in fact, that when they at last pulled up the major could not help remarking to Tony, "Does your sister do everything as well as she rides and plays piquet?"

"Alex? Oh yes. There's really nothing she can't do," Tony replied, as though having a sister who outshone most men at these endeavors were the most natural thing in the world. "Makes Alexander mad as fire too." He grinned and then added soberly, "It's a great pity. She would make a capital earl, certainly better than my brother, but there it is. I can't say I was best pleased when she turned up here like this, but so far it has done the trick and I've never seen her enjoying herself so much. Even if I could come up with the rest of the blunt I wouldn't have the heart to send her back, not just when she is getting the chance to see and do so many of the things she has dreamed about." Then, uncomfortably aware that he had revealed a good deal more than he meant to, Tony shut his mouth with a snap and, digging his heels into Caesar's flanks, urged his horse on to catch up with his sister, who had easily outdistanced the two of them.

Until this moment, Lord Wrotham had never stopped to consider the world from a feminine point of view. He had simply always assumed that his mother and the other women he had known were perfectly content to spend their lives devoting themselves to their clothes and the gossip of the *ton*. Indeed, many of the men of his acquaintance did little else themselves. If he himself was intolerably bored by it all, what must an intelligent woman be? At least he and a few others like him were able to go into the army or politics, but what choice had someone like Alex? Struck by this new perspective on the world, the major resolved to do everything in his power to ensure that she had the most stimulating, most interesting, most wonderful time in her life while she was still in the metropolis, which, considering her astounding success at the tables, would be all-too short a time. The major was discovering that he did not like the prospect of London without her.

Chapter 19

Lord Wrotham's attempt at providing diversion and amusement of a high order was entirely successful. All thoughts of Bonaparte, the impending conflict, and the necessary departure of Tony and the major were replaced by the pleasurable anticipation of the delights in store for Alex that evening. Despite a predilection for the classics and the tragedies of Sophocles and Euripides, Shakespeare was the English dramatist Alex most enjoyed. While *Henry the Fourth* was not her favorite of the Bard's plays, Falstaff being too uncomfortably similar to Alexander to be diverting, Alex could hardly contain herself until that evening.

Putting the last touches on her cravat in front of the looking glass, Alex mused again on the ease of a gentleman's life, free to attend a play whenever he liked without thinking about having proper companionship. And how simple it was to dress. To be sure, there was a great deal of discussing of tailors and the tying of cravats, but beyond that, gentlemen really had very little compared to ladies as far as dress was concerned.

It was sufficient for a gentleman to sport a well-cut coat. There was no worry if the décolletage was too low, the sleeves cut in last year's style, or the color decidedly passé. Still, oddly enough, and for just the briefest of moments, Alex wished she were donning a lovely filmy gown of green or some color that would show off her eyes, and with a neckline that would reveal her slender, graceful neck and shoulders— not that she had ever owned such a thing in her life. Furthermore, she could not imagine what had possessed her to think thoughts that were far more like Ally's then hers.

Enough of that. She would just have to be satisfied with looking distinguished instead of beautiful. Giving the auburn curls a final pat, she went downstairs to await Tony and Christopher who had both insisted on escorting her to the theater.

Alex might have been less than satisfied with her appearance, but she was alone in her opinion. Watching her as she sauntered toward them, Lord Wrotham was struck again by her graceful carriage and air of self-possession. In truth, Alexandra de Montmorency made a very handsome gentleman.

Unbidden there rose an image in the major's mind—a most disquieting image—of a delicate neck and white shoulders and the gentle swell that even the tight bandages could not quite conceal. He wondered idly what she would look like clad in delicate garments that would reveal the slender figure now obscured by the dark coat and starched cravat. It was a picture to make his throat tighten and take his breath away—a most awkward situation for one suddenly called upon to respond to Alex's friendly greeting: "Good evening, Wrotham. I saw in a copy of the *Times* that Mr. Bartley is to play the part of Falstaff. Do you know anything of him as an actor?"

Christopher stared blankly for a moment as he struggled to bring himself to reality. "No, not at all, that is, I am certain I have heard the name before, but . . . but I have been away from London so long that I am of no help as to what or who is *au courant*."

Alex noted his reaction with interest. What had occurred to fluster the man so, for undoubtedly he was flustered. It was hard to conceive of the cool and collected Major Lord Wrotham ever being disconcerted by anything. A second glance, stolen a few minutes later revealed that he had quickly recovered. Gone was the self-conscious look and the hint of a flush under the tan, but Alex was certain they had been there, and her conjectures as to what could possibly be the cause of his discomfiture kept her quiet all the way to the theater. However, her two companions, immersed in speculation as to the probable location and subsequent movement of Bonaparte's troops, failed to remark upon her unusual silence.

It was not until they arrived in their box that Tony and the major noticed Alex's silence, but now her lack of conversation arose from entirely different reasons. Beyond her initial gasp of "Oh, how wonderful!" she had sat absolutely dumb, engrossed by the scene and the activity all around her.

To the major, she looked like an excited child at her first circus, and the play had not yet even begun. Christopher had not been to the theater in an age. When he had attended, it had been with companions, especially females, who cared more about the impression they were making on the assembled audience than the spectacle they had come to see. In truth, the major found Alex's delighted absorption far more enthralling than the play itself and he spent a good deal of the first act watching it all reflected in her expressive face.

"Are you enjoying it, then?" he inquired as the curtain fell after the first half.

"Oh yes! I have read the play ever so many times, but it is nothing like seeing it come alive, is it?" she replied shyly.

The major was touched. To think that a woman who could travel about England alone and take on the *ton*—adopting a disguise, moreover, that was equally as skilled as any of the actors on stage—that she could still take such pleasure in a simple play was somehow very endearing. Too few members of society allowed themselves to be anything but thoroughly bored by it all. It was such a simple thing, but he suddenly realized how much her pleasure in the performance enhanced his.

"And I do think that Mr. Bartley is most clever in his portrayal of Falstaff," Alex continued. "He is extremely diverting without turning his part into mere buffoonery."

"Yes, I think that—" Wrotham was interrupted in midsentence by the sound of the door to their box opening. A gay voice cried, "Christopher! I vow 'tis too bad of you. Why if you had only told me you were going to the theater we could have made a party of it."

Alex watched in sympathetic amusement as the major, who had frozen at the sound of his mother's voice, forced a smile onto his rigid features and turned to greet her. "Hello, mother. Why, Hugh," he greeted his half brother with some surprise. "Whatever brings you here?"

"Well you may ask." The Earl of Claverdon, a rather sober,

heavyset man, certainly did appear extremely uncomfortable, and most definitely out of place in the fashionable throng. "I needed a new hunter and there were some business matters I was forced to attend to in the City, so here I am."

"And I told him positively that he could not spend the evening moldering away at home, that he must take me to the theater." The dowager countess patted her stepson's arm and smiled up at him in a coquettish way that only succeeded in making the poor man look all the more miserable. Then she turned to Alex. "You naughty boy, you promised to call on me. I have been quite pining at home waiting for you. But you young men are all the same, roving all about town without a thought for the ladies." She shook a playful finger at Alex before turning to Tony. "Now this fine-looking fellow is familiar to me."

"That is Anthony de Montmorency, Mother," Christopher explained patiently, but anyone who cared to observe could see that the patience was hard won and likely to evaporate at any moment.

"La, a family with two such handsome men is like to make a woman's head swim." The dowager countess advanced on the hapless Tony with a most beguiling smile, but happily, before the unfortunate Tony was forced to submit to the lady's flirtatious chatter—and before the major had throttled his mother—Hugh broke in to point out that the curtain was about to rise on the next act and they had better regain their seats.

Pouting prettily at her stepson, the countess bestowed a final dazzling smile on the de Montmorencys, admonished them both to call upon her, and then departed in a flutter of gauzy draperies, leaving behind a furious son and a heavy scent of patchouli.

"Women!" Christopher fumed. "They are nothing but vain parasites, every one of them after attention, wealth, or a title, or all three, and the worst of their sex are those in the *ton*. Give me honest Haymarket-ware anytime. At least with them you know what you are getting into. They only exact payment for services rendered, not for a lifetime. The rest are after everything but you—your possessions, your position, your—" he broke off suddenly, realizing that one of his companions was a member of the group he was so bitterly disparaging. The major turned to Alex. "I do beg your pardon, but . . ."

She smiled ruefully. "No need to apologize to me. Ever since I first took tea with Lady Ramsey and her daughters and heard them debating the qualities of prospective suitors and wagering as to the likelihood of their being brought up to scratch, as if they were no more than a hunter or a racehorse, I have had an aversion for most female company in particular, and the society that promotes that sort of thing in general. In my opinion, the marriage mart is just flesh peddling of another sort."

The major grinned as he added, "And not nearly as satisfying as the more honest trade I was referring to." Damn! He had done it again! Here he was feeling so at ease with her he was quite forgetting that, despite her clothes, Alex was a woman, and as gently bred as anyone he was likely to encounter in the *ton*, all of whom would have shrieked and fainted at the very mention of the existence of the bits of muslin that haunted the streets of London. Yet here she was quite calmly discussing it with him as though she were a brother officer.

The curtain rose and Alex turned to concentrate on the play unfolding below, but her companions had no eyes for the stage. Tony, having at last caught a glimpse of the fair Lucinda in a box opposite then, was plotting ways to run into her party as they left the theater, while the major's thoughts were entirely of the woman sitting next to him.

It appeared that Alex had even less use for the female sex than he did, yet the way the world was now constructed she was forced to endure the company of women or none at all. He'd been able to dampen the pretensions of most marriage-mad misses, and was now generally regarded as a hopeless bachelor, a state that discouraged all but the hardiest of pursuers. But a woman who disdained the society of much of her sex would, at best, be labeled blue or eccentric; at worst, she would cease to exist at all socially. Yet Alex obviously enjoyed good fellowship and rational conversation, both of which were denied those who kept to themselves.

Not for the first time, the major wondered what her life must have been like before she came to London. Her very enjoyment of the metropolis suggested a spirit that had long been stifled in the countryside. And not for the first time he wished he had been in Norfolk to do for her what her useless twin should have done—taken care to see that she was introduced to those who could share her interests. The major became so exercised at the thought of all of this that he was prepared to ride straight to Halewood and talk some sense into Alexander de Montmorency, dying though he might be. It was only the very real possibility that he would be ordered to the Continent at any moment that kept Lord Wrotham from doing so.

Chapter 20

It was only later, alone in her bedchamber, that Alex had a
chance to reflect on the evening's conversation. She had
been so wrapped up in the play that she hadn't paid much
attention to the bitterness in Lord Wrotham's voice and the
cynical gleam in his eyes as he had spoken so slightingly of
her sex. Now, alone with her thoughts, she recalled the scene
in vivid detail. It was more than bitterness that she had detected; there was also pain, the pain of disillusionment. Small
wonder, she supposed, with a harpy like the Dowager Countess of Claverdon for a mother. A woman so greedy for masculine attention would have had little love to spare for anyone
but herself, and certainly not for a small son.

The major must have been a very lonely little boy. Alex remembered her own happy childhood, which had been filled
with the love of her parents and the warmth and companionship of brothers and sisters. How unhappy she had been when
Alexander had begun to show his true nature, and how much
worse it must have been for the major to have the sole person
in his life be someone as self-centered as his mother obviously
was.

No wonder Lord Wrotham was not married. Now that she
stopped to consider it, Alex realized that he must have been
forced to offer a fair amount of resistance in order to maintain
his bachelor status. From the little she had observed at the
Norwich assemblies, most young misses could be quite determined in their pursuit of handsome young men who offered titles and the potential for a great deal of pin money.

Of course, much of this was the merest conjecture. Alex did

not know precisely how young the major had been when his father had died or his mother remarried. She only sensed that he was young from the attitude these events seemed to have engendered toward his mother. One might expect that such an experience would have made him distrustful of all of mankind, yet he had been quick to sense her needs and generous in his offers of assistance.

These were not the actions of a misanthrope, nor was his invitation to the play. In that, she had sensed a special concern for her happiness and amusement that bespoke a person alive to the hopes and dreams of others. How sad then, that such a person had suffered from a lack of such sensitivity on the part of someone who should have been close to him. It only took the briefest of observations to see that the Dowager Countess of Claverdon was sensitive to nothing but admiration of herself.

It was the oddest thing, but Alex found herself wishing that somehow she could erase the pain that she sensed in the major, could give him the disinterested kindness and concern that his mother and other women appeared to have denied him. She shook her head. It was a foolish thought and undoubtedly it was all imagination on her part. Anyway, what could a green girl from the wilds of Norfolk give a man such as Lord Wrotham? In one week of his adventurous existence he had seen more of the world than she had in her entire lifetime. Still, Alex resolved to observe him more closely in order to test the accuracy of her speculations.

During the ensuing days Alex had ample opportunity to do just that, for not only did Christopher stick close to her side at White's, encouraging one high flyer after another to take on the challenge of beating the seemingly invincible de Montmorency, he kept turning up at the Clarendon on the slimmest of pretexts, always with an offer of some project for her amusement. These ranged from taking her to see the equestrian feats at Astley's Amphitheater to witnessing the latest debates in Parliament over the raising of troops.

Prior to coming to London Alex had always been so occupied with the running of Halewood that she had had little time for anything else, and even if she had, as a single female she was restricted in her movements and amusements. Now for the first time in her life she was sharing new experiences, new impressions, with someone else, a person who could be relied upon to speak knowledgeably and to furnish interesting commentary. It was altogether a delightful experience and Alex began to view her increasing success at the gaming table with some dismay, for the closer she came to reaching her goal, the closer she was to returning home. However, whenever such unsettling thoughts came to her, she was quick to put them out of her mind so as to retain what wits she still had left about her.

These wits she put to observing Lord Wrotham during their various outings as closely as he had at first observed her. After several strolls along Bond Street and Piccadilly she was able to establish that scornful as he might be toward the fairer sex, the major was an object of supreme interest to them. This was borne out by discreet but flirtatious glances cast in his direction from underneath the brims of fashionable bonnets or behind coquettish parasols. If Lord Wrotham was aware of such attention, he gave not the least sign of it except a marked determination to pay attention to the discussion that he and Alex were sharing as they sauntered along.

This state of affairs was thrown into even clearer perspective one afternoon as they were cutting across the park at the height of the fashionable hour. They had nearly gained the gate when a gay voice trilled, "Christopher," and an elegant barouche drew alongside them. The Countess of Claverdon, clad in a carriage dress lavishly trimmed with ribbons and ruffles leaned out to accost them.

"How perfectly charming to come upon you like this when you are usually never to be found here at this time of day." The grim look on Wrotham's face was proof enough as to his reasons for avoiding such a public spot at such an hour. "You must ride with me a little way." Anticipating her son's response, she wagged a playful finger at him. "You cannot deny me the pleasure of showing off my handsome son. All the town tabbies will be so jealous, though of course no one believes I could possibly be old enough to have a son your age. And I am so delighted that you are accompanied by de Montmorency here, for it can only add to a lady's credit to have two such fine-looking gentlemen in her carriage."

The countess smiled smugly as they climbed in and then leaned forward to address Alex in confidential tones. "You know, one has to take advantage of Christopher's presence whenever one can, he is so elusive. All the young ladies complain of it. Here they are dying for a word or a look and he neglects them all most shamefully. Why, can you credit it, I am the only woman he is ever seen with in public!"

Alex was fumbling for a suitable reply, but luckily the countess, heedless of anyone but herself, rattled on. "It is a great deal too bad because he must marry. Think of the succession"—she turned to her son—"you may choose to ignore Lavinia Carstairs, though she is accounted a diamond of the first water, but you must have someone you know. Now this dreadful war is over you can . . ."

"Mama." The major sighed in exasperation. "The war is *not* over and I do not need to insure the succession. Osbert is perfectly capable of taking care of everything should anything happen to me, and his son is a likely-looking lad. Besides, I can not think that any of this is of any interest to de Montmorency here."

The countess was silenced, but only for a moment, then turning to Alex she inquired, "Surely you are not such an unnatural son. I feel certain you must have a young lady to whom you are devoted."

Out of the corner of her eye, Alex caught a glimpse of bright blue eyes brimming with amusement and the oddest wave of happiness washed over her. It was such a gratifying thing to share something with someone that for a moment she felt as though she and the major were by themselves alone in the park. Sharing the secret of her identity with him gave her a sense of intimacy such as she had never had, not even with anyone in her own family. "No," she stammered slightly. However, with the most heroic of efforts, she was able to maintain a straight face. "But then, I am somewhat younger than your son and have time yet before I should be thinking of such things." She shot a triumphant glance at the major. There, that should pay him back for doing his best to overset her.

Leaning down to flick an imaginary speck of dust off his highly polished Hessians, Wrotham managed to whisper "Touché" in her ear.

It was the gesture of a moment, but the warmth of his breath ruffling her hair, the closeness of his lips to her skin almost felt like a kiss. What a ridiculous notion! Alex angrily dismissed the thought the moment it occurred. Really, Alex, she admonished herself, the strain of the entire thing has gotten to you. Touched in your upper story is what you are. Still, she enjoyed the delightful feeling of conspiracy and friendship in spite of herself.

Having had more than enough of his mother the major begged her to let them down, which she did reluctantly. "It is so rare that I see you." She pouted prettily. "For you never attend any of the routs and balls to which I know you have been invited."

"If you know that, then you also know that I am far too busy, Mama. I am here in London at Wellington's express command and must devote myself to that," he replied evenly enough, but Alex, observing the muscle twitching in his jaw, knew the control he must be exerting over his temper.

No wonder the man had no love for her sex if his first experience with it was with someone as capricious and demanding as the countess. As soon as they were out of earshot the major echoed her thoughts. "You see what I mean? That is all they want—constant attention, someone to dance attendance on them from the moment they put up their hair and let down their skirts, and they are all in league with one another. They won't rest until you are caught in the parson's mousetrap, condemned for the rest of your life to wait upon them. It beats me why anyone gets leg-shackled." He stopped, embarrassed at having forgotten once again that it was a female to whom he was talking, but Alex seemed not to mind in the least.

"Me too." She was thoughtful for a moment. "Though why I feel that way I cannot explain. My parents were very much in love. Papa really never got over Mama's death. Oh, he tried, but they shared so much together that everything reminded him of her. He never stopped missing her."

"Really?" Christopher snorted. "They were lucky then and so were you. I have never known anyone who even liked the person they married after all was said and done, nor were they ever as interested in them as when they had been pursuing them."

"That is because they were enamored of the idea of it all rather than the person. I, for one, should never consider matrimony unless I were good friends with someone first."

"What? You do not believe in falling in love? I thought all young women dreamed of being swept away on a tide of passion."

"I do not. It sounds dreadfully uncomfortable to me. And besides, one cannot live out one's days on a tide of passion." She stopped to stare up at him curiously. "Why? Do you believe in love? Have you ever been in love?"

"I thought so once." The major laughed bitterly. "I suppose it was love. She loved my possessions and my estate until someone with more of both came along. For my part, I loved her beauty until I saw what was beneath it. I awoke from *that* dream quickly enough, and I am delighted to say I have never fallen for it again." But somehow he did not look happy about it. There was a bleakness in his eyes that made Alex long to replace it with the warmth and love she had known in her own family.

Sensing her scrutiny, the major turned and found the green eyes looking up at him with so much sympathy and understanding that he was at a loss for words. He hadn't even known the extent of his anger and hurt until he saw it reflected in her eyes. Somehow, just having someone understand it did a good deal toward easing the pain. "Never mind. You need not look so distressed." He laughed, both gratified and uneasy at her quickness of perception. "I soon got over it. I joined the regiment and discovered all the fellowship, the companionship a man could wish for."

"I'm glad," was the simple reply, but Alex was not convinced. Fellowship he might have had, but there was still a part of him that longed for something more—something he wanted but had never found, else why was he so affected by his mother? Most people would simply have dismissed her as a vain and silly woman, but the major seemed unable to do so. His barely concealed contempt for her and for women in general hinted at an anger and a disappointment that went deeper than that. It was as though he truly had longed for love and affection but had it denied him.

Why of all things, Alex wondered, did she entertain the

wish, fleeting though it was, that she could give him what he wanted? It would be so easy. He was charming and interesting, a man who cared passionately about things—his country, his comrades in arms, even a young woman masquerading as her brother in order to save her birthright. Alex had had great experience in taking care of people, from useless older brothers to rambunctious younger ones. She knew that ensuring the happiness and comfort of a grown man who possessed no outrageous eccentricities and who had been looking after himself for years would be simplicity itself.

The real question was why did she wish to do this? Surely it was just because she wished everyone could enjoy the love she had received in her family. She firmly put all such thoughts out of her mind, concentrating instead on what she hoped was to be her last evening at White's. With the major urging veteran gamesters in her direction, she had managed to win thousands of pounds at each sitting and all that was needed now was a few thousand more. She should have been overjoyed to think that after tonight her masquerade would be over. She could cast aside Alexander de Montmorency forever and resume her normal life—a prospect which did not elate her as much as it should have.

By now they had reached the Clarendon—a surprise to both of them, as each one had been so wrapped up in his own thoughts that neither one had been very conscious of their progress.

Christopher paused on the stairs, laying a hand on his companion's shoulder. "I must repair to my chambers to write up some reports for the Duke. Until tonight. It should be the last. Courage *mon brave*, you have almost reached your goal." He turned and was gone, leaving Alex to stare stupidly after him, a lump in her throat and unaccountable tears stinging her eyelids.

Chapter 21

The gaming room at White's was densely crowded by the time Anthony, Alex, and Christopher arrived. In order to see his sister through her final round, Anthony, who had been begging off more and more frequently to attend events where he was likely to encounter his adored Lucinda, had eschewed an opportunity to look for her at the Bellingwood's rout.

By now a respected regular, Alex was hailed by players at several tables and invited to join the play, but just as she was about to take her seat at the table adjoining General Scott's, she was accosted by a gaudily dressed man of indeterminate years who sported a rather boldly patterned waistcoat and the high color of one of Bacchus's more confirmed devotees. "Ssho, de Montmorenshy, I hear you're cleaning out the pocketsh of all the gentleman here," he slurred. "It'sh my turn now to show you that not everyone here ish easy game or my name ishn't Gilesh O'Hara."

Alex had never seen the man before and, if the expression of the onlookers were anything to go by, neither had anyone else. His aggressive air brooked no denial, and on her last night here, Alex was not about to do anything that would cause a stir. When he waved an unsteady hand toward a table in the corner and wove toward it she could do nothing but shrug and follow.

It rapidly became apparent that Giles O'Hara had grossly overestimated his card-playing abilities and it took the shortest of whiles for Alex to trounce him severely, winning all that remained of the money she needed. That accomplished, she heaved a sigh of relief and smiled pleasantly at her opponent. "I thank you for the game, sir, but I am afraid I must beg your indulgence in cutting it short as I am promised to Cathcart this evening."

With a roar O'Hara rose and pointed a wavering finger at her. "You'll not dismish me so easily, my fine young buck. Gilesh O'Hara is no pigeon to be plucked ash you have done all the othersh. No. You'll sit down and play an honesht game with me and then we shall shee who winsh."

An angry flush rose in Alex's cheeks and her fists clenched at her sides, but she managed to reply calmly enough. "Certainly. And I shall beat you as honestly as I just have done."

"Are you calling me a liar? No one callsh Gilesh O'Hara a liar to hish face and lives. Name your weaponsh and your secondsh."

By this time, the deathly hush that had fallen at the adjoining tables had spread throughout the room. Alex rose to face him, maintaining her outward composure although her eyes positively sparkled with anger. "Pistols," she replied promptly. Then she turned to Christopher. "And I beg Lord Wrotham to oblige."

His heart in his mouth, the major shot a quick glance at Tony, who appeared to be no more concerned by the entire episode than his sister was. "I shall be honored to do so." He bowed ever so slightly in Alex's direction.

"Thank you." Alex turned back to her accuser. "Very well, then, sir. I suggest that we repair to a suitable spot at daybreak. The sooner honor is satisfied, the better. As to the location, I leave its selection to the seconds." And without giving O'Hara time to reply she turned on her heel and strode toward the door, leaving the room abuzz behind her.

The first to recover was the major who, after establishing Wimbledon Common as the site for the encounter, grabbed Tony by the arm and hustled him toward the door, whispering urgently, "Whatever shall we do?"

"Do? Why nothing."

Christopher was not a little taken aback at the callous insouciance with which Alex's brother viewed the dreadful situation. "But we cannot let her do this!"

"Don't see how we can stop her, old fellow. Question of

honor you know, and she wouldn't thank you for doing so."
Then seeing that his words had done nothing to erase the
worry in the major's eyes or the tense set of his jaw, he laid a
hand on Wrotham's shoulder. "Relax, man. Alex is as fine a
shot as I have ever encountered. She should be. I taught her
myself down at Halewood. She is as steady as a rock and has
eyes like a hawk. I wish we had time to go to Manton's so you
could see what I mean. Taught her swordplay as well, though
she is not as good at that. Oh, she is a very pretty fighter, but
nothing out of the ordinary. I say the best thing we can do is
go home and get ourselves a bit of sleep as Alex will undoubtedly do. If I know anything about it, I would say that a man
like O'Hara is likely to stay up until the appointed hour getting
drunk as a lord and he won't even offer Alex a challenge worthy of her. Come. Let's toddle along then."

And they headed toward the door. Once outside, they hurried along the street to catch up with Alex, who had slowed
her pace in the hopes that they would. Difficult though it was
for him to credit, the major was struck by the fact that the air
of unconcern she had exhibited in the club still remained. She
greeted them both with a nonchalance that Christopher, for
one, was far from feeling.

The major studied her carefully. From the steady green eyes
to the smooth white forehead to the beautifully sculpted lips,
not a single feature betrayed the least sign of anxiety. Few
men of his acquaintance would have been as calm in such circumstances. Wrotham shook his head admiringly. "Are you
not concerned about this encounter?"

An impish smile flitted cross Alex's face. "Will you think it
very bold of me if I say no? Someone who displays such a sin-
gular lack of skill and concentration at cards is not likely to
suddenly acquire these traits once he has a pistol in his hand.
Besides, I am an even better shot than I am a card player."

The major laughed, but the tightness that gripped his stomach would not go away. He wanted to beg her to let him take
her place, but he knew that even if she could keep her honor
intact while allowing him to do that, she never would do so.
One look at the proud lift of the chin and her erect carriage
was enough to tell him that. All he could do was to continue

along to his lodgings and try as best he could to wait until dawn.

Oddly enough, Alex thought to herself, she was truly not worried. The worst of her adventure was over. She had only to deposit the last of her winnings at Hoare's bank to make her wild gamble successful. In contrast to the hopes and fears riding on her skill at the gaming tables, facing the mouth of a pistol in the hands of a drunken braggart was the merest nothing. Still, not wishing to be foolhardy in her confidence, she repaired immediately to bed the moment she reached the Clarendon, doing her best to compose herself for the upcoming duel.

It would have been naïve to hope for a solid night's rest before facing such a challenge, but she did manage to doze off once or twice before Lord Wrotham, who had been awake all night and pacing the floor, banged on her door.

Alex was unprepared for his strained and exhausted expression. Surely he had faced far worse situations many times over. Were the shadows under the eyes and the lines of fatigue concern for her situation? A strange feeling of warmth and gratitude swept over her at such a thought, making her "Good morning" unusually gruff. That such an out and outer as Lord Wrotham should care what happened to Lady Alexandra de Montmorency was most surprising and wonderful, and she was quite unprepared for the happiness it brought her.

"I have a carriage waiting downstairs." For his part, the major could not believe that anyone going to face even as doubtful an opponent as O'Hara could look as well rested as Alex. What an incredible woman—no, what an incredible person—she was! Christopher still found it difficult to believe that someone as courageous and intelligent, someone he admired and enjoyed as a friend could be a member of the sex that hitherto had caused him so much annoyance and pain.

"Good. I shall just get my cloak." Alex grabbed her cape, swung it over her shoulder, and headed out the door with the major in her wake.

The faintest blush of pink stained the sky as they reached the common, and wisps of mist rose from the ground lending an unearthly air to the entire scene. Real enough, however, were the deadly-looking pistols handed to the seconds for inspection and Giles O'Hara's bullying threat, "Now we'll show who's the honest man and who's the Captain Sharp. You shan't get away with this, de Montmorency."

Not deigning to reply, Alex shrugged, accepted her pistol from the major, and went to take up her position. She sighted carefully, took a deep breath, and waited calmly, her eyes on the white handkerchief being held aloft.

On the sideline, the major, standing next to Tony, who had arrived a few minutes before, was gnawing the inside of his lip in a desperate attempt to appear as calm as the woman facing the pistol.

The handkerchief fluttered. Knowing her opponent was less than steady, Alex forced herself to raise her pistol and take aim as coolly as if she were in the barn at Halewood. There was a flash and a loud report which allowed her to place her own shot precisely where she wished, hitting O'Hara's gun and sending it tumbling to the ground while he stood stupidly gazing at his empty hand.

Alex's marksmanship brought a round of cheers from the sprinkling of onlookers. She bowed and, not deigning to acknowledge O'Hara, turned her back to him and headed toward the carriage, barely aware of a stinging in her left arm.

Tony sprinted toward his sister, his face beaming. "By Jove, Alex, that was a simply splendid shot! Couldn't have done better myself."

"I had an excellent teacher," she replied modestly, though she was unable to hide her happy grin. Really, she was rather proud of herself. Now that she could allow herself to think about it, she was weak with relief, but her nerves had been cool and steady when the situation demanded it.

Too overwhelmed by a variety of confusing emotions, Wrotham was quite unable to say anything. First and foremost was relief that she was unharmed. Then there was tremendous admiration. It had been a magnificent shot, executed with the boldness of someone confident of her skill. Next, oddly enough, was pride—a pride that someone he had come to like had acquitted herself so very well, from the dignified response in the face of an outrageous insult to the brilliant conclusion of a dangerous episode. No man could have done better. Christopher was not entirely certain that even he could have made such a shot, but somehow, in his pleasure at Alex's success, he did not mind such a notion, strange though it was. But strangest of all had been the cold, paralyzing fear that had gripped his heart as he had watched her standing there, slim, straight, and proud in the cold dawn light. She was so brave—shouldering all the responsibilities that came her way without the slightest complaint—that he wanted more than anything to throw himself in front of her as she stood there, wrap his arms around her, and protect her from it all. Yet he could do nothing except stand and observe, hoping that the bullet would miss her.

When the first shot was fired, it had taken all Wrotham's strength to keep himself from running to catch her, so certain had he been that she would crumple to the ground. But no, she had stood her ground magnificently, taking advantage of O'Hara's wild shot the instant it occurred.

At last the major found his voice. "I suggest we repair to my chambers for a well-deserved breakfast. What do you say?"

"Capital idea." Tony beamed. "I am so hungry I could eat a cart horse. I shall see you at your lodgings then." He waved and turned toward the bush to which his mount was tethered.

Alex, closely followed by the major, climbed into his carriage. Wrotham rapped on the roof and they were off. Free at last to acknowledge the sting in her arm where her opponent's bullet had grazed it, Alex gingerly felt her sleeve, trying unobtrusively to assess the damage.

However, her slight motion did not escape the major's sharp eyes. "You're hurt!" In an instant he was on the seat beside her easing her arm out of her coat.

"It is nothing, the merest scratch." Alex tried to pull the coat back on, but he would have none of it. Without a thought beyond easing the pain that was evident in the way she winced, Christopher undid her cravat, opened her shirt, and slid it off her shoulder to the point where he could see the angry red weal against the smooth white skin.

Gently his hands explored the wound. "Yes." He sighed in relief. "The skin is barely broken." He pulled a clean handkerchief from his pocket and wrapped it around her arm, knotting it expertly. "There. A little of Radlett's salve and you'll be right as a trivet in no time." Then, suddenly aware of what he had done, he flushed a deep red under his tan. "I do beg your pardon. I did not mean . . . that is to say I had no intention of . . ."

Alex's eyes twinkled. "Think nothing of it. It is not every day that a man tears my clothes off, I assure you, but nor is it every day that I fight a duel. And, as your action was inspired by the most humanitarian of impulses, I can only thank you for doing so." Almost regretfully she pulled on her sleeve and endeavored to retie her cravat.

The major's hands had felt so warm, so comforting against her bare skin that the ache of the wound had almost disappeared. In fact, Alex wished for a brief moment that it had been worse, because it had been so very pleasant to feel his touch—a thought so unnerving that she was rendered completely incapable of managing her cravat.

"Here, let me. You are making mice feet of the whole thing." Christopher removed the cravat from Alex's nerveless grasp and, wrapping it around her neck, fashioned it efficiently and neatly into a creditable imitation of the way she had tied it that morning. "There." The major looked into the green eyes regarding him so trustfully, and for a moment he had an almost irresistible urge to kiss the gently parted lips and the delicate tip of her nose. Quickly banishing such unsettling thoughts, he murmured, "I am so glad you are safe."

"So am I," Alex replied softly, not taking her eyes from his. How strong his face was, with its straight nose and square jaw. Even the crinkles at the corners of his eyes from long hours of squinting at the sun lent it character. Yet there was a kindness, almost a tenderness in it as he looked down at her, his expression full of concern.

Here was unfamiliar ground and Alex, unused to such thoughts, hastily tried to direct them elsewhere. Laughing shakily, she continued, "Though I am not entirely surprised to find myself mostly all in one piece. From the moment he issued the challenge, I could tell that O'Hara was even a worse marksman than he was a card player, poor man. How do you suppose he ever managed an entrée to White's?"

Wrotham seized upon the change of subject gratefully. "God only knows. Someone must owe him something because he did not get there on his own."

Then, unable to think of anything further to say after the tensions and the revelations of the morning, they both fell silent, each staring blindly out the window, wrapped in thought and oblivious to the passing scene.

Chapter 22

Tony was eagerly awaiting them in Wrotham's chambers, Radlett having supplied him with a tankard of the best ale to be had in the environs. In fact, so exhilarated was he by the events of the morning that he was regaling the major's henchman with a minute-by-minute description of the morning's events when Alex and the major entered.

Alex could not help grinning at her brother's highly colored rendition of the encounter, but still she was pleased at his obvious pride in her abilities. How delightful it was to be able to sit down to a companionable rasher of eggs and discuss all the finer points of the affair, from the moment O'Hara had had the effrontery to challenge her until she had turned her back on him at Wimbledon Common. Somehow, Alex could not help comparing it all to the very dull tea parties she was occasionally forced to endure at home in Norfolk, which were sadly lacking in the exuberance and the generous spirit present at the moment. Casting back mentally, she realized that with the notable exception of her sister and her mother, Alex had never heard one woman praise another in her entire life as the major was now praising her. How she longed for all this—the camaraderie, the adventure, the actual living of life and the sharing of its dangers and challenges with other people—to go on forever, but she knew that she had only a week at the most to enjoy this and then it was back to Norfolk and her customary routine.

Now that she had won back the money Alexander owed and then some, every minute Alex spent in London was taking money from the children and Halewood. That morning before she had left for Wimbledon, she had penned a note to Ally, informing her of the success of her visit and requesting her to send Ned with the carriage and Trajan. At least dressed as a man she could enjoy some of the journey riding her horse until they were in the neighborhood of Halewood.

". . . think that we shall be shipping out within the week." Tony's voice broke into his sister's reverie.

"Have you been called up, then?" the major inquired.

"Yes." Tony looked sheepish, for not wanting to cause his sister worry, he had delayed telling her until absolutely necessary. "I would have told you, Alex, only I just found out about it and the duel put it clean out of my mind."

"Well, that should stop your complaining about having to rot in London while the Corsican monster is gobbling up all of Europe," his sister said, grinning in Tony's direction.

"Yes. It is time someone stopped him." But somehow Tony did not sound as excited by the prospect of action as he once would have.

Alex quirked a teasing eyebrow at her brother and he blushed vividly. "You see, Lucinda and her mother were counting on my escort to several upcoming routs, and now they will be forced to go alone," Tony confessed shamefacedly.

His sister took pity on him. "Having seen her I feel certain that she is the type of woman who admires a man who does his duty toward his country far more than she does the bucks who while away their useless existence on the town. You could hardly hope to impress her by remaining here while all of Europe is in danger."

"You think so?" Captain de Montmorency said, sounding relieved.

"Most definitely. I know I should feel that way. Don't you agree?" Alex turned to the major.

"Indubitably," he agreed, winking at Alex. "Where do you sail from?"

"Ramsgate."

"Ah yes. Wellington should be pleased that we are mobilizing at last."

"And so should you," Alex interjected. "For it seems as

though your efforts are at last having some effect. I hope it is not too little too late."

"So do I." The major sighed. Most sisters would have been greatly distressed at the thought of their brother's leaving for war, and certainly none could be as fond of a brother as Alex was of hers, but here she was calmly discussing his departure as though it were no more than a trip to Brighton. Examining her more closely, he could barely detect the worry in her eyes, but beyond that there was not the slightest indication that she was putting up a brave front. Christopher wished desperately that he could offer her some words of assurance and comfort, but in all honesty he could not. He knew, as any seasoned soldier knew, that the imminent struggle with Napoleon was bound to be a grim one and of epic proportions.

Striving for a lighter note, the major turned to Alex, inquiring, "Now that you have won what you set out to and have made yourself a name as a gamester to be reckoned with, shall you return to Norfolk or stay on to increase the family fortune?"

"Ah, it is high time I returned to see that all has not gone to rack and ruin in my absence. Ally is a dear and runs a household beautifully, but there is a great deal to be done about the estate—fences to be repaired, livestock to be purchased, cottages to be put to rights. Besides, if I were to remain here any longer I might be completely seduced by Dame Fortune." She smiled ruefully. "It is rather more exciting here than in Norfolk, you know."

"Certainly you make it so, fire-eater that you are." The major grinned.

"Now that is not fair," Alex protested. "The duel was none of my doing."

"Of course you did not start it, but given the opportunity, you took it eagerly enough. Clearly if you were presented with an opportunity for an existence more lively than the one you have in Norfolk you would have plunged yourself into one scrape after another."

"Too true," her brother said, laughing. "You don't want to offer Alex a challenge of any kind for she is like to forget that she is only made of flesh and bone and will take on anything, no matter how dangerous."

"I can see we shall have to offer you enough of interest in your last days here to keep you so stimulated you stay out of trouble when you return home." Wrotham smiled at Alex in a way that made her feel as though making her enjoy her remaining time in London was the most important thing in the world to him.

The major was as good as his word, thinking up one amusement after another until she was too distracted to consider her return home or her brother's imminent departure, which occurred not too many days thereafter. He called at the Clarendon one fine morning just as Alex and the major were returning from an early ride in the park, remarking sotto voce as they climbed the stairs to Alex's chambers, "I did not think it quite the thing for the regiment to see my brother clinging to me as we said farewell."

"As if I would," his sister began indignantly. "I am not such a poor creature." Nevertheless, her eyes were misty as she hugged him.

Watching them from his place by the fire, Wrotham felt a tug at his own heart as he saw their fondness and concern for each other. For the first time in his life he wished that there was someone who cared as much for him, someone to wish him a farewell and Godspeed when he left.

But the major had one more task to accomplish before taking up his own duties on the Continent. He was determined to escort Alex back to Norfolk despite her brother's assurance that there was no need to do so. "Awfully good of you, old fellow," Tony had responded gratefully to the major's suggestion, "but she is as capable as you or I and she won't thank you for not seeing that."

"I know." Christopher smiled ruefully. "And I know that it is entirely possible that she could handle anything that came her way as well as I could, but"—he paused, struggling for the words that would convey his thoughts—"it is just that if anything did happen that was at all upsetting to her, I should like to be there."

Tony nodded sympathetically. "So should I, but believe me, I have been feeling that way for years and nothing has yet come along that she has not been more than equal to."

"Yes. I expect that is so." The major had bidden good-bye

to Tony without further discussion, wishing him a pleasant journey and promising to look him up when he had made his way to the Continent, but he had continued to mull it over in his mind as he made his way to his own hotel.

Tony was undoubtedly correct in his assertion that Alex would in all likelihood continue to conquer every problem that came her way. After all, Wrotham had met very few men who were as resourceful as she was. However, that was not the issue. Her brother had entirely missed the point that the major had been trying to make, which was that he not only wanted to help her with an actual crisis, should it arise, he also wanted to spare her the responsibility of having to come up with ways to get herself out of any possible fixes. Sometimes, thinking of ways to solve problems was just as tiresome and draining as actually dealing with them.

The oddest thing was that he did not know whether he wanted to do this for Alex or for himself. Christopher had never before encountered someone he respected and admired as much as Lady Alexandra de Montmorency, and he wished, in some indefinable way, to show her this. But how was he to do this, other than helping her and encouraging her in the role that she had already selected for herself?

In addition, he liked to think that as their friendship had grown, perhaps she had come to feel the same way about him. He wanted her to like and trust him as much as he did her. He wanted to be the sort of person who was strong enough and clever enough to be able to be of material assistance to her, though being of assistance to someone as capable as Alex was quite a challenge. He wanted—the major, who had been striding blindly along Piccadilly, suddenly came to a halt. What did he want?

What he really wanted was for it to be as difficult for Alex to face returning to Norfolk as it was for him to face having her leave. That was it. He was going to miss her damnably—a most uncomfortable sensation, one he had never suffered before, and one he certainly did not wish to suffer alone.

Since his childhood, when his father had died and Christopher had discovered just how selfish and shallow a person his mother was, he had never allowed himself to count on anyone except himself for companionship, assistance, amusement, or

anything else. Even in the regiment, though he had been fond
of many of his fellows and now missed the general camaraderie, he did not feel the absence of anyone in particular.

For the most part, people had looked to him for advice and
leadership, but had been unable to give him those in return. It
was not like that with Alex. Once he had thrown her into the
company of lucrative gaming partners, she had handled everything on her own, and magnificently too. If anything, her escapade was her own adventure and she had allowed him to
participate as an onlooker—one whose experience and judgment were respected, but an onlooker just the same.

Now he wished to be more than just an onlooker. He wanted
to share it all with her. For the first time in his life he had encountered someone as equal to every situation as he was himself, and all of a sudden, the prospect of taking things on with
a partner was far more appealing than taking them on alone.

Revelations such as this would have been disquieting at any
time, but to experience them now, toward a member of the opposite sex, to be uncertain as to whether the feeling was mu-
tual, and just at the point when the entire affair was nearly at
an end, was most disconcerting. No, it was more than disconcerting, it was upsetting, in the extreme, which was why
Christopher was planning to escort Alex back to Norfolk no
matter what objections she might raise.

At least it did not all have to end quite so soon. He could
postpone their inevitable farewell for a few more days. The
major resumed his walk as passersby had begun to stare at him
while he stood, transfixed, on the pavement.

There was also one more reason that he wished to accompany Alex, but it was a reason that Christopher could not quite
acknowledge even to himself. Alexandra de Montmorency
was a very good-looking young man, but Lord Wrotham was
longing to see what sort of a woman she was.

Chapter 23

Having made up his mind to escort Alex back to Norfolk, the major set about his plan with his usual dispatch. Once he had ascertained that he had accomplished all that he could for Wellington in London and that his place was now at the Duke's side, he set Radlett to packing his kit and readying things for their departure for the Continent. "I have a little . . . uh . . . family business . . . to attend to here so I count on you to be my advance guard," he informed his man the next day. "I feel certain that by the time I arrive in Brussels you will have scrounged up a place for us to lay our heads. You can also leave word of my imminent arrival at Wellington's headquarters."

Radlett nodded noncommittally, but his mind was working furiously. What sort of *family business* could the major have? The batman could not remember when his master had ever done anything but seek to avoid all possible entanglements with his family. Directing a sharp glance at Wrotham, he detected the oddest air of self-consciousness about him, which was highly uncharacteristic. Radlett was intrigued. The major was a man who was sufficient unto himself, not given to involvements of any kind unless they occurred in the line of duty, but if an occasion such as that arose he had always been more than forthcoming to the person with whom he shared most of his existence—his batman. However, at this moment, his demeanor was that of a man bent on keeping a secret appointment or one involved in a clandestine affair of some sort.

More than a little curious, Radlett thought carefully back over their stay in London. Other than appointments with par-

liamentary officials and politicians likely to lend a sympathetic
ear to Wellington's cause, the major had not had any inter-
course with anyone, save for a few unwelcome encounters
with the Dowager Countess of Claverdon and his friendship
with the de Montmorencys, all of which were perfectly unex-
ceptional.

If he didn't know his master so well, Radlett would have
said that the major was acting as though a woman were involved, but the batman knew better than that. He himself had
seen the Dowager Countess of Claverdon more times than he
cared to remember, and she was enough to put a man like the
major off the entire sex forever—not that his master wasn't as
hot-blooded as the next man. Radlett had seen the looks cast in
Lord Wrotham's direction, and the lures dangled out for him
wherever they were. He had also seen the answering disgust in
the major's eyes. No, Lord Wrotham was not one to become
entangled with a female. A quick tumble with a woman who
expected nothing more than honest payment for services rendered was more in the major's style.

Still, with instincts developed over long years in the army,
Radlett couldn't dismiss his suspicions; in fact, he would have
bet a considerable sum that a woman was at the heart of his
master's odd behavior—and it wasn't the Dowager Countess
of Claverdon. He resolved to watch his master more closely in
search of further evidence to support his theory.

Certainly, the rest of the day the major exhibited a restless-
ness characteristic of a man undecided about something. This
was precisely the case, for Christopher, having made up his
mind, was now faced with the difficult task of presenting it to
Alex in a manner that would be acceptable to her—a most
challenging proposition where someone as confoundedly independent and self-sufficient as Lady Alexandra was concerned.

A great deal of pacing about his chambers was required before Wrotham had screwed up his courage enough to put it to
the touch, but at last, deciding that he was going to gain no
further inspiration from delaying any longer, he strode around
to the Clarendon. There he met Alex just as she was returning
from an obviously successful shopping expedition, if the boxes
in the arms of the footman she had commandeered were any
indication. Observing the major's eyes taking in the name of a

well-known Bond Street modiste on one of the boxes, she hastened to explain. "It is for Ally."

The major grinned at the vehemence of her tone. "And of course you would not think of buying anything for yourself there," he murmured so softly that only the two of them could hear.

The green eyes widened in surprise. "No. Why should I?"

"Why indeed? Because you might just enjoy doing something for yourself for a change."

"Oh, but *I* have had this perfectly splendid adventure."

Wrotham chuckled. He could not think of anyone who would consider undertaking a long, uncomfortable journey in disguise, being attacked by ruffians, and facing a duel a *splendid adventure*, and certainly no woman he had ever encountered would look at it as compensation for shopping on Bond Street—or any other street for that matter.

By now they had reached Alex's rooms and, thanking the footman, she took the boxes, carefully piling them in a corner.

"I see that there are numerous others benefiting from your guilty pleasure at having this delightful escapade all to yourself," the major remarked, strolling over to the fireplace where he propped one shoulder against the mantel.

"Oh yes. I have bought a bonnet for Ally, a doll for Abigail, more toy soldiers for Andrew, ribbons for Mrs. Throckmorton and Bessie, and *An Essay Toward the Improvement of Some of the Important Instruments of Surgery, and the Operations in Which They Are Employed* by William Jardine for Doctor Padgett," she announced, pleased with herself.

Christopher smiled as he resolved privately to find her something special that would always remind her of her visit to London. He stood silent, enjoying her anticipation of the pleasure her presents would bring and thinking rather wistfully that he could not remember when his mother or anyone else had thought of him in such a way. He wished more than ever to become acquainted with the rest of her family, to discover what such a life of warmth and affection was like, but how was he to begin to broach his plan? Wrotham heaved himself off the mantel and strode over to the window, gazing at the passing scene while he hoped for something to come to him.

Alex glanced curiously at the major. The man seemed defi-

nitely ill-at-ease—a state so unnatural in the cool and self-possessed Major Lord Wrotham that she could not help but wonder at it.

He looked up, saw her watching him, and flushed. "Alex,"
he began. Well, he had got that out at least, now what? "I am
aware that . . . er . . . that is—" Dammit, man, he scolded himself, just blurt it out and be done with it. "I know you do not
need it, I mean, that is, you made your way to London from
Norfolk without incident, but I should like to escort you back."

He was right. She *was* offended. The green eyes were
frosty, and she stiffened as she replied, "That is considerate of
you, sir, but I am not in the slightest need of your assistance or
protection."

Christopher's heart sank. He had gone about it all wrong,
but he would not give up. He wanted this too badly. "I *know*
that." Seeing the anger kindling in her eyes, he hurried on. "I
was not offering my protection or assistance, merely my company. Long journeys can be very tedious, you know."

"Oh." Now it was Alex's turn to be at a loss. At least he did
not think she was some helpless female, but she could not let
him ride all that way with her. Why, whatever would people
think?

"And you cannot pull propriety on me now. It won't fadge.
Traveling alone with a man is the merest nothing when compared to gambling with them night after night at White's."

It was a lucky shot for Alex had been about to do just that.
Flustered, she looked up to find him smiling at her in a way
that did nothing to dispel her confusion—quite the contrary.
The dark blue eyes fixed on her so intently seemed to see right
into her, to know how much she longed for him to accompany
her, to make their friendship last a little bit longer, and yet
how she was also made most dreadfully uncomfortable by that
longing. Strangely, the smile on his lips was intimate, conspir-
atorial, as if he too shared in her confused emotions.

Unable to tear her eyes away from his, Alex stood helplessly for some minutes, desperately cudgeling her brains for
some excuse. Nothing came. At last she was forced to acknowledge this. "Very well. If you truly wish to, though it
means you will be faced with the tedious return journey yourself."

Christopher's grin widened. He had won—not that someone like Alex would actually admit defeat. "I shall be happy to be so bored. I suspect that in a few weeks I shall be looking back with longing at my life's very dullest moments. After my time in London, the journey will give me time to collect my thoughts and gather my wits for the next challenge."

Alex was suddenly somber. For a moment she had forgotten that he too, along with Tony, would be throwing himself into the impending fray with Napoleon. It was surprising how much she disliked that thought. However, whether it was a war in Europe or seeking his fortune in some other part of the globe, it did not much matter, given the likelihood of her ever laying eyes on him again.

The future stretching before her, empty of the companionship they had shared over the past few weeks, seemed desolate indeed. What harm could it do to her to share a few more precious days with him? None, she told herself stoutly.

Recovering from her momentary uncertainty, Alex smiled. "The question of whether gambling at White's dressed as a man or journeying unchaperoned with a man is a moot one where *my* reputation is concerned. I haven't one." A wicked gleam stole into her eyes. "Or at least not the sort of one most females are desirous of protecting."

"There's my girl." Christopher laid an oddly comforting hand on her shoulder. "Believe me, you will see more of life this way." He could not help chuckling at the expectant look his words brought to her face. "Equal to any challenge, are you not? You must have been the despair of your nursemaids."

Alex nodded, her eyes dancing. "However, the coachmen and the stable boys were inordinately proud of me."

The major gave a shout of laughter. "And no doubt, to a man, they would lay down their lives for you. I can see I shall have some explaining to do to your coachman now."

Chapter 24

I f Christopher worried over the reaction of this devoted retainer, he need not have. Ned Coachman, subjecting the major to one long, appraising look when his approval of Wrotham's escort was requested, heaved a private sigh of relief and murmured to himself, a gentleman for Lady Alex at last. He thanked Providence, to whom he had long since given up praying, for providing a man who would be the equal to his mistress and who would look after her.

In fact, in Ned's highly critical opinion, Major Lord Wrotham was a gentleman who was more than equal to the task. From the bright blue eyes that looked straight at you, sizing you up in an instant, to the broad shoulders, athletic figure, and proud bearing, one could see that this was a man used to handling every situation, even the most perilous ones—a man accustomed to command. If he had been asked to dream up someone for Lady Alex, Ned admitted humbly to his Maker, he could not have done a better job himself, though it would never do to let on.

Oh he, Ned Brimblecombe, knew how the tabbies would talk if they were to hear of the major's escorting her home, but to his mind, it was worth it, for it meant that this splendid gentleman had more time to appreciate his mistress's finer qualities. Besides, the gossips back in Norfolk, none of whom could hold a candle to Lady Alex, had never had the least effect on his mistress's behavior anyway, nor was it likely they would now, should any of this happen to come out. Personally, he was willing to die to keep the entire escapade secret and he felt certain that Bessie and Mrs. Throckmorton felt the same.

No, Ned was not shocked that his mistress was traveling un-chaperoned with a man. For certain, the rest of the world would be, but Lady Alexandra de Montmorency lived her life by her own lights, and though it was a very different one from most of the niminy piminy misses in the neighborhood surrounding Halewood, it was nonetheless proper. To Ned's way of thinking, his mistress was a true lady—responsible, gracious, kind, and with a courage and understanding that none of the other women with their hoity-toity airs could even hope to appreciate.

So it was with a light heart that Ned directed the packing of the carriage the next morning, checked the wheels and straps, and examined the tack and the shoes of all the horses. His mistress was a lady who traveled light, and in no time they were off, the freshness of the early morning lying like a mist over the city.

The major and Alex rode on ahead, stretching the legs of their mounts and reveling in their escape from the confining streets of the city into the open green spaces of the country. "Ah," Alex sighed, running her fingers through her auburn curls as they drew up on Highgate Hill. "It is good to feel the breeze in one's hair again. London is all that is fascinating and offers more of interest to see and do than I have ever had offered me before, but it is good to be out in the fresh air once more. Imposing buildings are all very well, but I still prefer to be surrounded by trees and grass where I can hear myself think."

Christopher smiled. "So do I." How very different she was from every other female he had known. They had all loathed the countryside, from his mother, who bemoaned the dearth of *genteel companionship* which, translated, meant the lack of an admiring masculine audience, to his first love, who had not been able to bear the loss of the shops on Bond Street for any length of time—but then, Lady Alicia Darling's tastes had always been rigorously governed by the *ton*. After all, she had preferred a decrepit old duke to the handsome and ardent young Wrotham because a duke, no matter how feeble, was more fashionable.

It was certainly refreshing to enjoy the country air with someone who was not complaining of the wind disarranging the trimmings on her bonnet or the sun ruining her complexion. The major drew a deep breath of pure pleasure. What could be more delightful than sharing a ride through the woods and fields with someone who was enjoying it as much as he was?

Alex's voice broke into this happy reverie. "What?" he asked, turning to smile at her. What a picture she made, her cheeks pink with exertion, eyes shining with the pure joy of being alive on such a day.

"I said, shall we race to that church I see up ahead? Trajan is itching for a gallop."

In fact, Christopher was eager for one himself. It had been so long since he had done anything more strenuous than trotting sedately through Hyde Park, and such forced inactivity after a life in the army had left him starved for true exercise. "By all means," he replied. "You call it."

"One, two, three, go!" Alex shouted. They were off, leaning over their horses' necks as they tore down the road.

While the major had anticipated that Alex would be a worthy adversary, he had not expected that she would so easily take the lead. Despite her clothes, her daring, and her unusual upbringing, she was a woman after all. As Trajan's tail flicked Brutus's nose, Christopher realized he had severely underestimated her. Lady Alexandra was a bruising rider, make no mistake about it.

Lightly touching Brutus's flank with his heels, Wrotham leaned even lower over his mouth's neck and urged him forward. Slowly they gained on the other horse and rider. The major, who had unquestionably been the most accomplished horseman in his regiment, refused to believe that someone might possibly beat him. Giving Brutus every ounce of encouragement he could, Christopher held his breath as the horse moved first to Trajan's flank, his shoulder, his neck, his nose, and, with seconds to spare, edged out the other horse by a nostril.

"Now *that* is what I call riding!" A breathless Alex congratulated him, shaking her head in wonder. "Until now, I was the fastest person I knew. I can see that I was a victim of provincial outlook."

Wrotham, long accustomed to beating anyone and everyone

who challenged him on horseback, was unprepared for the rush of satisfaction that her obvious admiration brought him. All of a sudden, he found himself wanting to keep that look in her eyes forever by daring the boldest deeds, conquering the most difficult situations, winning at everything for her.

For her part, Alex was undergoing her own revelations. For as long as she had been grown up no one had bested her in anything. Losing was a rather humbling experience to bear at this point in her life. At the same time, she was glad that the person who had beaten her was the major. That this man she had come to like and admire had proven himself worthy of her regard, even at her own expense, made her happy and proud to be his friend.

Once she had attained her adulthood, Alex had never really had anyone to look up to. To be sure, Doctor Padgett had challenged her intellect, but he was woefully absentminded, and he was utterly cow-handed when it came to horsemanship of any kind. While it was true that Tony was her equal if not better in athletic pursuits, he readily admitted that his older sister possessed more in her cock-loft than he and his older brother put together. Furthermore, he could not be bothered with politics, finance, or anything that demanded such mental exertions as Alexandra delighted in.

So it was that Alex, slowly discovering that her companion was more than a match for her in many things, began to enjoy relaxing in the knowledge that should any mishap occur on their journey, he was just as capable of dealing with it as she was.

Now, having thoroughly invigorated themselves with this exertion, Christopher and Alex were content to let Ned catch up with them. They rode along companionably, reveling in the fineness of the day and a conversation that rambled along as comfortably as they did, changing from one topic to the next as their interests led them from the logistical problems of keeping troops supplied abroad to the effectiveness of draining and reclaiming cropland in Norfolk. Heedless to their surroundings, they passed through Finchley and Welwyn, pausing only briefly in Stevenage for a hasty meal of bread and cheese before proceeding toward Cambridge.

In the meantime, following at a respectful distance, Ned sat atop the coach, glancing up from the road as often as he could to observe his mistress and her companion.

Casting back as far as he could remember, the loyal servant concluded that he had never seen Lady Alexandra so animated and amused. To be sure, she often shared long discussions with Doctor Padgett or the vicar, but Ned had never seen her laugh as she was laughing now, and only her madcap brother Tony could have gotten her to go galloping over the country-side with him as she just had. It had done the old coachman's heart good to see the glow in her face when he had finally caught up with the two of them. He could hardly wait to get back to the cosy kitchen at Halewood to discuss this interesting state of affairs with Bessie and Mrs. Throckmorton. If anything, the two women would be even more delighted and intrigued with the turn of events than he.

The trio made good time and arrived in Cambridge at a rea-sonable hour. They again sought out the Rose and Crown where the major, overruling Alex's protestations that she would not mind the taproom, bespoke a private parlor. "This is not White's, you know," he responded to her assertion that she was quite equal to dining in a roomful of male company. He raised a hand, warding off further objections. "I know from experience that you can handle yourself creditably in a brawl should one occur, but I prefer not to run the risk. You haven't enough science to make me comfortable should any unpleas-antness erupt, as it often does, and you are called upon to de-fend yourself." Correctly interpreting the hopeful glint in her eyes, he laughed. "No, I shall not teach you. Your brother may educate you in the art of swords and pistols, but the world of the fancy is a rough one and I shall do nothing to encourage you in its pursuit."

Alex sighed. "I expect you are in the right of it, but still I do . . ."

"No!"

"Very well." Then, brightening, she continued, "You need not instruct me in the use of my fists, but could you teach me the footwork, for I feel that it could be most helpful should I find myself in any uncomfortable situations."

"You are incorrigible." The major shook his head, but there was a twinkle in his eye. "Besides, I thought that all your *un-*

comfortable situations would be over now that you have successfully accomplished your mission."

"One never knows," she replied with a darkling look. "I
have yet to pay back the odious Sir Ralph."

They dined most pleasantly and Alex, listening to the
sounds of revelry coming from below, was forced to admit the
wisdom of the major's decision. However, not wishing to appear fainthearted, she told herself that the quiet of the private
parlor was much more conducive to intelligent conversation,
for which she thanked the major. "I shall make the most of discussions such as this for they will be sorely lacking in the days
to come—not that Ally and the children are not all that is
amusing, but our topics of conversation are rather confined to
household matters." She smiled at him over the generous helping of turbot in cream sauce that she was happily consuming.

The entire evening was so pleasant that each of them was
most reluctant to end it, but there was a day's journey yet
ahead of them and an early start was necessary if they were to
stop on the road for Alex to transform herself into Lady
Alexandra and still reach Halewood at a decent hour. Even so,
they lingered for the longest time outside the door to Alex's
bedchamber, candles sputtering in their hands.

Looking down at his companion in the flickering candlelight, noting that it caught the red glints in her hair and made
her green eyes appear enormous, the major found himself
fighting off the urge to kiss her. In the shadows she appeared
so absurdly youthful, so defenseless, that he longed to fold her
in his arms and hold her, to whisper all sorts of tender and
comforting things in her ear, to assure her that her life would
be safe and happy ever after.

It was the impulse of a moment that was cast off as quickly
as it had appeared, but he could not help being taken aback by
it, never having experienced such protective feelings in his
life, and certainly not toward any woman.

Gazing up at the major, Alex was struck by the curiously intent look in his eyes. Suddenly shy, she stared down at her gut-
tering candle, her other hand uneasily fingering the buttons of
her coat. Then with a laugh that sounded hideously false even
to her own ears, she blurted out, "If I continue to stand here

any longer, my candle will be quite burned out and I shall have to make my way in the dark."

The major, as disconcerted as she was, agreed with an abruptness and awkwardness that was uncharacteristic, "Yes, well, good night." Then, as she closed the door behind her, he whispered softly, "Sleep well, Alexandra."

Chapter 25

Sleep, however, did not come easily to either one of them. Despite her fatigue and muscles aching after an unaccustomed day in the saddle, Alex lay on her bed wide awake staring at the ceiling—not that she could see a thing, but somehow she just could not close her eyes and drift off the way she knew she needed to. I must be getting soft, she muttered to herself as she stretched one leg to relieve its soreness, discounting entirely the lack of exercise she had been forced to endure for the past few weeks. However, it was not discomfort that was keeping her awake so much as her thoughts.

What a wonderful day it had been! She had never known such easy companionship, had never laughed so much, ridden so hard, or discussed so many things in such depth and now, just having discovered that such happiness existed, she must soon bid it all good-bye. No use repining, she admonished herself as she rolled over in search of a more comfortable position. This time Alex, ordinarily a very self-controlled person, was unable to make herself do any such thing and her thoughts only slid into more dangerous directions: the impressive picture the major had made as he rode beside her, the squareness of his shoulders, the strength in his legs, the blueness of his eyes, and the way they crinkled in the corners whenever he laughed or teased her.

Suddenly, and most unaccountably, Alex wished that the carriage dress she had brought to change into the next day were just a little bit more fashionable, a little bit more becoming, and not as creased as it must be after being packed at the bottom of her baggage for so long. She was about to leap out of bed to extract it from her trunk and hang it out, but caution got the better of her. She had been successful in her escapade thus far, no need to threaten all she had won by taking foolish chances now.

Thank heavens I have *some* sense left, she comforted herself. For in truth, the thoughts that had just been running through her head had been running along lines as foolish as the thoughts of her nearest neighbor, Lady Warburton, and her bevy of silly coquettish daughters usually did, making Alex wonder if she had taken leave of her wits.

Unbelievably enough, sleep at last did come, but it was uneasy, she dreamt of vast battlefields filled with men, horses, and cannons, and of both Anthony and the major being swallowed up by masses of enemy soldiers. All in all, Alex was delighted to be awakened by the warmth and light of the morning sunshine that stole through the window and tickled her face.

She leapt out of bed and hurried to the washstand, eager to put all upsetting thoughts and fears of the previous night behind her. Then, recalling at least one of her concerns from the evening before, she dug into he trunk, pulled out her serviceable gray bombazine carriage dress, and gave it several hearty shakes before gently and carefully laying it back on top of her things. Her bonnet, equally practical and uninspiring, was also extracted.

Having had to dispense with a bandbox in order to maintain her disguise, Alex had selected the smallest and least prepossessing item of headgear she owned, which she now surveyed with intense dissatisfaction. Just for a moment she wished she could look forward to donning the elegant white satin carriage dress that she had admired as they had ridden in Hyde Park not so long ago; it had sported a matching pelisse of white twilled sarcenet complemented by an exquisite white satin hat with pomona green plumes. Although it was quite unlike Alex to notice such a thing, its wearer had been so lovely with her pink-and-white complexion, retroussé nose, and glossy dark curls dancing under the brim of her bonnet that everyone, even the major, had been unable to tear their eyes from her.

Silly goose, Alex muttered fiercely to herself as she struggled to banish such treacherous and unfamiliar thoughts from her mind. You know that it is a great deal more fun, and certainly more comfortable to ride astride a horse in breeches, to feel free to walk into whatever establishment you please without the least thought of whether it is proper, than it is to ride tamely in the park in a barouche accompanied by some ape-leader as a companion.

Closing her trunk, she hastily finished dressing and hurried downstairs to the taproom where Wrotham was already digging into an enormous rasher of ham and eggs. The welcoming smile on his face when he looked up and saw Alex was enough to banish even the worst fit of the dismals and she felt her ill humor vanishing magically as she took her place in the chair Christopher indicated.

Casting a cautious eye around the room, the major spoke softly, "As the crowd is a good deal more quiet at this hour then it was yesterday evening, I felt no qualms about having our breakfast here. I even took the liberty of ordering for you. It is a good deal more expedient and I know you are anxious to reach Halewood as soon as possible."

"Yes. Thank you." Alex took the plate of eggs that he had served her from the platter next to him. However, nothing could have been further from the truth. Suddenly, she wished Halewood—with its daily cares and deadly dull routine—were a million miles away. Despite her best efforts to keep her mind alive with books and journals, she knew her spirit had little room to grow there. She wanted to go on forever seeing new things, sharing them with someone who looked at the world as she did and asked the same questions of it.

However, being Alex, she resolved to make the most of what she had and, smiling gratefully at the major, she ate her breakfast, paid her shot, and went to see the horses put to as quickly and as efficiently as if she did not wish to prolong every possible minute of their journey.

It was another glorious day, and for the most part, they rode silently, enjoying the rich green fields dotted here and there with fruit trees just coming into blossom, the soft fresh morning air broken only by the burst of song from some bird intent on attracting a mate.

All too soon they reached Coltishall, where Alex would do her best to reassemble herself as Lady Alexandra de Montmorency and where it was agreed that Christopher would stay the night while she drove on to Halewood.

Once again Alex had tried to dissuade the major from escorting her the entire way. After all, what could possibly befall her within a few miles of her home, but much to her relief, he would have none of it.

"No. I shall not rest easy until I have seen you restored to your brothers and sisters and am assured that everything concerning the debt has been settled to your satisfaction," he had replied firmly. There had been a look in his eye that brooked no argument and that augured ill for anyone who threatened to overset the ultimate success of Alex's escapade. In fact, Alex could not recall when she had ever seen the major looking so severe. With a tiny shock, she realized that if indeed complications did arise, he was bound and determined to eliminate them for her. It was a novel idea and so too was the feeling of happiness that flooded through her at the thought of it.

Christopher even insisted on mounting guard while Ned drove the coach into a thick copse and Alex, with the shades on the coach windows open only a crack to allow enough light for her to see, struggled into her dress, fumbling with the fastenings as best she could. Lord the skirts felt cumbersome after the freedom of breeches! Finally, having smoothed her hair as much as possible, and feeling about to make sure she had left nothing undone, she firmly grasped the handle, opened the door, and jumped down.

At the edge of the trees the major sat quietly on Brutus, staring off into the distance until the swish of skirts on the grass made him look around. She was much smaller, more delicate than he had realized as she stood there in a soft gray dress that made her copper curls glow redder than ever. Without the padding on her shoulders she looked so slender and her bosom, released from its confining bands and now gently rounded, emphasized the slimness of her waist and hips. How could he ever, even for one minute, have thought that Alex de Montmorency was a man?

She drew closer, glancing up at him shyly, uneasily, the green eyes huge and anxious in her face. Christopher cast about desperately for something to say to relieve the awkwardness of the moment, to reassure her and to reassure himself. "I imagine that Trajan will rue this transformation even more than you do, seeing that an existence as a lady's mount will be confining to him. Knowing you, though, I feel certain you still occasionally throw caution to the winds and ride at the same breakneck speed that gave me such a run for my money yesterday."

The impish grin reappeared and with it, the twinkle in her eyes. Once again she was his same old Alex. "*Occasionally*, I fear, is not the word. Riding at *breakneck speed* as you call it, is a necessity for me or I should go mad."

The major cocked a quizzical eyebrow.

"Well, you try wearing skirts and cajoling servants and children all day," Alex retorted huffily, "and see if you are not a candidate for Bedlam in no short space of time."

"The skirts I give you," he conceded, "but as to cajoling children, you forget where I have been spending my time recently, though I am sure that the members of our illustrious governing body would quite fail to see it that way. But come, let me escort you to your carriage. Undoubtedly the servants and children are waiting eagerly for you to cajole them again."

The major leapt down and taking Brutus's reins in one hand, offered her his other arm. Again he was struck by her grace and slenderness. Alex was tall for a woman, her head reaching well above his shoulder, and he was a man of considerable height. That, however, in no way detracted from her essential femininity. Staring down at her, he wondered all over again how he could have been so taken in by her deception.

As if reading his thoughts, Alex replied, "I am not all that stupid, you know. I realized that in order to be Alexander I had to do more than don his clothes. I aped his walk, his way of holding his arms—oh, a thousand little things." Seeing that he remained unconvinced Alex withdrew her hand from his arm and swaggered forward, the Earl of Halewood once more.

The effect was so comical that Christopher laughed until tears streamed from his eyes. Wiping them away with his sleeve, he gasped, "No, you are not in the least bit stupid, but I swear you will be the death of me." He caught up to her and offered her his arm again. She accepted it, but not without a grimace. "No, do not pull such a long face at me, my girl," he admonished her. "The charade is not yet over, nor will it be unless you can behave something like a lady again and, much as you dislike it, the sooner you begin practicing at it, the better." And so, teasing and laughing, each trying to put the impending separation out of mind, they reached Alex's carriage.

"Take care of yourself. I trust you will not discover anything too disturbing when you arrive." The major handed her into the coach and then, leaning in through the open doorway, he added softly, "And remember, I shall be there tomorrow." He closed the door, flung himself on Brutus, and with a wave, was off, leaving Alex alone with her thoughts as the carriage made its way sedately toward Halewood.

Chapter 26

Christopher had not been far wrong in his guess; Alex's return had been eagerly awaited by those remaining at Halewood. Every day since they had received the letter announcing her return, Andrew had pestered Ally to hazard a guess as to when they could reasonably expect their older sister's arrival. At last, even the ever-patient Althea was exasperated with him. "You are a clever boy, Andrew—you figure it out. If it takes two days for Ned to get to London and an equal time to get back, and it takes time to pack and for the horses to rest, you tell me."

"Tell me, tell me," Abigail had chanted and Andrew, feeling that it was now incumbent upon him to predict his sister's return, found ways to pass by the windows overlooking the drive at least several times a day. Thus it was that the carriage was still the merest speck entering the gates of the long gravel drive when he raced into the schoolroom where Althea was overseeing Abigail's clumsy attempts at sewing, shouting, "She's here! She's here!"

As little enamored of feminine pursuits as her eldest sister, Abigail hastily dropped the miserable tangle of embroidery cotton and linen and scrambled after her brother. Sighing gently and shaking her head over her sister's cavalier disregard for such things, Althea laid down her own exquisitely executed needlework and headed downstairs to welcome Alex.

By the time she reached the front hall, quite a crowd had already assembled. The servants, headed by Jamison, the butler, and Mrs. Throckmorton, were quite as eager for Alex's return as her family was. Despite the careful collusion of the housekeeper, the butler, the coachman, and Bessie, the entire household had somehow come by the notion that Lady Alexandra's absence had a great deal to do with the future of all of them and, though it was generally believed that she had gone to visit relatives in Brighton in order to seek relief from pecuniary difficulties, they anxiously awaited news of the success of her mission. It had not occurred to anyone to doubt that she would return with the solution to their problems, but still they were glad to have her back to reassure them that their lives would continue along in the same comfortable pattern that they always had.

Seeing them all gathered under the gray stone portico, eagerly awaiting her arrival, went a long way to assuaging some of the sense of loss that Alex had felt at her parting from the major. In truth, she had missed everyone at Halewood, and after the noise and dirt of London she did feel a certain sense of peace and security wash over as she gazed over the rich green fields on either side of the drive, and stared at the lovely facade of her home, its bricks glowing warm and red and the diamond panes twinkling in the slanting rays of the afternoon sun.

"Alex, Alex, I jumped the hedge by the Hanger Wood!" Andrew, unable to contain himself any longer, ran down the steps to greet her.

Not to be outdone, Abigail hurried closely behind, bursting with news of her own equestrian progress. Following at a more sedate pace, Althea smiled at her sister over the children's heads, murmuring, "One would think they had not done any lessons at all, but I assure you they have."

"Oh, Alex, have you brought us something?" Spying some interesting and unfamiliar packages in the carriage, Andrew could not restrain himself.

Alex laughed. "Yes, you dreadful child, but I am not entirely certain that you deserve them. Does he, Ally?"

Andrew and Abigail held their breaths, hoping that their older sister would forget about the muddied frocks, the broken window, and the tarts stolen still warm from the kitchen.

Surveying their anxious faces, Ally was silent for a moment, her eyes bright with mischief. "Well . . ." She hesitated until she thought Andrew would burst from the suspense. "I think they deserve a *little* something. They have been quite diligent in their schoolwork." Heaving enormous sighs of relief, the two children clustered around Alex as she reached inside for two delightfully wrapped parcels.

"And I have something for you as well, Ally, only you must not let anyone see where it came from. Thank you so much for all you have done." She handed a striped bandbox to her sister who, upon seeing the name of the shop emblazoned across its lid, gasped and turned quite pale with excitement.

"Oh, Alex, Madame Céleste! It must have been shockingly dear!"

"And only a small fraction of what you deserve for taking charge of all this." Alex smiled at her sister's surprise and delight. "But on to more serious matters. What of Alexander? Is he alive? I assume you would have written of any changes."

"Only just," Althea responded soberly. "Doctor Padgett and Bessie have worked miracles, but he cannot continue for much longer. First come in and refresh yourself after the journey and then you may visit him."

So, swept along by a tide of siblings anxious to hear of her adventures and eager to share theirs, Alex was soon ensconced in the library with tea and biscuits at her side, listening to complaints that lessons had not been nearly so interesting since she had gone, that Cook had scalded her hand and been unable to use it for two days, that Farmer Trimble's pigs had broken out of their fence and taken a great deal of time and effort to catch, and caused much damage. However, conscious of the fading light, Alex soon excused herself and headed back to the carriage which Ned had kept ready for her.

Upon reaching Mrs. Bates's cottage she was greeted ecstatically by Bessie. "Oh, Miss Alex, it is *that* good to see you!" Then pausing, she continued in a whisper, a grave expression clouding her ordinarily sunny features, "I am afraid Master Alexander is doing poorly. He continues feverish and he is not always aware of the things around him. I did the best I could— we all did, but . . ."

"I know, Bessie, I know. I am just grateful you managed to keep him alive until I returned. The exposure he suffered was severe, and what with the life he had been living, it is a credit to you and Doctor Padgett that he survived at all." Alex headed for the tiny room at the back of the cottage where the sounds of labored breathing were proof that the sick man still struggled on.

She paused at the door. "Bye the bye, I was so eager to see everyone that I stopped first at Halewood, where I gave it out that I had left you in the village making a few necessary purchases for me. I have now come to fetch you and to visit some of the tenants."

Bessie bobbed her head. "Very good, miss. I shall remember. I do not think there is a soul who suspects anything."

Even though she had done her best to fortify herself for this meeting, Alex was unprepared for her brother's pathetic appearance. Once a florid, rather hefty man, the Earl of Halewood was a shadow of his former self. The bright auburn hair was graying and lank. Flesh hung loosely on his frame and the high-bridged nose jutted sharply above sunken, pallid cheeks, while the hands that clutched the covers were clawlike.

"Oh, Alexander," his twin whispered, sinking to a stool by his bedside. There was no response. How could he have brought such a thing on himself? she wondered, gazing down at the wreck of her brother. Even before his exposure to the storm, his life of dissipation had made him appear ten years older than his sister. Now he looked positively ancient, as though he were her father or even grandfather instead of her twin.

Alex had no idea how long she sat in the deepening twilight staring unseeing at the figure in the bed. Bessie stole softly in with a candle and then with a meager dinner, which Alex declined. Finally the man in the bed stirred and muttered. She leaned over. "Alexander?"

The eyelids flickered and then opened. The green eyes, so like her own, stared up at her uncomprehending for a moment and then with dawning recognition. "Alex?" he whispered.

"I'm here." Tears welled up in her eyes and rolled down her cheeks. There was a rustle in the bedclothes as one hand moved weakly. She grasped it with her own and felt it go limp as something like a sigh escaped her brother's lips. He was so still she hardly needed to feel for the nonexistent pulse to know he was gone. In truth, he had been gone from her for a long time. Her twin had died years ago when the self-indulgent, selfish youth had taken over the adventurous boy who had been her constant playmate.

Alex bowed her head and wept, not so much for her immediate loss as for the loss of someone who could have done,
could have been so much more. She wept for the spirit that
seemed to have been bent on destroying itself and very nearly
many others along with it. And she wept, just a little bit, for
the life that could have been, the closeness that could have
been if he had not grown up into a selfish lout.

At last, wiping her eyes, she rose and went to find Bessie.
The maid, seeing it all in her mistress's face, hurried to her
side. "Don't take on so, my lady; 'tis for the best, you know. It
is a wonder he held on this long, but I expect somehow he was
waiting for you. Come along now. I shall tell Ned to take us
home and we'll send for Doctor Padgett."

And, sliding the cloak on Alex's shoulders, the maid hurried
to call Ned, who appeared instantly to help the two women
into the carriage.

All the way home, Alex tried her best to blot out the vision
of Alexander, gray, faded, and frail, lying on the bed gasping
for breath, and replaced it instead with images of him as a boy,
his green eyes bright with mischief and the ready smile lighting his face underneath his unruly shock of flaming hair.
These were succeeded by the older Alexander, florid, petulant,
frequently drunk, and always selfish to the core. By the time
they had reached Halewood Alex was calm, glad that everything had worked out as it had, and relieved that Alexander
had been stopped before he had completely brought them to
rack and ruin. He had led them to the brink and that was close
enough for Alex. She was also thankful to have arrived home
in time to spend his last minutes by his side.

It was only as she and Bessie climbed the steps to her chamber and Alex gratefully accepted the maid's assistance in
readying her for bed that Alex realized just how tired she was.
It had quite a day, quite a journey, in fact, and the soft bed
waiting for her appeared most inviting.

Alex sank with relief into the pillows. Tomorrow she would
face the loathsome Cranbourne and throw his money in his
face—odious pig. And tomorrow, her stomach gave a queer
little flutter, the major would arrive. Immeasurably cheered by
this last happy thought, she drifted off into a deep slumber.

Chapter 27

Alex woke to the faint rattle of the under housemaid lighting the fire in her chamber. She grabbed for her wrapper and leapt from the bed. Full daylight was streaming into the room. Good heavens, she thought, splashing her face with the water the maid had just brought up, it must be nigh on eight o'clock! Forgetting everything except her wish to settle Alexander's debts with Sir Ralph as quickly as possible, she threw on her clothes with even less thought for her appearance than usual, ran a brush hastily through her curls, and hurried downstairs to the morning room, stopping briefly in the library to snatch up a pen and paper from her desk.

Althea was still in the morning room, nibbling some toast and lingering over a pot of chocolate. A liberal sprinkling of toast crumbs and empty plates attested to the former presence of the children. "Good morning," her sister greeted her with a smile. "The children could wait for you no longer and they have gone off to see Ginger's latest litter of kittens before they begin their lessons." Then lowering her voice, she continued hesitantly, "Alexander . . . the service . . . have you thought any more about it than you did last night?"

Alex, in the middle of gulping the fresh steaming chocolate that had just been brought her, nodded. "Yes. And I have decided that, if I possibly can, I shall do nothing until I have repaid Sir Ralph. I prefer to have him think that Alexander is alive, though elsewhere, when I deal with him."

Ally nodded, her expression of distaste a mirror of her sister's. "I quite agree. He is not in the least gentlemanly."

But then who among Alexander's associates was? Alex

muttered to herself. She set down her cup and, with a resolute dip of her pen into the ink, quickly wrote to Sir Ralph requesting an interview with him at his earliest convenience. She handed it to the footman who, having responded instantly to her pull on the bell, promised to deliver it with all possible speed. "And now"—Alex poured herself more chocolate and leaned back in her chair—"we have only to sit back and await the appearance of his odiousness."

Ally's stifled giggle was cut short by Abigail and Andrew, who erupted into the room, each eager to be the first with the news. "Alex, Alex, there is a soldier in the hall," Abigail, who had edged into the room just in front of her brother, announced. "He says that he is a friend of Tony's. . . ."

"But I don't see how that could be since he's not in the same regiment," her brother continued.

"How do you know that?" his younger sister demanded. "He's a soldier and Tony's a soldier, and . . ."

"Tony's uniform is red, you silly goose, and the major's is a Hussar uniform and is blue."

"Oh," Abigail replied, crestfallen.

"Never mind, love. I am sure I did not know that either." Ally gave her sister a comforting hug.

"I wonder if . . ." Andrew began, but all speculation was cut short by the arrival oft the major himself. Lord, the man was more handsome than she had remembered, Alex thought to herself, and it had not yet been an entire day since she had last set eyes on him.

"I hope that you will excuse me for arriving unannounced and at such an early hour," he began apologetically, eyeing the attractive family group appreciatively. Seeing Alex with the light flooding in from the windows behind her, looking the picture of fresh femininity, and flanked by her siblings, it was hard to believe that he had ever known her in London, had ever seen her lazing back in her chair surveying the company at White's with a cynical eye, had ever sauntered down Bond Street with her or watched anxiously as she fought a duel. "But I was passing through and knew Tony would wish for me to look you up." Christopher stole a glance at Alex, who looked to be faintly amused. She would never have accepted the taradiddle that someone just happened to be "passing through" their little out-of-the-way corner of Norfolk, but the absurdity of it did not appear to strike the others.

"Were you in Spain with Tony, then?" Andrew wanted to know. "You are a Hussar and he's a guard."

The major smiled. No flies on this one. The lad was as sharp as his eldest sister. "You are quite right, but quarters are sometimes scarce and we are forced to share them with lowly foot soldiers. Yes, we were in Spain but I did not meet your brother there. I came across him in London, where we talked of old times and discussed what is to come. He has gone off to the Continent already, but he knew I had business here before I rejoined Wellington so he asked me to look you up." The major glanced again at Alex to see how she was taking it. She nodded slightly and smiled.

"You are with Wellington?" Andrew was round-eyed with awe.

"Well, yes, but merely as an errand boy, I assure you."

"What is he like? Are the stories about him true?"

"Whoa, lad." The major laughed, but he could not help feeling touched by the worshipful light in the boy's eyes. "As I say, I am nothing more than a messenger, so I can tell you only what I know of him from a distance, but I can say that there is no one whose orders I would rather follow than his. Soldiers are rather skeptical fellows you know, but they have seen proof time and time again of the soundness of his strategies. If the Iron Duke tells them to do something, they do it gladly, no questions asked. I don't know what stories you have heard. Usually by the time something becomes a story there is not a grain of truth left in it, but if you have heard that he is as honest and hardworking a soldier as you'll ever hope to find, impatient with self-serving politicians, and devoted to his troops, then what you have heard is entirely correct."

"I knew it!" Andrew crowed. "Do you think he'll whip Boney?"

The major was silent for a moment, a grave expression settling over his features. "Yes," he responded slowly, "but it will be a very near thing and many brave men will perish on both sides."

"But Napoleon has only just gathered his army and Tony says that the fellows in his regiment are part of one of the finest fighting forces in the world," Andrew protested.

"That is most definitely true, but there are some equally splendid soldiers on the other side and many of our veterans of the Peninsula are off in America at the moment. There is no doubt it will be a match of Titans."

"Oh, how I wish I were older! Tell me, what is it like? Tony talks about his regiment, but he doesn't say much about the fighting. However, you are in the cavalry, you see everything. Were you at Badajoz or Ciudad Rodrigo?"

The major was amused to note that Andrew's younger sister was watching him as intently as her brother. "No." Seeing Andrew's face fall, and hating to disappoint the lad, he hastened to add, "But I was at Talavera and Salamanca." The major was inordinately pleased to see that his reputation rose once again in the boy's estimation.

"You were? Oh please, could you tell us about it?"

At this point Alex, knowing her little brother and his insatiable curiosity in such matters, interrupted the barrage of questions. "Perhaps our visitor would like some refreshment and a moment to catch his breath, Andrew." Alex pulled the bell and turned to the major. "I do hope you will spend some time with us, in which case, perhaps you would like to see your room."

"That is very kind of you. I . . ."

"Oh, please stay," the children chorused, anxious that this fascinating visitor not be allowed to escape before he had regaled them with exploits of daring and glory.

Alex could not help smiling at her siblings' enthusiasm and at the major's surprise and pleasure at their unabashed interest. There was nothing as flattering as the admiration in a child's eyes, unmarred as yet by selfish or self-centered motives of any sort. And, if the major's bemused expression was any indication, such genuine appreciation was a rare and welcome occurrence in his life. "Why, thank you. My business is not so urgent that I could not at least spend the night."

"Why do you not show the major to his quarters and he can refresh himself." Alex nodded at the children. "We shall put him in the guest bedchamber in the west wing, I think. It has been recently aired and has the nicest view."

Abigail and Andrew were at Christopher's side in an instant. "It's much the prettiest room," Abigail volunteered, holding out her hand.

Andrew, not to be outdone, offered to take the other hand. "Come alone and then we'll show you the stables."

"Just let me inquire as to what the major would like—coffee, chocolate, or some breakfast—before you lead him off," Alex broke in before they could drag him away.

"Coffee would be most welcome, thank you." Christopher smiled, rose, and taking the hands of each of his guides, allowed himself to be led off.

"I wonder if he is accustomed to children," Ally murmured as the trio exited the room, "or at least children who are as exuberant as Abigail and Andrew."

"Never fear. They are good children and their conversation is often far more interesting than that of many adults one is forced to entertain," her sister reassured her.

Christopher was discovering the truth of this as he followed his guides to the west wing. Not only were they genuinely interested in him as a person, they were ingeniously ready to share with him a great deal about themselves, their family, Halewood, and the surrounding countryside. He had not known that so much information could be retained and articulated by such young minds and, quite to his surprise, he found himself entirely captivated and highly entertained by their startlingly fresh view of the world.

Wrotham had come to Halewood because he had unwillingly become utterly fascinated by Alexandra. He wanted to learn more about a woman who acquitted herself better than most men at the gaming table, on the dueling field, in conversation, and at just about anything else he could think of. He wanted to learn more about a woman who could win his friendship and respect—something no woman ever had. To sum it all up, having enjoyed her as much as he had ever enjoyed any one of his male acquaintances, he looked forward with pleasure and anticipation to learning more about Alex as a woman. Now it appeared that he was going to reap unsuspected pleasure from his visit as he became acquainted with the rest of the family.

The rest of the family certainly appeared determined to make his acquaintance. Having conducted the major to his chamber, Andrew seemed loath to leave him. "Would you like to see the stables, sir? We don't have many horses, but my brother Alexander keeps some bang-up hunters, and Alexandra's Trajan is a prime bit of blood. Perhaps you would like to see to your horse as well, though Ned is the best when it comes to horses." To Abigail's protestation that they should follow Alex's order explicitly and leave the visitor alone to refresh himself, Andrew scoffingly observed that the major did not look in the least bit fagged, and to someone who had served in the Peninsula, any journey here must seem the merest jaunt. "Isn't that so, sir?" Andrew looked up earnestly for confirmation from the major.

"Oh, indubitably." The blue eyes twinkled at him. "I shall just leave my kit here, but I would like to have some of that coffee your sister promised me before we inspect the delights of Halewood."

"Andrew," his sister hissed, tugging insistently at her brother's sleeve, "he might want to . . ."

"I know, I know," her brother whispered back in a lordly manner. Then straightening to his full height and putting on his most adult demeanor, he turned to Christopher. "We shall await you in the morning room. Do please make yourself comfortable."

"Thank you." It was all the major could do not to laugh, and despite his most valiant efforts, he could not keep his lips from twitching. At the moment, the lad was the spitting image of his oldest sister.

Reverting immediately to his former exuberant self, Andrew urged, "But do hurry, won't you?" With a wave they were off, scampering down the long corridor, their golden curls glowing as they raced through each shaft of light thrown by the tall windows that pierced the gloom of the long hall.

Smiling to himself, the major strolled to the window and gazed out over the green expanse of lawn. What a marvel this family was—and what a contrast it offered to his own lonely childhood, with no companions except the servants and a mother who would sweep him up in a perfumed embrace when there were visitors, but who otherwise ignored him until he was old enough to offer escort and admiration. Here at Halewood these children were obviously loved and enjoyed, their needs recognized as equal to those of the other household members, and what charming creatures were the result of such caring and concern.

Chapter 28

The major's initial favorable impressions of the lively household only increased as he became better acquainted with it. Everyone from Althea and the children to Mrs. Throckmorton and Bessie, on down to the grooms treated him with unaffected friendliness and genuine interest. He could see that this open and relaxed atmosphere was owing directly to the mistress of the household, who was looked up to by one and all—and it was obvious to even the most casual observers that the respect so visibly given to her was accorded because of her judgment and knowledge rather than her social position. It was a respect warmed with the utmost affection, as evident from the protective way in which Ned had escorted her home to the solicitous regard so subtly expressed by Mrs. Throckmorton and Bessie. These two dedicated women hovered around Lady Alexandra, each in her own particular way—Mrs. Throckmorton, insisting that everything possible was done to ensure the major's utmost comfort, and Bessie, showing by look and manner that her mistress was someone worthy of the highest admiration. If there was deference in anyone's manner, it was for Alexandra's accomplishments and for the care she took to maintain the well-being of those around her.

Watching her with the children as she accompanied them on their tour of the stables, Christopher could well understand why all this was so. She treated them as she treated everyone else, as people whose thoughts, opinions, and feelings were worthy of her time and consideration. The result was that

Abby and Andrew regarded her as a friend—an adult friend, but a friend nevertheless.

As he listened to Abigail's descriptions of the picnics they had held in the meadow, and Andrew's reminiscences of the adventures they had had in the woods or rowing about on the pond, the major could not suppress a pang of envy for the rich and delightful life they enjoyed. Once again, visions of his own desolate childhood arose in his mind's eye and he felt the same old anger at his mother for ignoring him so completely.

"Do you have any brothers or sisters?" Andrew asked innocently enough as he tossed a ball for the lively little terrier who had been accompanying them.

"No. Or at least not while I was growing up. I now have a half brother."

"Then who did you play with?" the boy wondered.

"Well, no one precisely," Christopher was forced to admit.

"That's sad." Abigail, her childish features solemn at the thought of such an unhappy circumstance.

Yes, it had been sad, Christopher reflected later that afternoon as he accompanied Alex on a tour of the estate, but fortunately, it was not until now when he saw what childhood and family life could be that he realized what he had missed.

Heretofore he would have thought days in the country spent taking care of an estate would have been dull beyond belief, and he had always been delighted that he could leave his own lands in the competent hands of Mr. Beamish while he pursued the more exciting existence of a military life, but now, riding with Alex to survey the fields burgeoning with fresh young crops, checking fences, talking with tenants, and inspecting livestock, he realized that he had been wrong. There was as much challenge and satisfaction to be gained from such things as from life as a soldier, and none of the painful destruction to which he had forced himself to become accustomed.

Earlier, tossing Alex into her saddle as they had prepared to ride out, he had had a fleeting thought of how very pleasant it would be to do such a thing every day—to trot along together, companionably discussing the merits of one prize bull over another, or planting rye as opposed to wheat, the possible effect of the corn laws, or anything that might come to mind.

She had grimaced as he helped her mount. "I apologize. If I

had been in London now you should not be called to do any such thing. In breeches it is the simplest matter to climb on Trajan's back." She sighed regretfully.

"True. But you would not look as lovely as you do now."

The major spoke without even thinking, for she did look beautiful. The slate gray riding habit clung to her slender figure, revealing the soft curves, its severe color enhancing the delicacy of her complexion and the glorious red highlights in the curls that peeped out beneath her jaunty hat.

It was the merest observation on Christopher's part, but, as he observed the color wash over her face and saw the confusion in her eyes, he realized the full implications of what he had said. Until this moment, with the exception of one or two fleeting reflections on his part, they had just been two friends. Now they were a man and a woman, friends just the same, but with that difference finally acknowledged between them.

For her part, Alex was much less capable of articulating her own welter of thoughts. Too bemused by the incredible idea that someone, anyone, considered her beautiful, she could only sit silently, transfixed by the warmth of his voice and the admiration in his dark blue eyes. She was overwhelmed by the odd feelings that engulfed her—feelings she had never known before, feelings she could not even begin to identify or explain, feelings that left her breathless and not a little disconcerted.

"I beg your pardon." The major's anxious voice seemed to come from miles away. "I suppose it *was* rather presumptuous of me. I did not mean to insult you in any way."

Alex grinned ruefully. Now he was almost as ill at ease as she was. How perfectly ridiculous. Here they were, two adults who had shared danger and adventure without a by-your-leave, and now they were as awkward as schoolchildren—more so, because children never fell victim to such silliness. "No, I am not the least insulted, though I do think you ought to be concerned for yourself. No one has ever thought that of me before." She tilted her head, squinting up at the sky. "I daresay it is the sun—it has coddled your brains."

He gave a crack of laughter. "Not likely, Miss Skeptic. I have endured far worse than this on a daily basis in the Peninsula. What, has no one called you beautiful before?"

Alex snorted and shook her head.

"It is not that my wits are addled, it is that you have never dealt with a man of spirit before. We soldiers laugh at death every day; why then should we fear the wrath of a brilliant, independent, adventurous, and self-possessed woman? Don't look so astonished, Alexandra. You know that it takes great courage even to talk to a woman as terrifyingly self-assured as you are, but to admire her to her very face, why I wonder that even I, battle-hardened veteran that I am, dare to do so."

She laughed at his extravagant words, but Christopher could see that they had given her pause. He drew alongside her and added more gently, "It is not owing to any lack of loveliness on your part, you know; it is just that you are so many other things that it almost seems an insult to your character and intelligence to call attention to something that, in comparison, is so superficial. I am sure if I had been thinking about it at all, I should never have dared to say such a thing, but I was not and I just spoke the thought that came into my mind. But come, show me around Halewood and then I can admire something that you truly do set store by—your agricultural knowledge and your skill as a landlord."

The awkwardness over between them, they rode along conversing as comfortably as always: noting a fence that needed mending here, a roof to be patched there, pausing to consider the possibility of draining some more land, each enjoying what the other had to offer to the discussion, and each thinking how pleasant and how rare it was to be able to share so many things with another person after so many years of being all on one's own.

The sun was beginning to sink in the sky when they finally returned to Halewood, invigorated by the sight of the vast expanses of green countryside, the freshness of the air, and the exercise.

The butler, who had been keeping an eye out for his mistress in order to warn her that she had a visitor, thought he had never seen her look so happy as she did now. Grasping her gloves and crop in one hand, her other on the major's arm, she strolled laughing and chatting across the gravel drive and up the front steps. She looked positively radiant and Jamison did not relish dispelling that look with the information that Sir Ralph Cranbourne awaited her in the library.

Chapter 29

Not wanting to spoil his mistress's day, which had begun so propitiously, the butler had done his best to discourage the visitor with a deliberate vagueness as to the expected time of Lady Alexandra's return, but to no avail. "I shall wait for her," was the brusque reply to Jamison's suggestion that his mistress might not return until late afternoon.

That had been an hour ago and the caller's natural ill temper had not improved with the wait. The entire staff distrusted Sir Ralph and to a man, they suspected him of sinister motives and were most uneasy when he was present. It was bad enough to have him acquainted with Lord Alexander, Jamison thought as he led the man to the library, but that he should have doings with her ladyship was outside of enough.

Seeing the look on Alex's face at the butler's announcement, the major drew his own conclusions. Familiar with the entire background of her escapade, he had been able to deduce her feelings toward her creditor. It was enough to guess the extent of her dislike by the faint expression of disgust in her eyes and the tightening of her lips.

Not entirely certain of the best way to help Alex, Christopher nevertheless resolved to be near at hand should she need him. With a meaningful glance at the butler, he inquired if perhaps some refreshment might be served to him before he changed out of his riding clothes.

Catching the drift of the major's thoughts, Jamison responded gratefully, "Yes, sir, of course, sir. Perhaps his lordship would like to wait in the *morning room* and I shall have a tankard of ale brought to him directly, that is if ale is . . ."

"Ale would be most satisfactory, thank you," Wrotham replied, nodding appreciatively and following the butler, who led him to the morning room and indicated the chair most advantageously positioned for the overhearing of anything that might take place in the library.

Meanwhile Alex, acknowledging Sir Ralph's presence with the curtest of nods as she swept into the room, immediately strode over to the desk, where she had locked her winnings in anticipation of the moment. Extracting the key, kept carefully hidden in the book of sermons that lay under a pile of papers on the corner of the desk, she opened the drawer and pulled out a wad of notes, which she held out to her caller. "There, Sir Ralph, I believe that this will cover my brother's obligations to you. He would, of course, give them to you himself, but he is away at the moment and as he is most anxious to settle accounts with you, he instructed me to discharge his debts in his place."

Unable to come up with a reply suitable to this surprising turn of events, the baffled creditor extended his hand wordlessly. "You may count the notes if you wish, but it is all there," Alex continued haughtily.

The remark was a mistake. Sir Ralph Cranbourne had been looked down upon his entire life. That his lack of acceptance by his aristocratic neighbors had solely to do with his own low tastes, unsavory reputation, and ungentlemanly behavior was something that simply had never occurred to him. All he saw was Lady Alexandra de Montmorency, bearer of an illustrious name, sister to a drunken gamester who had been as spurned by society as Sir Ralph had been, looking down her nose at him as though he were the merest insect crawling across her carpet.

Sir Ralph felt the rage rise within him. He wanted to throttle her, to destroy that cool elegance, to humble that air of self-assurance. With a supreme effort he willed the fury down and smiling sardonically, rose to his feet to face her.

"Oh no, my *dear* Lady Alexandra. You fail to interpret the situation correctly. The debt was for one hundred thousand pounds *or* your hand in marriage. I have no need for the money; I am a wealthy man already. However, I *do* need a wife, and I find that you are precisely what I had in mind."

"You would not dare," Alex hissed, trying desperately to conceal her gasp of shock and horror. Her first instinct was to run, to escape from the odious presence of such a despicable man, but she knew instinctively that her detachment and poise were the most formidable weapons she had against such a miserable worm. "You have no power over me. I am of age. I am my own mistress. Now get out before I have you thrown out."

It was the last straw. Sir Ralph grabbed her and pulled her to him, thrusting himself against her rigid body, his fleshy lips pressing against hers.

No one had ever touched Alex so, and for a moment she was paralyzed with shock and distaste. A wave of nausea swept over her as she smelled the liquor on his hot breath. Closing her eyes, she fought for self-control, her thoughts racing frantically. To struggle would be to react. To react would be to acknowledge that he had power over her and besides, strong as she was, she felt quite unequal to overcoming or even breaking free of someone who outweighed her by several stone. She could not cry out as he had his lips clamped to hers, his hand at the back of her neck holding her head so that she could not even twist it. At last she marshaled her wits and, raising one foot, brought it down with all the force she could muster on the inside arch of his foot.

As a defense it was not particularly brilliant and Alex would have preferred something much more decisive, but it was enough to make him gasp and loosen his grip just as the major, his face dark with anger, came hurtling into the library. "Unhand the lady, you dog," he ordered through clenched teeth.

Already inflamed beyond all caution, Sir Ralph sprang at the intruder, his hands grabbing for the major's throat. Not even deigning to raise his fists, Christopher stepped coolly to one side, allowing his would-be attacker to crash headlong to the floor, where he lay for a moment gasping for breath.

The major strolled over to the prone Sir Ralph. "I suggest you leave as quickly and quietly as you came or you will find yourself without your precious money and in the hands of the authorities."

"This affair is none of yours," Sir Ralph snarled, rising unsteadily to his feet. "You have no right to interfere in an affair of honor. The lady is mine."

Christopher snorted. "*Dishonor*, more like. What right have I to interfere? I have the right of any gentleman to thwart a villain and protect a lady—a lady, I may say, who belongs to no one but herself. I am sure that her brother, who asked that I call on her, would agree with me. Now I suggest that you allow Jamison here"—he waved in the direction of the door, where the butler, with all the stateliness of a long line of privileged retainers to the de Montmorencys, stood holding the caller's hat and gloves—"to show you out."

Not until the door had closed behind Sir Ralph did Christopher turn to Alex, who stood rooted to the spot, too outraged and disgusted to react. "Alex?" he whispered softly. "Are you all right?"

She nodded dumbly.

"My poor girl. He is a nasty character, is he not? I should not even have let you be alone with him." The major moved closer to her, trying to read the thoughts behind the glazed look in her eyes. In many ways it resembled the expression he had seen in the faces of young soldiers after their first battle. He took one limp hand in a warm, reassuring grasp. "It is over now, Alex. You have won. You are free from that scoundrel."

She gasped, shuddered, and raised her hands to her face. Silent tears trickled down through her fingers.

"Come, my girl." Ever-so gently he pulled her to him until her head was resting on his shoulder.

"It was . . . it was dreadful," Alex sobbed. "I could not get away, he was so odious, so . . . oh how could he!"

"Hush, hush." The major stroked the auburn curls. "You *did* get away. You had already freed yourself when I arrived."

She pulled away, gazing up at him with eyes swimming in tears. "I have never . . . it was so awful," she began.

Christopher's heart turned over at the misery in her voice. More than anything he wanted to sweep her off her feet and into his arms, promising that nothing would ever happen to upset her so again, that he would always protect her and take care of her. It broke his heart to see her look as lost and bewildered as she did at this moment, but he knew that what she really needed was not a champion and protector as much as her own self-confidence restored. Perhaps for the first time in her adult life she had been powerless, and the most help he could offer her now would be to give her back that belief in herself, no matter how much he might long to comfort her and have her cling to him for support.

It was such a magical sensation to hold her, to be so close to her, to feel the silkiness of her hair brushing against his cheek, her heart pounding against his chest, that he dared not move for risk of breaking the spell. Enfolding her in his arms felt so perfect—as though he had been hungering for something all his life and just now been satisfied, as if he had only been a part of something that was now complete.

He could have stood there forever reveling in the scent of rose water in her hair and the warmth of her under his hands, but she needed something else from him now. As he had done with so many battle-weary young soldiers, he strove to think of something that would help rebuild the world that had just come crashing down around her. "You *did* say the man was odious. I have seen some scoundrelly fellows in my time—the raff and scaff of Europe in fact—but I have yet to clap eyes on such a one as he. No wonder you were so eager to discharge Alexander's debt, though Sir Ralph was certainly dismayed by your coming up with the ready so promptly. Undoubtedly, he was looking forward to months of pleasure threatening you all with dire consequences if you did not pay. I'd have given a monkey to see his face when you offered up the blunt."

Alex raised her head from the reassuringly broad shoulder, a thoughtful frown wrinkling her brow. "Yes, he was rather put out about it, and I must say, I enjoyed stealing a march on him. I suppose I should have left the room then, but he was so disgusting, had so obviously come to gloat, that I told him to count it if he wished. I rather think that was the wrong thing to say."

Christopher clapped a hand to his forehead. "Wrong thing to say? It was madness! I only wonder that you are alive." He looked down at her. "You are a fire-eater, you know. I thank God I do not have you in my regiment, as I would constantly be having to keep your from flinging yourself in the cannon's mouth."

The green eyes regarded him gravely. "I suppose I *was* taking a risk."

"I should say so! I, for one, would never be alone in a room with a rogue like that. He is a very nasty piece of work and as dangerous and unpredictable as a snake or a wounded boar."

"I daresay, I mean, well . . . I am very lucky that you were around." The words came out haltingly and the major could see how much it cost her to get them out, but how very much he wished to hear them. Funny thing that—for years he had done his level best to stop women from counting on him, from making demands of him, and now he wished more than anything in the world that this one would. However, other things were at stake here beside his own hopes and wishes. The major shrugged as casually as if they were discussing a hand of piquet as he replied, "Far from it. You had already gotten the best of him. I merely came in as a rear-guard to stop him from even thinking about falling back and regrouping."

Christopher could see that she did not entirely believe this, but she was grateful to him for seeing things that way. "I do hope he is convinced"—Alex grimaced—"for I have the strongest disinclination for ever crossing paths with him again. Would you really have sent for the authorities?"

The major grinned. "The only *authorities* I was referring to were these." He held up his fists. "I know little enough of the law or of this county to know if he even could have been detained, much less punished, but it sounded good at the time."

"*I* certainly believed you." An answering smile flickered across Alex's lips, and then she was serious again. "But indeed, I do thank you for looking out after me. I do not know . . ."

The major reached for one slim white hand and raised it to his lips. "Believe me, Lady Alexandra, I am honored to be of service to a lady as redoubtable as you. I only wish I could do more."

It was a courtly, old-fashioned gesture, but one that was highly appropriate. After all, he had come rushing in like a *preux chevalier*, Alex thought, and oddly enough, she had liked it. How wonderful it was to have someone else shoulder her problems for a change, and how strong, safe, secure, and even loving his arms had felt around her. She could have stayed within them forever, savoring the delicious sense of peace and security he gave her.

But she must not think such a thing. The man loathed females, and with justification, from what she had seen of his mother. Besides, he was a soldier, ready to depart the very next day for a conflict that was bound to test every soldier engaged in it to the very limits of his endurance and abilities.

Now it was Alex, uncomfortably aware of the two dark blue eyes fixed on her with an intensity she could not quite fathom, who strove to bring lightness back into the conversation. "You are most kind. The least I can do to repay all your kindness is to see to your comforts. I shall instruct Jamison to see to it that you are provided with a bath and whatever else you need before dinner." She smiled and hurried from the library, her thoughts and emotions in complete and utter turmoil.

Chapter 30

~

It was a turmoil that continued through dinner and a desultory game of piquet in the drawing room while Althea amused them all by playing the harp. Try though she would, Alexandra could not keep her mind or her eyes on the cards. They kept straying to Wrotham's beautifully shaped hands, bringing disturbing memories of their warmth and strength as they had held her. Occasionally she would glance up to find him watching her intently, as though he were trying to read her mind or commit her face to memory. At last, hoping to dispel these disquieting thoughts by removing herself from the source of them, Alex excused herself relatively early and headed for the less disturbing isolation of her bedchamber.

This ploy, though it took her away from Wrotham's unsettling presence, did nothing to expunge him from her imagination. In fact, once in bed, she was at liberty to relive the entire day without interruption.

How ridiculously glad she had been to see him, after only a few hours out of his presence. What a joy it had been to show him around Halewood, sharing all her hopes and fears, and how terrible and wonderful her experiences had been that afternoon. Here she was, never having been held by a man outside of her family, embraced in the space of a few minutes by both the most loathsome and the most admirable men she had yet encountered. To go from utter disgust and revulsion to such sweetness and delight was truly to run the gamut of emotions and, strangely enough, those emotions that were actually the most upsetting were the ones she had experienced in the major's arms, for they were the most threatening to everything that she had hitherto taken quite for granted.

Never having come across any men, except the doctor and the vicar, who were more like fathers than anything else, with whom she could converse the least bit intelligently, Alex had taken it as a matter of course that she would never meet anyone who held any attraction for her, and had consequently envisioned for herself a quiet, fulfilling life in the country, managing the estate.

Now she suddenly found herself yearning for something more. Alex was not sure precisely what that was, but ever since she had known the major, the life she had so confidently planned out for herself had increasingly begun to seem rather empty. At first she had attributed this new perception of her future to the expanded vision that her trip to London had given her, but now, happy to be back at Halewood, she knew that it was her friendship with the major, not the many delights of the metropolis, that she would miss so sorely. The most upsetting part of it was that ridding her life of that emptiness required the presence of someone who was going out of her life forever the following morning, someone who was off to another continent and a war and very likely without the least thought for her in his mind.

There Alexandra, for all her cleverness and perception, was quite mistaken. Only a few steps behind her in quitting the drawing room, the major also had sought an early repose, but he too was beset by reflections on the events of the day and thoughts of what the next one would bring. He was even less successful than Alex at sorting out the welter of emotions that was playing such havoc with his mind and heart.

Like Alex, he had planned a future uncomplicated by any emotional entanglements. Now, for the first time in his life, he was discovering what it was to care for someone else's happiness and to want to do something to ensure that happiness. The damnable part of it was that he could do nothing, for it was imperative that he leave for Brussels the next morning—not that Alex would have allowed him to help her anyway. Here was the moment he had been longing for, when he could leave his frustrating assignment of wooing the cautious and hidebound members of Parliament and return to a life where there was action, where one felt as though one were accomplishing something. Yet now, a small part of him longed to remain at Halewood with Alex. The thought of not seeing her each day, not knowing how she was doing, was unpleasant in the extreme.

Christopher had grown so accustomed to looking out after her—not that she needed it in the least—that he knew he would miss it. He had grown very fond of the little wrinkle that appeared between her eyebrows when she was puzzling something out, the glint in the green eyes when she took on some new challenge, and the dimple that hovered at the corner of her mouth when she was amused. Now he was going to have to say farewell to all of that, perhaps forever.

All of a sudden the major was stirred by the most absurd desire to tell Alex all this, to promise her that he would come back and make sure that Sir Ralph never bothered her again, that Althea would have a brilliant Season, and that the children would be provided with all the adventures and excitement they could possibly want. Whatever was wrong with him? Not even the most beautiful of the women who had thrown themselves at his head had ever awakened the least desire in him, much less any inclination to take care of them; yet here he was, longing for nothing more than to hold Alex in his arms again and promise her the world. The more he considered it the more the idea appealed to him. Not only did he want to comfort her, he wanted to hold her until she felt desire stir within, to kiss her until her eyes shone with passion instead of tears.

You are a fool, Wrotham, he admonished himself sternly. It is all this anticipation of battle that is making a sentimental idiot out of you. Besides, what makes you think it the least likely that she would wish you to act this way, even if you were to do so? Nothing. Lady Alexandra enjoys taking care of herself, and she won't thank you for meddling in her life any more than you already have. With that bracing thought, Christopher blew out his candle, buried his head in the pillows, and willed himself into a restless slumber.

He was up betimes the next day, though there was very little preparation necessary for his journey. He had decided to ride to Harwich and catch a packet from there to Ostend—a simple enough plan in itself, but remarkably difficult to execute, entailing as it did a farewell to Alex. He said his good-byes to Althea and the children, promising them that he would look up Anthony and write them about anything truly interesting that happened. Then he turned to Alex and discovered that he could not leave her this way, surrounded as she was by family and servants. "Why not ride a little way with me?" he inquired, hoping that he did not sound as desperate as he felt. "Undoubtedly you and Trajan will be needing exercise today; you might as well get it now."

A brilliant smile broke through the grave expression on Alex's face. "What a capital idea. I shall just run and change. I won't be a minute."

It was a promise that only Alex, of all the women he had ever known, could make with any degree of truth in it, the major reflected as he strolled to the stables to request the saddling of Trajan.

The day was a glorious one, but this time the flowering hedgerows and freshness of the air went unnoticed by both riders as they steered their horses down the road, their minds wholly occupied with their parting and the major's uncertain future.

After traveling a mile or two in silence, Christopher could stand it no longer. He reined in Brutus, jumped off, and turned to help Alex down. For some time he stood there bemused, his hands on her waist. He had meant only to thank her, to wish her well and then ride off, but something inside of him wanted more than that. "Alex," he began, but looking down into the green depths of her eyes, he could think of nothing more to say. How could he put into words all that her friendship had meant to him, the many things she had made him feel that he had never felt before? Christopher felt inadequate to capture all that in mere words. "Take care of yourself," he whispered huskily as he drew her into his arms.

He kissed her forehead gently, cupping her chin with his hand, and then brought his mouth softly down on hers. It was meant to be an affectionate kiss, nothing more, but her lips quivered under his and he suddenly found himself crushing her to him, moving his lips against hers as though he would devour them. It was as though holding her close, kissing her, tasting her, would resolve all the conflicting emotions that were causing him so much confusion, could satisfy the strange new longings that seemed to have taken him over completely.

Then, just as suddenly, a picture flashed into his mind of Alex, struggling in Cranbourne's grip, Alex with tears of fury and indignation crying "How could he?" Stricken, Wrotham released her. "I am so sorry," he apologized shamefacedly. "I didn't mean . . . I . . ."

"It's all right," Alex whispered tremulously, dashing away a tear.

"I would never for the world upset you, I beg . . ."

"I know, I know, and you haven't upset me. It's just . . . it's just—Oh, do be careful, Christopher," she begged.

The major could have laughed with relief. It was just concern for his safety, not dismay at his presumption that was upsetting her. He smiled down at her. "How can you doubt me, you who have fought at my side? It is *I* who should worry about *you*. After all, you are the one who indulges in the truly reckless behavior."

Alex gave him a watery smile.

"Now let me help you up. I know, I know—you wish you were wearing breeches, but it is a cruel and unfair world, my girl." He flung her on Trajan and mounted his own horse, then turned to smile at her once more. "Now no more adventures for the time being. Neither Tony nor I will be around to help you out of any more of your scrapes."

"Of all the unjust—" she began indignantly, but with a wink of one bright blue eye and a quick dig of his heels, the major was off in a cloud of dust, leaving her to stare furiously after him. "Odious man!" Alex shouted at his retreating figure, and then to her utter shame and dismay, she found herself sobbing helplessly. This will not do, Alex, she scolded herself. It will not do at all. If Wrotham were to have even the slightest suspicion that you were such a weak-willed ninny, such a watering pot, he would be ashamed that he had ever befriended you.

But Christopher, galloping hell for leather down the road, was having his own problems. What with the dust and all, he had the worst lump in his throat that no amount of swallowing seemed to dislodge, and a stinging in his eyes that no amount of blinking could relieve.

Chapter 31

As best she could after Wrotham's departure, Alex stepped back into her old routine. At the outset, preparations for Alexander's funeral had occupied her time and kept her mind from returning too often to thoughts of the major and his welfare. Now that Sir Ralph had been dealt with, she felt at liberty to announce her brother's death, to accept the condolences of the neighborhood, and proceed with the matters at hand. Naturally, someone as rackety as her brother had made no provisions for anything, but her father's will, which had entrusted the estate as well as the care of his brothers and sisters to his firstborn, had also provided instructions in case something untoward should happen to Alexander and thus Alex, if still unmarried, was left a goodly portion of income from the estate and the management of it until such a time as Anthony could take it over.

As news trickled over from the Continent, the likelihood of Anthony's fulfillment of his role as master of Halewood became less and less assured. Reports of Napoleon's continued amassing of forces and building of fortification, in addition to the strengthening of the Allied armies in Belgium, left no doubt that an encounter of titanic proportions between the opposing armies was imminent though as yet unpredictable. Filled with concern for both her brother and the major, Alex pored over newspapers as though her life depended on it. In fact, so absorbed did she become in the events unfolding on the Continent that she wore an unaccustomed air of abstraction that was evident even to the lowliest stable boy.

"The mistress is worritin' herself to a shadow," one of the

lads commented to Ned as he rubbed down Trajan one after-noon after Lady Alexandra had returned from one of her long, lonely rides about the countryside.

"It's a right worrying time for all of us, lad," had been the coachman's noncommittal reply, but he, perhaps better than anyone, knew the reasons behind the mistress's pallor and lack of appetite. He had seen the way her eyes lit up whenever they fell on Lord Wrotham, how companionship with the major had brought new radiance to her face and an extra lilt in her voice. It was only natural that the loss of his company and concern for his welfare should rob her of that. The old servant longed to do something to help her, but what, outside of assassinating the Corsican monster, could he do to dispel the strain from her eyes or the anxiety from her face? To be sure, she also had her brother to consider, but though Anthony was as dear to her as anyone, nothing and no one had made Lady Alexandra bloom as she had when the major had been with her. It is a crying shame, that it is, the devoted retainer often muttered to him-self. She finally finds a man who is up to her weight and mea-sure and he has to go off and fight this cursed war.

But old Ned was not the only observant member of the household. Everyone felt the loss of the major's presence, short-lived though it had been. He had brought a vitality and energy that affected more than just the mistress of the house. "Such a kind gentleman," Bessie remarked to Mrs. Throck-morton over her mending one evening, "spending time with the children and all, and being so interested in everything and everyone."

The housekeeper nodded in agreement, though in her opin-ion, kindness had nothing to do with it. A shrewd observer herself, she had seen the admiration in the major's eyes as they followed the mistress, and she had been aware of the unspoken communication that seemed to exist between the two of them. Why, it was as though Alex and Lord Wrotham had been friends for years.

Even Althea, though she would never have discussed it with the servants, much less her formidable sister, was aware that the major had been a great more for Alex than a friend of Tony's. The more she considered it, the more Ally realized that she had never seen her sister so gay and full of life as when the major had been at Halewood, nor had she ever known Alex to be prey to such a fit of the dismals as she had been since he had been gone.

Thus it was not a complete surprise to Ally when Alex one day announced her intention to go to Brussels. "Well, so many people who have loved ones in the army are going," Alex said defensively. "Even Lady Meacham and her daughters have gone. Of course, they have given it out that they are concerned for Teddy who, even though he is the heir, joined the Life Guards. Why, you know as well as I that she thinks it her best chance to pop off her daughters all at once when there are so many eligible officers about who will do anything to put off thinking about the battle likely to ensue. Besides, what with the masses of soldiers involved, if there is a battle, how can we be sure that anyone will be able to look after Anthony should anything happen?"

Ally was no less fond of her brother than Alex, nor any less concerned, but it would never have occurred to her to go to such lengths, nor was she at all fooled into the belief that it was purely for Anthony's sake that Alex was haring off again. Nevertheless, she replied quietly, "Yes, I suppose you have a point there, but you cannot go alone this time."

"Yes I shall. I don't plan to go as a woman, after all."

"Alex, not again!"

"But just consider, Ally, how much more easily I shall be able to move among the troops, how much less likely I am to attract attention if I am a man rather than a woman. If people here ask, you may say that I have gone to look after Tony as he is now head of the family. It is perfectly unexceptionable, you know—they just won't know I am doing it in breeches."

Althea gave up. It was always useless to remonstrate with Alex anyway, and even more so when her jaw was set as it was now, and there was that gleam in her eye. "Very well. I shall see to it that bandages are made and medicines gathered, for I suppose you are not going to consult with Doctor Padgett."

Alex had the grace to look sheepish. Doctor Padgett had not been best pleased with her first escapade, but he had recognized that she was at *point non plus* and he could come up with no other way to procure her a hundred thousand pounds.

Now he was likely to dissuade her by offering to contact a fellow physician he knew attached to some regiment or to send some promising assistant he had heard of in her place.

"No," Alex replied airily, "he has quite enough to do around here and it would never do to go putting ideas of glory and adventure into his head."

In fact no one in the household was particularly surprised at Alex's latest plan. She was given to queer starts, but they were all so well meant and usually turned out for the best, so it didn't occur to anyone to object. After all, hadn't she just come back from her last journey with the means to save Halewood? Naturally, she was concerned for her brother now that Lord Alexander was gone.

Thus it was that not too many days later Alex found herself standing on the deck of a packet boat bound for Ostend. She and Ned had journeyed to Harwich and found, much as she suspected they might, that any number of craft were ferrying back and forth between Harwich and Ostend.

As she stood by the rail gazing out over rolling gray seas, wind whipping her hair, Alex finally stopped to reflect on her latest escapade. After the major had left she had moved as if in a dream, her actions guided by emotions she could not quite fathom and was loath to acknowledge. However, here in the harsh beauty of the open water, with nothing but sea and sky to distract her, she was forced to admit to herself that she was in love with Lord Wrotham. And what was worse was that she, for all her intelligence and independence, was behaving no better than Lady Meacham and her daughters. No, she rationalized, she was not actually pursuing the major. All she wanted was to know that he was alive and well. Once assured of that, she was quite prepared to return to Norfolk and take up where she left off.

No she wasn't. Alex shook her had angrily, furious at herself for her weakness and self-deception. In truth she wanted the adventure they had shared together to go on and on forever. She wanted to be able to look over her shoulder and find him right there beside her, blue eyes alert and watchful, ready to take on any challenge. She wanted to be able to look up from the newspaper and discuss the latest questions of the day with him. And she wanted, at least once more in her life, to feel the strength of his arms around her, giving her the sense of absolute peace and security that had washed over her when he had held her in the library.

More unnerving, but even more intriguing were the sensations he had awakened when he had kissed her. Alex had never known what it was to ache with such longing for . . . she didn't know precisely for what it as that she longed, but the most delicious feeling of languor had swept through her when his mouth had come down on hers, and she had wanted nothing more than to stay there forever held close to his chest with his lips gently exploring hers, his hands warming her, caressing her.

Entertaining such thoughts will do you no good, my girl, she admonished herself. He detests women, and the only reason he suffers your company is that he still thinks of you more as a man than a woman. Still, no matter how hopeless and dangerously tantalizing such dreams were, she could at least grant herself the pleasure of knowing he was safe—or not. Alex would not allow herself to consider that possibility. In truth, she was not her usual coolly rational self, but someone driven by an elemental need to be near a loved one who was in danger, whether that loved one was aware of her presence or not.

So confusing and overwhelming were the thoughts and emotions buffeting her as she stood there at the rail that it seemed only the space of an hour before land came into view and the shouts of the sailors and passengers preparing to disembark interrupted her reverie. Even after they had docked, Alex could not shrug off her dreamlike state, and she docilely followed Ned to the waiting carriage. Ordinarily, she would have been agog at the prospect of her first step onto foreign shores, but now, trancelike, she merely sat bemused by her own conflicting feelings as Ned threaded his way through the crowded streets of Ostend to the square, where he was able to procure rooms at a respectable-looking hotel.

The rain that had been threatening all day had finally broken, and chilled to the bone, Alex was more than content to settle into her chamber with a bowl of hearty soup for her supper. Exhausted by the past days of furious packing and planning, and worn out with worry over whatever was to come, she fell immediately into a heavy slumber.

Many miles away, wetter and even more chilled and exhausted than Alex, Christopher too was trying to rest. He had spent three full days in the saddle, the first reconnoitering for possible French positions or movements in and around Mons, the second attempting to carry dispatches between the English forces at Quatre Bras and the Prussians retreating from Ligny, and the third establishing communications among the Anglo Dutch troops as they took up their positions around the village of Waterloo.

Now, having found a small space for Brutus and himself in a stable near the inn where Wellington had set up headquarters, and too tired even to eat, he collapsed onto a pile of straw next to his equally spent horse.

However, tired as he was and much as he longed for the welcome oblivion of sleep, even a few hours of it, the major lay there listening to the rain dripping from the roof and thinking of Alex. How much he had wanted to say to her the day he had left. How he wished he could make her see what vitality, what zest, what delight she had brought to his life. Ordinary things and everyday routines suddenly seemed to have meaning for him. The old nagging sense of being at odds with the world had disappeared.

For so many years on the eve of a battle he had gone to bed not caring much whether he lived or died the next day, his main concern being that he conduct himself with bravery and distinction. Now he could hardly bear the thought that he might never see her again, might never be able to hold her again, might not ever be able to tell her how much he loved her, or that he loved her at all. Why had he not told her that? Christopher clenched his fists in frustration, but deep inside he knew that he had not because for Alex the idea of love and romance, the feelings between a man and a woman, were too new to be broached hurriedly and then dropped while he went off to war, perhaps never to return. At least this way he would spare her pain. If he were killed or horribly wounded she would continue to think of him as a good friend and nothing more. It was better this way, but how difficult it was when he wanted to be so much more than a good friend. He wanted to be everything for her, as she had so rapidly and so surprisingly become everything for him.

Christopher sat up and fished around in his pocket for a piece of paper, pulling out a dispatch that had lost its value by the time he had finally tracked down Blucher. "Dearest Alex," he scrawled with the pencil he always carried with him. At least if he were found perhaps the letter would reach her, let her know that he wanted . . . what did he want? He knew, of course—had known, but been unable to vocalize it, for ages. He wanted her to be his wife, to share the rest of his life with him. How simple it all seemed now, and how confusing it had been only a little while ago. He stopped. This was no better than speaking before he left her would have been. Better to leave things as they were. He thrust the paper back in his pocket and lay back on the straw picturing her as he had last seen her, her curls glinting copper in the sun, her green eyes dark with concern for him . . . and at last he slept.

Chapter 32

〜

The sleep that had overtaken Alex the moment she laid her head on the pillow evaporated quickly enough with the first light of day. Eager to be off now that she was so close to Brussels, she was delighted to discover upon her descent from her chamber that Ned had already ordered the horses to be put to and had paid their shot. "Begging your pardon, my la—er, lord, but I knew you would want to be on the way as there is rumor of a battle having been fought, leastways that is if I understand what them stable lads be saying."

"Thank you, Ned." Alex summoned up a wan smile for the old man, whose grizzled face betrayed such concern for her happiness and well-being. "You are quite correct in thinking that I wish to be in Brussels before nightfall. What with so many people of all nations converging on the place, I should think there is scarce a room to be had and I should like to find the most commodious quarters possible, lest . . ." Her voice faltered for a moment. She cleared her throat angrily. "Lest we are forced by circumstances to remain there some time."

"Now, now, no call to think that way." The old man shook his head sternly before mounting the box.

The day had dawned beautiful, clear and bright after the rain of the previous afternoon and evening, making the brilliant green countryside appear even more lush and not so very different from the vast expanses of her native Norfolk. But Alex, more concerned with the military state of affairs than the geographical, had eyes only for the steady but increasing trickle of travelers approaching them. The closer she and Ned got to the capital, the more it appeared that these were refugees who had piled their household belongings onto farm carts and wagons and were fleeing to safety. Alex's heart sank. Knowing how attached the farmers in Norfolk were to their land, she felt certain that only a conflict of monumental proportions could dislodge these peasants from their homes.

When they finally arrived in Brussels as part of a mass of horses and vehicles that were pouring into the city as equal numbers were pouring out, it was a scene of indescribable confusion. Everywhere there were soldiers, exhausted, dirty, and wounded, slumped in doorways, their eyes glazed with fatigue. The citizens, from scullery maids to highborn ladies, were doing their best to bring water and dressings to those in most urgent need, but they were helpless in the face of the sheer numbers.

Over the general hubbub of shouts and cries and the creaking of heavy wagon wheels rose a distant booming thunder. Once she paid attention to it, Alex realized that the booms were far too incessant to be thunder. It was cannon fire. She clung anxiously to the carriage door, peering out through the window, desperately scanning faces and uniforms as they inched along, propelled more by the mass of humanity than by any knowledge of where they were heading.

Finally, desperate to get his mistress settled, Ned caught the attention of an unmistakably English groom who was hurrying along, clutching a roll of bandages. He directed them to the Hotel d'Angleterre in the rue de la Madeleine, where a harassed hotelier, informing them that General Sir Thomas Picton himself had deigned to accept the hospitality of his hostelry not two nights before, demanded an exorbitant price for their lodging. There was nothing for it but to pay and be grateful they had any place at all.

Alex did her best to discover the state of affairs from the chambermaid, but the poor girl, entirely nonplussed by the world events unfolding in her once-quiet city, and awed by the English milord, could only stammer incoherently. Alex had better luck, however, with her host who, having provided refreshment and repose for the illustrious general and his staff, had taken it upon himself to keep abreast of events.

Yes, there had been a battle and no, he could not say precisely who had won, but it appeared that perhaps the French had, for Wellington had fallen back to the little village of Waterloo. That had been the day before yesterday. Nothing decisive that he could see had happened the next day, but the weather had been so miserable that he felt most sorry for the poor men on both sides, out in the cold, the wet, and the mud. Today they had heard the sound of cannon fire a little before noon, and later, the stream of wounded had begun to appear in vastly greater numbers than before. Was Monsieur looking for someone, a brother, perhaps? The town was filled with families—wives, sweethearts, sisters, parents—all eagerly awaiting news, but look, the sun was falling low in the sky and still the booming kept on, still the wounded came. Best for Monsieur to eat something and wait until further news arrived.

This was precisely what Alex was forced to do. Though the food was dry as sawdust in her throat, she willed herself to eat it, well aware that she would need all her strength in the hours to come. That finished, she went to find Ned who, concerned that in the general confusion and distress someone might make off with the carriage and horses, could not be persuaded to accompany her in search of news. "I've got a cold pork pie that Cook gave me and some cider as will suit me just fine," he assured Alex when she came in search of him sometime later.

By now, dusk had well and truly enveloped the city, but still the cannonade continued. At last, unable to bear the inactivity anymore, Alex pulled some of the bandages she had brought from the carriage as well as a flask of water and went out on the street with the others who were attempting the monumental task of attending to the wounds.

For what seemed like hours she poured water delicately between parched lips and bound wounds as best she could, concentrating only on accomplishing each task at hand—staunching the blood from a saber cut over an artilleryman's eye, binding the shattered hand of a young cavalry officer in the hopes that it would do until more expert help was found. It was only by dealing with each of these as a job to be completed and not allowing herself even to think of the pain and suffering of those she was helping—and those she could not help—that Alex was able to keep from breaking down completely at the sight of so many wounded and exhausted men.

The night had well and truly fallen when suddenly Alex was

aware of a change. It was so subtle that at first she was not quite able to pinpoint it and then she realized—it was the silence. Pouring the last drop of water she had left between the lips of an enormous Highlander with a bloody bandage wrapped around his head, she turned and hurried back to the hotel.

"Now!" she hissed to Ned, who was dozing by the carriage.

The coachman, instantly alert, rose to his feet. "Are you certain it is safe? Neither Master Tony nor the major would thank me for letting you . . ."

"Listen for yourself. It is silent. However, we shall proceed with caution. I have gathered from the few soldiers I have been able to help that the center of Wellington's forces was at a place called Mont St. Jean, just outside the village of Waterloo. We shall make for that. Surely with all the wounded pouring in it will not be difficult to find."

Nor was it. The difficulty was in making headway through the crowds of wounded soldiers staggering on foot and loaded in wagons and carriages, and maneuvering around abandoned supply wagons and deserted cannon. The road was a quagmire, softened by the rain the previous day and the traffic of horses and artillery today. At last they came to the vast expanse of the battlefield. Alex's breath caught in her throat at the sight of so much carnage and destruction. It seemed impossible that anyone had survived, but they had. Here and there were remaining regiments bivouacked on the very ground they had fought over, snatching what respite they could from the horrors of the day.

Unable to cope with the question of whether Christopher was even alive after such a day, Alex had resolved first to seek out her brother. Coming at last upon a group of riflemen, Ned asked if they knew where the regiments of the Guards were to be found. They were directed on ahead to the farm at La Belle Alliance where those who had survived onslaught after onslaught of Ney's cavalry had rushed in their final charge. Proceeding slowly along the road, they came at last to the smoldering remains of the farm, and Alex, seeing groups of soldiers in the uniforms of the Guards bivouacking in the nearby orchard, finally opened the door of the carriage and got out, telling herself again and again, remember, you are

Alexander. No matter what happens, no matter how upsetting the news, you are Alexander.

Gulping a deep breath of air still acrid from the smoke of the battle, she made her way toward one group gathered around a pitiful fire. With as detached an air as she could muster, Alex asked for Anthony. After conferring with his comrades, one soldier, a brawny young lad whose eyes were red-rimmed with fatigue, gestured off to the right, where those remaining in her brother's battalion had gathered. Her heart in her mouth, Alex strolled over, searching the weary faces for her brother's. At last she saw someone who resembled Tony leaning wearily against a gun carriage with two fellow officers.

"Tony?"

All of them stared at her. The man in the middle with a slight cut over the left eye looked so like her younger brother, with the finely shaped head and fair hair, but now, peering at the features gaunt with fatigue and blackened with powder, Alex was not so sure.

"Alex?" The middle Guardsman stared at her incredulously. "What the devil are you doing here?"

"I say," one of the other officers protested, "that is rather a cool reception for someone who has obviously come in search of you."

Tony blinked. "What, you, here?"

"Ned and I have brought you some water and provisions," Alex replied as calmly as if she had just brought him a hamper on the hunting field.

Understanding slowly replaced the vague look and Tony straightened. "I do beg your pardon, Alex, but I had not expected you, you see, and we have had a dashed rough day." He strode toward her with something more like his usual springy step. "But show us what you've got. Come on, lads." And Tony followed his sister as she turned and led him to the carriage, where the hungry soldiers fell on the provisions so carefully packed at Halewood.

Alex sat in silence as they attacked the bread and cheese, the cold pies, and ale with all the concentration of men who had not given food a thought for the past twenty-four hours. Satiated at last, Tony turned to his sister with a lopsided grin. "I shan't ask, but . . ."

"No, don't." In her anxiety to discover more about the major Alex cut him short, then she hesitated, not quite sure how to proceed. Finally realizing that it was ridiculous for a female dressed in men's clothes standing in the midst of a field surrounded by the wreckage of one of the world's great battles to be overcome by missishness, she blurted, "Do you know where Chri—I mean, the major might possibly be?"

Tony, who seemed to consider this the most natural question in the world stopped and considered for a moment. "Difficult to say. As one of Wellington's aides he could have been anywhere. Wellington and Blucher met here not so long ago and then Wellington and his staff, or what was left of it, headed back towards Waterloo."

"Ah." Alex fell silent until her brother, who at times was gifted with rare flashes of insight, continued, "I daresay that he would welcome some of your provisions as well. Why do you not head back in the direction of Waterloo. We shall be merry as grigs now that you have fed and watered us."

"Yes." Seeing that some of the customary vitality was beginning to return to her brother's face, Alex was eager to be gone. "Yes, I believe I shall do that." Climbing once more into the carriage, she turned and leaned out the window. "I can be found at the Hotel d'Angleterre." Tony nodded and waved.

Jolting once more over the rough road back toward Waterloo, Alex was beset by doubts and fears. Was she mad? What would the major think of her chasing after him like some—some hussy? What would he think of her . . . that was, if he was even alive. What was it that Tony had said about Wellington's staff? "What was left of it." All she wished to know was that he was alive, Alex told herself. She did not even need to talk to him—a glance to assure herself that he was all in one piece after this terrible day was all she needed. If he was not, well then, no one would be the wiser, but at least she would know one way or the other and she could return to Halewood in peace—or if not in peace, then at least resigned.

The carriage made its way slowly back toward Waterloo, Alex so intent on seeking out Christopher that she shut her mind to the moans coming from the heaps of bodies everywhere. The men in need of aid seemed limitless and there was no way she could help them all, but all of a sudden, the carriage, which had been proceeding slowly but surely, came to a halt.

Alex leaned out. By the moonlight she could see that a man in the green uniform of the Ninety-fifth Rifles had crawled out into the middle of the road. Grabbing a flask of water, Alex leapt out and ran over to him. Gently she rolled him over and held the flask to his lips. His breath came in shallow gasps and he reached for the flask greedily, wincing with the effort. Looking down to discover the cause of this, Alex observed a dark stain spreading across his chest. Hastily she opened his shirt searching for the wound, hoping to staunch the flow, but even as she thought about returning to the carriage for some bandages, he gave a final groan and his head fell back.

Alex just sat there stunned, holding him and hoping that he had felt some comfort at the last, hoping that he had not felt alone, that he had known that someone cared and, though she hardly dared admit it, hoping that if such a thing had happened to Christopher, there had been somebody there to hold him.

For the longest time she just sat there with the dead soldier's head in her arms, paralyzed by the poignancy of it all, until the sound of a lone horse galloping along the road roused her. The hoofbeats slowed, but Alex was so wrapped up in her own thoughts that she did not even look up until the horse stopped beside her and its rider dismounted.

She looked up at the horseman, whose tattered and muddy uniform was testament to the day he had spent. Blood was oozing from a cut on his head, his face was grimy and lined with fatigue, but the dark blue eyes were as alert as ever. "Christopher?" she gasped. Gently laying the rifleman down, Alex stood up.

A beam of moonlight touched the copper curls, proving to the exhausted Hussar that he had not gone completely mad after all, that it was indeed his own Alex who stood in front of him. Such had been the unbelievable horror and intensity of the past few days that he did not even stop to wonder how she came to be there. Suffice to say that she was there when he needed her most, her presence no more miraculous than his own survival, despite having had two horses shot out from underneath him and an unexploded shell land within feet of him as he carried orders to the poor fellows defending La Haye Sainte.

With a groan he wrapped his arms around her, whispering her name over and over. To hold her and to feel her heart beating against his after so much death and destruction was indescribable. He stood there reveling in the closeness of her, the strength in her slender body, and the sense of peace and security her presence gave him. Never in his life had he allowed himself to count on another human being, not even his fellow soldiers, yet here she was at his most desperate hour without his even asking for it. He did not know of another person who could have accomplished what she had and yet here she was, almost as cool and collected as she had been that first night when he had seen her at White's.

Christopher unwrapped one arm and tilted her chin so he could look deep into the green eyes that scanned his face worriedly. He wanted to tell her all that she had given him—faith, trust, love—he wanted to tell her how magnificent she was, to thank her for, oh, so many things, but nothing would come out except "I love you, Alex," as he brought his lips down on hers. He pulled her more tightly to him. "I love you. I love you."

Christopher rained kisses on her cheeks, her eyelids, her forehead, until he had to stop to catch his breath. Then suddenly it occurred to him that he might not be the reason she was here. After all, Tony had left for the Continent even before he had. Fool that he was! Their encounter might have been the merest coincidence. But surely she felt the way he did. How would he be able to feel so certain of the rightness of it all if all the love were on his side alone. Gently the major grasped her shoulders and put her away from him. "Tony?" He hardly dared ask.

"Tired, but alive at La Belle Alliance."

Then surely if Tony's safety had been her only concern she would have stayed by him or brought him with her. He had to know. "Then where were you going?" Christopher held his breath.

"To Wellington's headquarters to . . ."

"To?" he prompted her gently.

Alex hesitated. He had been so glad to see her, had even spoken the words she had longed to hear, but how much of that had just been a reaction to all that he had gone through? She wanted him to love her, wanted it more than anything in the world, but she needed to be sure that it was love and not just relief, joy, or gratitude at being alive. "I . . . I was coming to see if you were . . . if you were . . ." She could not go on. All the strain, the worry that she had successfully held at bay when she needed to, suddenly overcame her and tears stung her eyes.

"Then you *did* come to find me after all." The major sighed with relief, allowing himself to let out the breath he had been holding, waiting for her answer.

Alex looked up and saw her own answer in the blue eyes smiling down at her with such love and tenderness, as though she were all he needed in life. "Yes, Christopher, I did."

And they clung to each other at last, aware only of the comfort of each other's arms, the magic of each other's touch, and the joy of having found such completeness—a completeness that neither one had ever dared hope to find.